The Blogger

The
Blogger

The Fifth in the DCI Jeff Temple Series

James Raven

ROBERT HALE · LONDON

ISBN 978-0-7198-1894-3

Robert Hale Limited
Clerkenwell House
Clerkenwell Green
London EC1R 0HT

www.halebooks.com

2 4 6 8 10 9 7 5 3 1

Typeset in Palatino
Printed and bound in Great Britain by CPI Antony Rowe
Chippenham and Eastbourne

*Dedicated to my Mum and Dad
for buying me a typewriter for Christmas
when I was fourteen.*

'Technology and social media have brought power back to the people.'

Mark McKinnon, US Political Advisor.

*

**Extract from a report commissioned by the UK's
Intelligence and Security Committee into the threat posed
by the growth in online activism.**

'We would like to draw the committee's attention to what we perceive to be a disturbing trend in respect of online – or cyber – activists. There is now clear evidence that they are having an increasing impact on public opinion, both in the UK and worldwide. This has been determined by a detailed analysis of the blogs and social media channels through which they run their campaigns and communicate their messages. The study covered 200 of the most prominent social justice blogs, 200 independent political blogs, and 200 issue-specific blogs. Interestingly, those blogs run by high-profile individuals appear to be the most successful when it comes to reaching and gathering followers. We have identified a number of UK based bloggers whose reach now far exceeds the total readership of all national newspapers. This means they are becoming increasingly influential – and therefore a serious threat to conventionally organised political and corporate forces.'

Dated 23 June 2015

CHAPTER 1

DANIEL PRINCE HAD no reason to believe that he was about to die. The thought never entered his head as he watched himself on TV and basked in the glory of his latest, most stunning, success.

The events that had been taking place in London were helping him to achieve a level of fame and notoriety that surpassed his wildest dreams. He was unquestionably the man of the moment, and it therefore didn't occur to him that he might not live long enough to enjoy it.

In fact, these final few minutes of his life were spent trying to come to terms with everything that had happened. From yesterday's mass protest in the capital to today's sudden announcement that four high-flying ministers had been forced to resign from the government, creating a full-blown crisis.

Prince was struggling to take it all in as he sat glued to his wall-mounted plasma screen while sipping at his fourth glass of wine. He was feeling light-headed, and dizzy with excitement.

The BBC were running an interview he had given earlier, one of many that had been shown on rolling news bulletins around the globe over the past two days. The same questions were being fired at him, this time by a bespectacled reporter in a dark grey suit and open neck shirt.

'What's your reaction to what has happened, Mr Prince?'

'What would you like to say to those people who responded to your call and took to the streets?'

'How do you answer those in authority who are unnerved by the fact that you appear to wield so much influence?'

His replies were weighted with carefully chosen phrases such as 'the power of the people', and 'this is true democracy at work'.

But he cringed at the sound of his own voice, which was high-pitched and somehow lacking in gravitas. He put it down to nerves. The tidal wave of attention had overwhelmed him, and it was clear from his on-screen demeanour that he was ill at ease. He squinted and swallowed too much, and there were too many pauses between sentences. He came across as less than confident, almost apologetic, and that wasn't the impression he'd wanted to convey.

It didn't help that he looked older than his thirty-three years, and his face appeared pale and gaunt. Plus, the camera added at least ten unflattering pounds to his already bulky frame.

Not that any of that really mattered. He wasn't the focus of attention because of how he looked and sounded. It was because of what he'd done.

Over the past forty-eight hours, his online profile had soared into the stratosphere, and he'd been thrust into the mainstream limelight alongside film stars, politicians, and infamous criminals. One newspaper had gone so far as to claim that he was now one of the most influential bloggers in the world.

It was bound to have a huge impact on his life. Or rather, on *their* lives. Beth, his fiancée, had always supported and encouraged him. She'd been there from the start and had helped him to mount his various campaigns. As someone who valued her privacy, she'd been content to remain in the background. But he knew he wouldn't have achieved so much if she hadn't been by his side throughout.

He looked at his watch. It was coming up to 10 p.m. Beth was due to arrive at Southampton Central station in about an hour. He'd spoken to her earlier when she'd called him from Manchester to tell him that she'd been following the news and was proud of him.

'I love you more than ever, Danny Boy,' she'd said. 'And you deserve a really big kiss when I get home.'

'I'll be expecting more than just a kiss,' he'd responded. 'I haven't seen you all weekend and I can't wait to get my grubby hands on you.'

She'd laughed. 'Well, that's good to know. I don't want you to lose interest in me now that you're a hot-shot celebrity.'

On the TV the interview ended, so he started surfing the channels until he saw that he was the subject of a studio-based discussion programme. One of the guests, a middle-aged guy in a grey suit, was in full flow.

'Social media has made celebrities of people who would never before have found an audience, and Daniel Prince is one of them. Most of us don't go online just to be entertained. We want to be informed, inspired, empowered. That's why bloggers who strike the right note are attracting such large numbers of followers.'

Another guest, a woman in her thirties, responded. 'It's no wonder Daniel Prince was able to encourage so many people to go out and protest. The statistics speak for themselves. He has eight million followers on Twitter, half a million fans on Facebook, and his People-Power blog gets over ten million page views a month.'

Back to the man in the grey suit. 'Over the past decade we've seen an explosion in the popularity of blogging. There are now over 300,000,000 blogs covering everything from fashion to politics. The ones that are trending now are those that campaign for worthy causes and social justice. That's because people are disgruntled, disillusioned and disengaged with governments, politicians and big business. They feel they're being let down by those in power, and the blogs provide a platform for them to express their outrage and anger.'

He's spot on there, Daniel thought. The world was changing faster than ever thanks to social media, and people now wanted more control over the events that were shaping their lives. They were becoming less tolerant of corrupt politicians and corporate dominance. And of a decision-making process that they rightly felt was distorted by self-interest.

Daniel was convinced that power was gradually shifting back to the people, and not before time.

He got up from the sofa to pour another glass of wine and have a final cigarette before Beth got back. He didn't want her to know that he'd started smoking again. He gave up two months ago, but had succumbed to temptation on Friday night when the pressure had begun to build. Today was Sunday, and in that time he'd got through almost three packs of Marlboro Lights, a shameful total of fifty-five fags.

He went out onto the balcony before lighting up. It wasn't a particularly cold night, considering it was late November, so he didn't feel the need to put a coat on over his sweater.

The flat was on the tenth floor of a twelve storey, upmarket block overlooking Southampton's River Itchen. The views were spectacular, especially at night when he could even see the distant lights on the Isle of Wight.

He drew the acrid smoke deep into his lungs, and then smiled to himself as he stared out across the city.

His mother would have been proud of him. From an early age she had always told him to do the right thing, and to try to make a difference in the world. Well, he was certainly doing that.

He was suddenly reminded of how he'd felt six years ago when he'd notched up his first success as an online activist – by forcing the closure of the care home in which his mother had died from neglect. Then, as now, he'd been filled with an invigorating sense of accomplishment. It was like being plugged into the electricity mains; his body positively fizzed with the endless rush of adrenaline.

Thankfully the wine was helping him to relax, and with luck it would also help him to get to sleep tonight. He'd been awake for almost seventy-two hours, and he didn't doubt that tomorrow was going to be just as hectic as today and yesterday.

He'd already committed to giving interviews to CNN, Sky and Euronews. And he was pretty sure that other broadcasters would be contacting him as the events in the capital continued to unfold.

Before he knew it, he had emptied his glass and finished his cigarette. He flicked the butt out into the night and went back inside, sliding the glass door shut behind him.

He checked his watch again, and decided to call Beth on her mobile to see if she was likely to be delayed. He couldn't wait to see her and not just so that they could make love. He was anxious to talk to her about what had happened, and to share his thoughts about what it would mean for them in the coming weeks and months.

But just as he was reaching for his phone, the doorbell rang. It took him by surprise because he wasn't expecting anyone, and the concierge downstairs in the lobby hadn't called up to tell him he had a visitor.

He felt his spirits soar at the thought that Beth had got back early to surprise him. It was just the sort of thing she would do.

He was so excited suddenly that he forgot about the cigarette butts he'd left in the ashtray and the smell of smoke on his breath. And as he rushed to answer the door a wide grin lit up his tired features.

It looked as though it was going to be the perfect end to an amazing day.

CHAPTER 2

THE TRAIN WAS passing Basingstoke when Beth Fletcher's mobile phone rang. A name from her contacts list appeared in the little display window – Tabitha Ferguson, esteemed editor of *Female* magazine.

Beth knew instinctively why she was calling and her heart sank. She thought about not answering, but knew she couldn't afford to piss off the woman who had given her so much work these past few years.

'Hi, Tabitha,' she said breezily. 'How are you?'

'Much better now that I'm finally through to my favourite freelance contributor,' Tabitha said. 'I've been trying for ages.'

'I'm on a train. The signal keeps cutting out.'

'That explains it then. Where are you going?'

'Home. I spent the weekend in Manchester with my father. He's not well.'

'I'm sorry to hear that, Beth.'

'Thank you.'

Tabitha cleared her throat before continuing. 'You might have guessed why I'm calling. It's about your boyfriend, Daniel.'

'What about him?' As if she didn't know.

'Are you serious? He's all over the news again. They're saying he's responsible for yesterday's protests here in London and for finally convincing those politicians to step down. Every editor in the country wants to find out more about him.'

'And does that include you?'

'Of course. But what I want is your perspective on things; the girlfriend of the man who's shaking up the establishment and mobilizing the British public.'

'Well, I wouldn't go that far.'

'Come on, Beth. You know yourself that this has been building for a long time. With each campaign Daniel Prince has attracted a bigger, more vociferous following. He forced those football clubs to back down when they decided to put up ticket prices. Then he put so much pressure on Barclays Bank that they had to withdraw those obscene bonuses for their top people. And what about his rant against Tesco? It cost them millions in lost revenue.'

Beth felt herself smile. 'I suppose he has been on a roll this past year.'

'You can say that again. Your bloke has managed to achieve what most online activists find impossible – he's convinced a huge number of people to listen to him. This is serious stuff, Beth, and our readers will be fascinated to know about you and your relationship with him.'

'So you want to interview me?'

'No. I want you to write a piece for us. If you can do it by Wednesday we can get it into the next edition.'

Beth had never turned down a commission, but she was tempted to make an exception this time. As a freelance writer, she specialized in articles for women's magazines, everything from fashion to relationship issues. But she steered clear of personalizing her work, preferring to be an objective, impartial narrator. This aversion to opening up her own life to the anonymous masses had been with her since she embarked on a career in journalism ten years ago.

'Look, I know you don't like being part of the story,' Tabitha said. 'I get that and respect it. But this is special. It's a one-off, and I'm willing to pay you twice the usual rate.'

Beth dragged in a long breath and conceded that it'd be foolish to reject such a generous offer just because she didn't like to write about herself. And it made sense to stay on good terms with the woman who happened to be one of her main sources of income.

'Very well,' Beth said, after a beat. 'You've talked me into it.'

'That's fantastic, Beth. I'll call you first thing in the morning and brief you on exactly what we want. It'll include some photographs of the two of you together, so best send me a selection, and I'll pick out a couple.'

'Sure thing.'

'Do you think Daniel will be OK with it?'

'I'm sure he will. Unlike me, he's not one to shy away from a bit of self-publicity.'

After the call ended, Beth switched on her iPad and went online. She brought up the BBC live news feed just in time to catch the headlines.

'Our top story tonight is the resignations of four senior members of the government, including the Foreign Secretary,' the presenter said. 'They've stepped down following the mass protest on Saturday that brought part of London to a standstill. It's estimated that 40,000 people converged on Downing

Street to demand that the Prime Minster sack his colleagues in the wake of the new tax scandal.

'The protesters are now claiming that the sudden resignations are a victory for people power and in particular for Daniel Prince, the online activist and blogger who whipped up their anger and urged them to take to the streets.'

They cut to footage of Daniel standing with the demonstrators in Whitehall. In a voiceover, the presenter explained how for weeks the MPs had been resisting calls to step down. This was after a tabloid broke the news that they had all been avoiding tax that was payable on large sums of money hidden in offshore accounts.

They agreed to finally stump it up, prompting the PM to stand by them, and the clamour for their heads started to die down.

But Daniel was outraged and decided to launch his own online campaign against them through his People-Power blog. He drummed up support through Facebook, Twitter and a host of other networking sites.

When that wasn't enough to get them out, he took a calculated risk, and for the first time urged his followers to join him in a public demonstration. No one, least of all Daniel, expected so many people to turn up for it. But arrive they did, and in their tens of thousands.

It was well-deserved recognition for his tireless campaigning on behalf of worthwhile causes. And Beth decided that when she got home she was going to show him just how proud she was.

The train arrived at Southampton Central, slightly ahead of schedule at 10.45. Fifteen minutes later, a taxi delivered Beth to the ultra-modern Riverview apartment complex.

'What the hell is going on?' she said as she stared through the window at the cluster of emergency vehicles in front of the high-rise block in which she and Daniel shared a flat.

'Something pretty serious by the look of it,' the driver said.

There were three police cars and an ambulance. Lights were

flashing and men in high-vis jackets were rushing around.

Beth paid the driver and got out. She stood on the pavement holding her small leather case, a frown creasing her brow.

She was wearing a red coat over a black polo sweater and jeans, but that didn't stop the damp air from raising goose bumps on her flesh.

The entrance to the block was directly in front of her. There was a clutch of uniforms outside, and through the tinted windows she could see more activity in the brightly-lit lobby. All around her was the distorted sound of radio chatter.

Over to her right, a police privacy screen had been set up around a small section of the paving area. Her frown deepened as she wondered what was behind it.

'Can I help you, madam?'

The question was posed by a burly police officer who came up behind her.

'I live in this block,' Beth said, bemused. 'What's happened?'

He gestured for her to move towards the entrance. 'Would you mind going straight through to the lobby? An officer inside will speak to you.'

The coppers who were gathered in front of the glass doors parted to let her through. She had never seen the spacious lobby so crowded. As well as the uniforms, there were about a dozen people in casual clothes. She recognized several of them as fellow residents, including William and Faye Connor, their neighbours on the tenth floor.

George Reese, the portly concierge, seized her attention by calling out her name.

'Miss Fletcher. Over here.'

He was standing in front of the reception desk, a familiar figure with his shiny bald head and ill-fitting blue blazer.

Beth started walking towards him, but then stopped suddenly when she heard someone say, 'Oh my god. She's Prince's girlfriend.'

Her head snapped towards the voice, which belonged to a middle-aged woman with whom she was vaguely acquainted.

'Excuse me,' Beth said. 'Why did you say that?'

The woman didn't answer. Instead her eyes dropped like lead weights and she fixed her stricken gaze on the floor. The man she'd been talking to did the same.

Beth experienced a blast of anxiety and then felt her throat constrict when she saw that everyone else in the lobby was looking at her.

Before she could react, she was approached by a tall policewoman who pressed her lips together in an awkward smile and said, 'Are you Beth Fletcher?'

Beth nodded and felt her stomach contract.

'Would you mind stepping into the office behind the reception desk, Miss Fletcher? I need to talk to you.'

'Why?' Beth said. 'What's going on?'

The policewoman reached out to grip Beth's elbow. 'I'm afraid there's been an incident involving your partner, Mr Prince. I need to—'

'I don't understand,' Beth broke in. 'Daniel's upstairs in our flat. He's waiting for me to arrive home.'

A shadow passed over the officer's features, confirming for Beth that something was terribly wrong.

'Has there been an accident?' she said, her voice cracking with emotion.

'I think we should talk about it in the office, Miss Fletcher.'

Beth's heart gave a frightened beat as she suddenly put two and two together. She spun round and looked through the window at the emergency vehicles outside. Her eyes then zoned in on the privacy screen that had been set up on the forecourt.

'Daniel's been hurt, hasn't he?' she screamed. 'He's out there.'

The officer started to speak, but Beth didn't wait to hear what she had to say.

She dropped her case and dashed towards the doors, ignoring calls for her to stop.

Outside, she shouldered her way through the group of startled coppers and ran towards the screen. It was a flimsy frame that had been put together with plastic poles and nylon sheeting.

A part of it collapsed as soon as Beth touched it, revealing a sight that would haunt her for the rest of her life.

A white-suited forensic officer was kneeling over a man's body lying on the paving stones.

The man was in a dreadful state. It looked as though part of his skull had been crushed. His eyes bulged open and his swollen tongue was poking between thin blue lips. His torso was twisted sideways, arms and legs awkwardly splayed. His sweater and jeans were drenched in blood. More blood was splattered across the paving slabs.

It took a moment for Beth to realize that it was Daniel, and her senses went into lockdown.

The shock to her system was such that she wasn't able to scream. Her mouth fell open and her eyes rolled upwards in their sockets.

Then she passed out and collapsed on the ground, a couple of feet from her dead fiancé.

CHAPTER 3

As BETH FLETCHER was making her grim discovery, DCI Jeff Temple was inserting the concierge's emergency key into the door of Daniel Prince's flat. A moment later he was inside, followed by two uniformed officers.

Temple was surprised at the sheer size of the place. It was open plan, with a huge living room and bright, modern kitchen. The lights were already on and so was the wall-mounted television. The furniture looked expensive, and nothing struck Temple as being out of the ordinary, or out of place.

He signalled for the uniforms to check the other rooms, just to make sure there was no one in them. He then noticed that the sliding door leading to the balcony was wide open. That was obviously where the cold draught was coming from.

He crossed the room and stepped outside. The flat had a million dollar view of the city and the River Itchen, on which the moon was casting a cold glow. He peered over the glass balustrade and saw the blue flashing lights of the emergency vehicles ten floors below.

He could also see a bunch of yellow police jackets crowding around a spot close to where Daniel Prince had landed. From this distance he couldn't make out what was going on, but whatever it was, it looked as though the team had it covered.

Ninety minutes had passed since Prince had fallen to his death, presumably from this very balcony. It was a long way down and hardly surprising that the poor man's body had been crushed on impact with the paving slabs.

Temple had only just arrived. He'd come straight up to the flat after a cursory glance at the unsightly mess on the ground, which had turned his stomach and sent a rush of heat up his back. It was the last thing he'd expected to see late on a Sunday night.

Control had called just as he'd been about to go to bed. They'd told him there'd been a suspicious death, probably a suicide, and he was being informed because the identity of the victim was sure to attract a lot of attention.

At first he hadn't recognized the name. But then it came to him that Daniel Prince was the man credited with the downfall of the latest bunch of contemptible politicians. He'd been appearing on news bulletins for days.

It was enough to convince Temple that he ought to visit the scene himself rather than send one of his detectives. If the city was about to be hit by a media firestorm then he needed to be involved from the start in his capacity as head of Hampshire's Major Investigations Team.

Angel, his live-in girlfriend and MIT colleague, had offered to come with him, but as she was already in bed, he'd told her to stay put.

'I'd rather you got some sleep, sweetheart,' he'd said. 'If we do have a high-profile murder on our hands, then I want you and the rest of the team to be wide awake and raring to go first thing in the morning.'

But so far there was no evidence to suggest that this was anything other than a straightforward suicide. According to the bald-headed concierge, Prince had almost certainly been alone in the flat this evening. His girlfriend was away and no one had paid him a visit.

As Temple stepped back inside, the uniforms confirmed that the flat was empty.

'Then have a good look around,' he said. 'But be careful what you touch. And let's get forensics up here.'

He stood in the centre of the living room to gather his thoughts and take everything in. If the flat said anything about the couple who lived here, it was that they had good taste and enjoyed their creature comforts.

There were two white leather sofas facing each other across a marble-topped coffee table. The carpet was deep and luxurious, and a 52-inch flat-screen TV dominated one wall.

A breakfast bar separated the living area from the kitchen, and on it stood an almost empty bottle of white wine.

Temple walked over for a closer look. Next to the bottle was an ashtray containing at least ten cigarette butts. The obvious conclusion to draw was that Daniel Prince had been smoking and drinking heavily just before he fell to his death.

Was that because he'd been anxious, depressed or frightened about something? Something that screwed with his mind and drove him to suicide?

Temple wondered if perhaps he'd found it impossible to cope with the sudden, intense glare of publicity. Before this weekend, Prince had been a reasonably well-known blogger and activist in the UK. Temple had seen him on Newsnight a couple of times and had read some of the stuff he'd written for the newspapers.

But his latest campaign against the politicians had lifted his profile to a whole new level. He was suddenly famous – or infamous – depending how you looked at it.

And it wasn't unknown for people who are propelled into the limelight to freak out and top themselves.

He wondered what Prince had been thinking as he walked out onto the balcony. Had he been planning to throw himself over, or was it a spur-of-the-moment decision, prompted perhaps by too many glasses of wine?

He was about to join the search of the rest of the flat when one of the uniforms appeared in the doorway.

'I've just checked out the main bedroom, sir,' the officer said. 'I've found something that you should see. And don't worry – I haven't touched it.'

Temple followed the officer along the hallway and into a bright and airy bedroom.

The officer pointed to the king size bed. 'There it is, sir. On the pillow.'

Temple didn't know it then, but that was the moment things started to get complicated.

CHAPTER 4

BETH REGAINED CONSCIOUSNESS in the back of the ambulance. There was a moment, just a moment, when she thought she was waking from an awful nightmare.

But the hideous reality returned like a crushing weight as soon as she realized where she was. She let out a scream that was more animal than human, and the paramedics had to hold her down until she stopped struggling and fell silent.

'You fainted, Miss Fletcher,' a woman's soothing voice said. 'You've had a terrible shock, and we're going to give you a sedative to help you cope. Please try to relax.'

She didn't feel the needle go into her arm. She was too far gone for that. But she did feel the tension leave her muscles as the medication entered her bloodstream. It brought with it a sickening wave of despair, and the first flood of tears.

'Daniel can't be dead,' she cried out. 'I have to go and see him.'

She sat up quickly, and it made her dizzy. Her head felt swollen, and she found it hard to focus through stinging tears.

She saw that the rear doors were open, and a copper in a fluorescent jacket was peering in. Beyond him, more uniforms were milling around in front of the apartment block.

The paramedic put a hand on her leg and said, 'You should stay here at least for a few more minutes. Give the sedative time to take effect. We're not going anywhere.'

Beth pushed the hand away and swung her legs off the stretcher.

'I can't,' she said. 'I need to know what's happened to Daniel.'

She spooled back in her mind to what she'd seen before she blacked out. Daniel's broken body. The blood on the ground.

His battered skull caught in the glare of the police arc lamp.

She closed her eyes and shook her head, hoping the image would retreat. But it stayed with her like a gruesome hologram floating in her mind. Her throat tightened, and for a few moments she had to fight to get air into her lungs.

The paramedic gripped her shoulder. 'You shouldn't torture yourself. There's nothing you can do for him.'

Beth opened her eyes and blinked the tears away. 'I'm fine,' she said. 'Please don't try to stop me.'

She stood up and took a deep breath. Then she noticed that the police officer was holding out a hand and offering to help her down from the ambulance.

Once outside, she managed to stop sobbing, and her vision began to clear. Her eyes were drawn immediately to the police privacy screen about fifteen metres away.

'I need to see Daniel,' she said.

'That's really not a good idea.'

'But what happened to him? Was he attacked?'

The officer didn't respond, so Beth gave him a hard stare.

'I have a right to know,' she said. 'He's my fiancé.'

The officer's face clouded. 'Mr Prince appears to have fallen from your flat's balcony. It happened just over an hour ago.'

Beth gasped as if a punch had taken her breath away. She felt her legs wobble and it was as though the ground had shifted from beneath her.

The officer took her by the arm to hold her steady, and she began to cry as he led her back into the building. She barely noticed the people around her as the tears prickled her eyes, and the sobs racked her body.

The next few minutes passed in a daze of blind, gut-wrenching emotion. She was only vaguely aware of being steered through the lobby into the back office. There she was given a chair and offered a mug of tea by George, the concierge.

'It's hot and sweet, my dear,' he said. 'You should try to drink it.'

'I don't want it.'

She looked up at him and saw that his eyes were plaintive and forlorn.

He withdrew the mug and shook his head. 'I can't believe what's happened. It's horrendous, and I feel for you. Mr Prince was such a nice man.'

Beth felt her heart give a kick. She was about to respond when George stepped back and his place was taken by the policewoman she had spoken to earlier.

'Hello again, Miss Fletcher,' she said. 'Is there anyone we can call? A relative, perhaps?'

Beth sucked in a ragged breath and wiped her eyes with a tissue from her coat pocket.

'No, there isn't,' she said. 'My father's in Manchester, and he's ill. My mother's no longer alive.'

'A brother or sister?'

'I don't have any.'

'A friend then?'

Beth squeezed her eyes shut, and tears trickled from under closed lids.

'I can't think of anyone right now.'

'Well, don't worry,' the officer said. 'Your neighbours, Mr

and Mrs Connor, have said you can spend the night with them in their flat. They're outside. Is that all right with you?'

She gave a barely perceptible nod and leaned forward to bury her face in her hands. Her head was spinning, and she was struggling to hold on to reality.

Was it really possible that Daniel was dead? How in God's name could he have fallen from the balcony?

It made no sense.

Questions flooded her mind, but they served only to further confuse and distress her.

She heard a man's voice suddenly and lifted her head to see that the policewoman had moved aside and a guy in a neatly pressed grey suit was now standing before her.

'I'm Detective Chief Inspector Jeff Temple,' he said. 'Is it OK if I have a word with you?'

He was in his mid to late forties, with a friendly, stubble-coated face. His eyes were dull and ringed with fatigue, and his brow a concertina of lines.

Beth didn't respond to his question, just watched him pull over a chair and sit in front of her.

'I can appreciate how shocked and upset you are,' he said. 'I understand you just arrived back from Manchester and that you've been told what has happened to your fiancé, Mr Prince.'

He was leaning forward, and she could feel the odourless breath of his words on her face.

She scrunched up her brow and said, 'I was told he fell from the balcony. But that can't be right. It's impossible.'

Temple bit down on his bottom lip and breathed in through his nose, causing his nostrils to flare.

Beth could almost see his mind working as he tried to decide what to say and how to say it. After a few beats he spoke in a voice that was almost a whisper.

'It seems that Mr Prince took his own life by jumping from the balcony, Miss Fletcher.'

Her heart exploded. 'No … he wouldn't do that. He had no reason to. Daniel was happy. We were going to get married next year.'

25

'I'm really sorry.'

She raised her voice. 'You've got it wrong. Daniel would never have killed himself. That's ridiculous.'

The detective cleared his throat. 'So you weren't aware that he'd been having suicidal thoughts for some time?'

Beth opened her mouth to speak, but no words came out. Every muscle and sinew in her body froze.

Temple reached into his jacket pocket and produced a small transparent bag containing a sheet of white paper.

'We found a note, Miss Fletcher. Mr Prince left it on your pillow upstairs. I think you should read it.'

CHAPTER 5

TEMPLE HAD TO swallow to clear a lump from his throat. The pained expression on Beth Fletcher's face as she read the note almost moved him to tears.

Over twenty years on the force and he still wasn't immune to the reactions of those whose loved ones had died suddenly and tragically. Suicide added a cruel dimension to the emotional impact, and in most cases it made it harder for them to come to terms with their loss.

He could tell that Beth was still in a state of raw shock and would be until the grief set in. He watched her take in the last rambling thoughts of her dead fiancé.

She was an attractive woman, he realized, with a slim figure and a mop of dark, wavy hair that kissed her shoulders. Her large brown eyes were swollen and moist, and tracks of mascara were running down her cheeks.

'But this is all wrong,' Beth said suddenly, without taking her eyes off the letter, which was sealed in an evidence bag. 'Daniel wasn't depressed. It's absurd.'

Temple couldn't help thinking that her boyfriend had been a selfish bastard. He just couldn't sympathize with people who chose to commit suicide, knowing they'd leave behind a trail of utter devastation.

'There's no way he wrote this,' Beth said. 'And if he had, he would have written it by hand – not typed it, for God's sake.'

'We checked the laptop in the study, Miss Fletcher. That note was still on the screen. It was the last thing he typed just before he …'

'He didn't jump, Inspector,' she yelled, the words rising hysterically in her throat. 'I don't care what you think or what it says in this note. Daniel would never have killed himself. He enjoyed life. And today he was happier than ever. He was on a high when I spoke to him.'

'That's often the way with people who take their own lives,' Temple said. 'They hide their true feelings right up until the last moment.'

She shook her head. 'I would have known if something was wrong. He would have told me if he'd been depressed. But he didn't and he wasn't.'

Temple wished he'd been given a pound for every time someone had said that to him. He would have been a rich man by now.

'Perhaps he couldn't cope with all the attention that was suddenly being heaped on him,' he said. 'He'd been smoking and drinking heavily this evening by the look of it.'

Beth frowned. 'But Daniel doesn't smoke. He gave up months ago. And he only ever has the occasional glass of wine.'

Temple's heart went out to the poor woman. She was in denial, and he could hardly blame her. It was a familiar reaction in these circumstances, and he had seen it more often than he cared to remember.

'Look, at this stage we can only speculate as to what happened,' he said. 'It'll be up to the coroner to determine Mr Prince's state of mind and the cause of his death.'

'It wasn't suicide,' Beth insisted, her voice breaking. 'I can tell you that for sure. And there's no way he would have fallen from the balcony.'

Temple braced himself. He could see where this was going.

'Daniel must have been pushed to his death,' Beth said. 'He was murdered, and you should be out there now trying to find out who did it.'

She broke down then in a paroxysm of tears. The policewoman stepped forward and put a hand on her shoulder to try to comfort her.

Temple took back the note from her limp hand and stood up from the chair. He muttered another condolence and then said, 'Best if we leave it there and talk again later. Meanwhile, if there's anything you need from your flat then just let one of the officers know.'

Temple went back into the lobby and returned the suicide note to a forensic officer so it could be checked for fingerprints. He then asked the sergeant in charge to brief him on what information his team had so far gathered.

For now it was still a suspicious death inquiry, despite the discovery of the suicide note. That meant interviewing potential witnesses, finding out all they could about the victim, and carrying out a forensic sweep of the flat.

Sergeant Bill Mackay, a gruff Scot whom Temple had known for years, was on top of things as always. He read from his notes as he explained that no one had yet come forward to say they'd seen Prince fall. But the concierge did hear the body smash onto the forecourt.

'He told me it sounded like a gun going off,' Mackay said. 'So he went out to investigate, and there was Prince. He called it in straight away.'

'I noticed security cameras either side of the entrance,' Temple said. 'Have we checked them yet?'

'We have. There are two. One focuses on the doors and the other on the forecourt and road. It was this second camera that captured the moment of impact and it makes for pretty unpleasant viewing.'

'I bet. I don't suppose it sheds any light on what might have happened.'

'I'm afraid not. D'you want to see it?'

'Later. What about neighbours? Did anyone see or hear anything?'

'We're still going door-to-door, but I don't think we'll get a result there. It's not the kind of night to be standing out on the balcony.'

Mackay pointed to a couple standing apart from the group of residents in the lobby. They looked to be in their thirties and were clearly distraught.

'That's Mr and Mrs Connor. They live next door to Prince's flat on the tenth floor. They were apparently watching television when it happened and knew nothing about it until we rang the bell. They've said that his girlfriend can stay with them tonight. She hasn't got any relatives she can go and stay with. Her father's her next of kin and he's living in Manchester.'

'What about Prince? Any family we should be contacting?'

'It's a matter of record apparently that his parents are dead and he has no siblings.'

Temple bit down on the inside of his cheek and straightened his back to release the tension forming between his shoulder blades.

'When I arrived, the concierge told me Prince hadn't had any visitors this evening,' he said. 'How can he be so sure of that?'

'There's only the one entrance and visitors have to check in at the desk,' Mackay explained. 'The concierge then phones the residents to check if they want them to go up.'

'There must be other access points to the building.'

'There's a fire escape and service entrance at the back, but security cameras cover those and the concierge monitors them. He says no one entered the building during the evening who wasn't a resident, and nobody left it after Prince hit the ground. When we arrived we sealed it off, so we know who's come and gone.'

'What about a parking area?'

'There's a car park on the ground floor and only residents

have access. There's a camera at the entrance. No cars arrived or left after four p.m. apparently and the only way in and out is a door into the lobby.'

Temple mulled this over and said, 'How many flats on each floor?'

'Four, but the Connors are the closest. You'll have noticed that the balconies are all separated, so the residents have to lean over the balustrades if they want to see what their neighbours are up to.'

'Do we know how long Prince has lived here?'

'He and his girlfriend moved in two years ago. He bought the flat outright with money his mother left him when she died.'

'Did he get on with the other residents?'

'Apparently so. They regarded him as a bit of a celebrity because of his TV appearances and campaigning. They say he was pleasant and quietly spoken. However, the concierge did mention that Prince fell out big time with one guy.'

'Oh? What was that about?'

Mackay shrugged. 'I haven't yet been given the details. He told one of the PCs just a few minutes ago. All I've got here is a name – Hari Basu. He lives on the eighth floor.'

'We should speak to him then.'

Temple looked at his watch. It was now well past midnight, and he realized he wasn't going home any time soon.

'We need to wrap things up here as quickly as we can,' he said. 'It'll mean keeping people up until we've taken statements, but that can't be helped. I don't want everyone buggering off to work before we've spoken to them.'

'I've put in a request for more officers,' Mackay said. 'I've also alerted the media department, and they're sending someone along. I'm guessing it's only a matter of time before the vultures descend.'

Temple nodded. 'Good call. That's why we have to cover all the angles before we declare this a suicide.'

Mackay furrowed his brow. 'Do you really think there's any doubt, sir? I mean, he did leave a note.'

'I'm pretty confident that's what happened, Sergeant. But Prince's girlfriend doesn't believe it. She's convinced he was pushed off the balcony. When she goes public with that the papers will stir it up and put us on the spot. So we have to be a hundred per cent sure we're right before we discount foul play.'

CHAPTER 6

THE LEVEL OF activity both inside and outside the apartment block increased as more people arrived on the scene.

Among them were the Hampshire pathologist, Dr Frank Matherson, and detective sergeant Dave Vaughan, who worked under Temple on the Major Investigations Team.

DS Vaughan was forty, with a wiry physique and sharp mind. He didn't need to be told what to do. He got straight to work, liaising with the forensics crew and arranging for statements to be taken.

Temple went outside to speak to Matherson, who was in the process of examining Prince's body.

The grey-haired pathologist was kitted out in the full forensic garb – white suit, gloves, shoe covers and mask.

He had moved the body slightly, revealing the full, gruesome extent of the man's injuries. A part of Prince's brain had been pushed through the back of his shattered skull, and his right shoulder had been torn out of the socket.

Temple watched as Matherson lifted Prince's sweater to peer underneath, and he saw that at least two ribs were protruding through the flesh. There were copious amounts of blood on the body and the ground around it.

After a moment, Matherson stood up and heaved an almighty sigh. He looked tired and drawn, and Temple guessed he'd been roused from his bed to come here.

At six foot, Matherson was several inches taller than Temple and around a decade older. The pair had a high regard for each other, and Temple had lost count of the number of cases they'd worked on together.

'Is there any doubt as to the cause of death?' Temple asked him.

Matherson removed his mask and shook his head. 'He suffered massive internal and external injuries as a result of the fall. As you can see, the back of his skull was crushed on impact. There are multiple bone fractures, and I've no doubt there's significant damage to the internal organs, including the kidney and spleen. It's all consistent with a drop from ten floors up, which is about a hundred feet, or thirty-odd metres.'

'Can you tell from how he landed if he jumped, fell or was pushed?'

Matherson produced a tepid smile. 'I wish it were that simple, Jeff. In these cases it never is. It looks to me as though he landed on his back, the point of impact being the shoulders. A lot of jumpers land feet first, but not those who dive or let themselves fall forward. And there's also the possibility that from such a height he could have rolled over in mid-air.'

'So what more might you learn at the post-mortem?'

'Probably not much. Toxicology might throw up something interesting like drugs or high levels of alcohol. But if any wounds were inflicted before he came down, they might not be easy to detect, considering the state of the body.'

Nothing Matherson had said came as a surprise to Temple. Jumpers invariably presented a challenge to those whose job it was to deal with the aftermath.

He looked up at the glass-fronted block towering above them. Most of the lights were on in the flats, and several people were standing on their balconies, peering down on what was going on.

He counted up ten floors to Prince's flat, and it made him shudder. Prince would have plummeted to the ground in a matter of seconds. He'd landed only about five metres out from the block and roughly the same distance from the road in front of the building.

'Have you been up to the flat in question?' Matherson asked.

'I have, and I can tell you the deceased left a suicide note.'

'Really? So why do I sense that you're harbouring doubts?'

'It's not me. His girlfriend doesn't buy it. She's convinced he was pushed.'

Matherson shrugged. 'Natural reaction. Nobody wants to believe their loved ones are so unhappy they'd rather be dead.'

Temple looked again at the dead man and had to force back a wave of nausea. It had been a while since he'd seen a body so badly broken.

'We can give the go-ahead for him to be moved now,' Matherson said. 'I'll carry out the post-mortem first thing in the morning.'

Temple thanked him and went back into the lobby. He was making a beeline for DS Vaughan when his mobile rang. He saw from the caller ID that it was his boss, Chief Superintendent Mike Beresford.

'Hello, skipper,' he said. 'I expected to hear from you before now.'

Beresford sounded apologetic. 'I only just got your message, Jeff. We spent the day at my daughter's house in Dorset. She lives in a mobile phone black spot, and I forgot to leave her home number with Control. We're on our way back now.'

'Well, no harm done. I just wanted you to know what's happening.'

'I already know. You aren't the only person who's been trying to contact me. I just had the Chief Constable on the line, demanding to know what we're doing.'

'News travels fast.'

'You're not kidding. Someone must have put Prince's name out there within minutes of him hitting the concrete. The chief got a call soon after from a high-ranking official at the Home Office. Prince's death has got the powers-that-be in a flap apparently.'

'Why's that?'

'Because it's happened on the same day that he effectively

forced four government ministers to resign.'

'But it looks like he took a swan dive from his tenth floor balcony,' Temple said. 'Nobody's fault but his own.'

'Well, let's hope that is what happened. If not then we're likely to have a problem.'

'Care to explain, guv?'

'I should have thought that was obvious, Jeff. Daniel Prince is – or rather, was – one of a growing band of superstar bloggers. He has a massive online following, and he's been able to influence public opinion on a range of controversial issues. That's made him a right royal pain in the bum for the government and big business. It's also made him a target for those who fear that people like Prince are becoming too popular – and therefore too powerful. So if for whatever reason somebody did murder him then the conspiracy theorists are going to have a field day.'

'You mean they might accuse the government and the big corporations of being behind it?'

'Precisely. The public will jump to that conclusion anyway because the default position now is never to trust those in power. That in turn will put enormous pressure on us as we try to find out what happened. It'll probably also ensure that Prince becomes even more popular in death than he was while he was alive.'

Temple grunted into the phone. 'I can see why it could make things difficult.'

'So tell me what you've got,' Beresford said. 'The Chief Constable wants me to get back to him right away.'

Temple put Beresford in the picture and tried to reassure him by saying that Prince had left a note.

'But his girlfriend thinks he was pushed,' he said. 'So expect her to shout it from the rooftops.'

'That would be a concern if there wasn't a note,' Beresford said. 'But since there is one she'll just come across as a grieving girlfriend in denial.'

'I'll talk to her again in a while,' Temple said. 'The poor woman's still in shock.'

'Then try to persuade her to accept the facts. And as soon as you're happy that it was suicide, I want it announced to the media. I'll organize a press conference for later. Are the press there yet?'

'No, but I'm expecting them to turn up at any minute.'

'Well, stay on top of things, Jeff. Make sure we don't miss anything, and I'll be there within the hour.'

CHAPTER 7

BETH REMAINED IN the office behind reception as she tried to come to terms with what was happening.

Shock and grief had battered her senses into submission, and the time passed in a deadening blur. Her eyes were inflamed from crying and a fire burned in her head.

The policewoman stayed by her side, uttering meaningless platitudes, but nothing she said could dull the pain that was almost physical.

The note she'd been shown kept appearing in her mind. She already knew it by heart, and each word was like a needle to her brain.

My darling Beth ... Please forgive me for taking the cowardly way out. I've been seriously depressed and having suicidal thoughts for months. I can't bear to go on and I'm so very sorry. I feel bad for leaving you, but I know that in the long run you'll be better off without me ... Love you always ... Daniel xxx

She just didn't understand. Daniel hadn't been depressed and he'd never mentioned having suicidal thoughts. He'd been happy and content and had been looking forward to getting married.

The note was a lie. It must have been written by someone

else. But who would have done such a thing and why?

The fact that she might never know the truth filled her with dread. It would only add to her anguish and intensify her grief. But how could she ever find out how and why Daniel had died if the police were convinced he'd killed himself? They wouldn't bother to search for whoever had typed up the suicide note; the same person – or persons – who must have pushed him to his death.

A dark blanket of despair was smothering her, and she felt the tears building behind her eyes again.

'Shall I send for the paramedics?' the policewoman said. 'They're still outside, and perhaps there's something more they can give you.'

Beth shook her head. She knew there was nothing anyone could do to ease her suffering. She would have to endure the agony of losing the man she had loved since they first met seven years ago when they were both trying to make their mark as journalists.

She was working at the time for a daily broadsheet, and he was a freelance hack who did casual shifts for various newspapers, including hers. They met three weeks after she had ended a previous relationship that had hit the rocks.

Daniel hadn't had a steady girlfriend for some time, so there was nothing to hold them back when they realized they liked each other.

Within a year they were living together in a rented flat in the capital. But neither of them were native Londoners. She'd been born and raised in Manchester, and he hailed from Southampton. After his mother died, she'd left him a tidy sum so they opted to invest it in a property on the South coast, having decided that London was an OK place to work in, but not to live in.

It had helped that by then they were both freelance operators – she a writer for women's magazines, he a successful blogger.

The next phase of their life plan was to have a June wedding. The venue – a quaint hotel in the New Forest – was already booked, and the money put aside in a joint bank account.

But now it wasn't going to happen. Her dreams had been shattered and her life wrecked. She didn't feel she could go on. She didn't *want* to go on.

A howl of anguish escaped from her throat suddenly, and her face collapsed under a flood of tears. She cried for what must have been a full minute. When she eventually managed to get control of herself again, she used the heels of her palms to wipe her eyes.

The heat in the room was suddenly stifling, and yet cold goose bumps rippled across her flesh.

She felt a hand on her shoulder, and the policewoman asked her if she was ready to go upstairs with Mr and Mrs Connor. She looked up and saw that her neighbours had joined them in the little office.

'I want to go to my own flat,' she said, but the officer told her that wasn't possible.

'It'll probably just be for tonight, Miss Fletcher. Mr and Mrs Connor have said that you can stay with them. They have a spare bedroom.'

Beth squinted at the couple. Faye Connor was petite and curvy, with long hair the colour of dried grass, and brown eyes that had a cat-like slant.

Her husband William was tall and thin, with hair that was receding at the front but long at the back.

They'd moved in next door six months ago and had gone out of their way to be pleasant and neighbourly.

But Beth didn't want to spend the night in their flat. She didn't want them sharing her grief. But she knew she had no choice. There was nowhere else to go, and she had no family or close friends on hand to help her through this.

She was alone now and would be for the foreseeable future.

CHAPTER 8

TEMPLE WATCHED AS Beth Fletcher was led across the crowded lobby to the lift, sandwiched between the couple who had offered to take her in for the night.

The wife had an arm around Beth's shoulders, and the husband was carrying her small suitcase.

Temple could see that Beth was struggling to hold it together, and a dull gaze had settled in her watery eyes.

The sight of her caused his insides to knot up. It made him think about what he himself had gone through after his wife Erin had died of cancer. The grief had been like a brick in his heart, weighing him down so that he could barely function.

It took him five years to finally emerge from the depths of despair, and it only happened after he met and fell in love with a detective twelve years his junior named Angelica Metcalfe, or Angel for short.

He wondered how long it would take Beth Fletcher to find happiness again, or if in fact she ever would.

As she stepped into the lift, she lifted her head and looked straight at him. But he wasn't sure she could see him through the tears that sparkled in her eyes.

After the lift doors slid shut, Temple told DS Vaughan that they could use the office behind reception to have a word with the concierge.

'The chief super will be here soon and he wants to announce to the press that Daniel Prince killed himself,' he said. 'So let's get on and satisfy ourselves that he did.'

George Reese was a sad-looking man with huge bags under his eyes. His face was a grey, washed-out colour and his bald head shone with perspiration. He stood at about five foot six and was somewhere in his early fifties.

As he sat on the chair facing them, Temple noted that his hands were clasped in an anxious knot.

'How are you feeling, Mr Reese?' he said. 'You've had quite

a shocking experience.'

'I'm fine apart from the fact that I can't stop my heart from pounding. I keep hearing him fall. It was so loud. And when I saw him lying there I thought I was going to be sick.'

'Well, we won't keep you long. I'm sure you'll be wanting to get home.'

'I've talked to head office and they're sending someone to cover for me.'

He went on to confirm that he'd been on duty since 5 p.m. and that he always worked the night shift.

'My wife walked out on me fourteen months ago,' he explained. 'If I'm here keeping myself busy I don't miss her so much.'

Temple asked him to go over much of what he'd already told them, but he didn't have a problem with that because he was in no hurry to get away.

He said that he was probably the last person to see Daniel Prince alive.

'He was out most of the day giving newspaper and television interviews,' he said. 'He arrived back here about six and like always, he stopped at the desk for a chat. He told me he was knackered and said he was expecting Beth to get back from Manchester at about eleven.'

'Was he acting like a man who was preparing to throw himself off a balcony?' Temple asked.

'Certainly not. He seemed in good spirits and said he couldn't believe that those ministers had finally resigned. He was really excited about it.'

'Did he say anything else?' Vaughan asked him.

Reese shook his head. 'No. That was about it. He said goodnight and went upstairs.'

'What about before today? Had he ever given the impression that he was suffering from depression and having suicidal thoughts?'

'No way. If he was depressed then he hid it well. Seems to me he had everything to live for, especially after what he'd managed to achieve.'

'You told me earlier that he had no visitors this evening,' Temple said. 'Are you sure about that?'

'I'm positive. All visitors have to come past me.'

'Did anyone else in the block have visitors?'

'No, which is not unusual for a Sunday. In fact, it was really quiet right up until … well, you know.'

'Am I right in assuming that the security cameras record everything inside and outside the lobby?' Temple said.

Reese gestured towards an array of digital surveillance equipment built into one of the office walls.

'We keep the recordings for a week before deleting them. Your people have already taken the discs.'

'What about the fire escape and service entrance?' Temple said. 'Are they monitored?'

'Of course, along with the garage. The fire exit is also alarmed and the service entrance is kept locked, so nobody can enter or leave the building through them without me knowing.'

'I gather Mr Prince was quite a popular resident,' Vaughan said.

'He was indeed. And so is Miss Fletcher. They made a lovely couple.' Tears welled up in his eyes as he spoke.

Temple leaned forward in his chair. 'You told one of the constables that Mr Prince fell out with another resident.'

Reese nodded and lowered his voice conspiratorially. 'That's Mr Basu. He works in the docks and lives on the eighth floor. They had a disagreement at a Hallowe'en party last year given by one of the other residents. It almost came to blows apparently, and Mr Basu made threats against Mr Prince.'

'Do you know why?'

He shrugged. 'Well, I wasn't there, but I was told that they had an argument over what Mr Prince did. You know, the blogging and campaigning. Mr Basu accused him and people like him of stirring up trouble. That's really all I know, I'm afraid.'

'We'll talk to him about it ourselves,' Temple said. 'Meanwhile, what about other residents in the block? Are there any who were particularly close to Mr Prince? Someone he might have confided in?'

Reese squeezed his eyes as he thought about it.

'Well, I know he went for the occasional drink with Mr Kessel,' he said. 'They used the bar across the road.'

Temple took out his notebook and pen.

'Can you give me Mr Kessel's full name, please?'

'Yes. It's Joseph. He lives on the fifth floor, and he's from Israel.' He smiled. 'We have quite an eclectic mix of nationalities in this building, Inspector.'

Temple made a note of the name and said, 'Do you know if Mr Kessel is in?'

'I know he isn't, actually. He went out about seven this evening. It'll be on the security footage. He told me he wouldn't be back until the morning. It means he doesn't yet know about his friend.'

'Do you have his contact details?'

'They'll be on the computer along with those of all the other residents.'

'And how many residents are there exactly?'

'Sixty-five people and forty-eight flats,' Reese answered. 'About half are renting and the others are owner-occupiers. And five flats are currently empty.'

Temple traded a glance with Vaughan.

'A lot of potential suspects then,' he said. 'Seems like we've got our work cut out for us.'

CHAPTER 9

TEMPLE AND VAUGHAN left the concierge in his office to make himself a cup of tea and went back into the lobby.

What he'd told them about Prince being upbeat earlier in the evening had given Temple something to think about. It tallied with what Beth Fletcher had said about her boyfriend's mood when they spoke on the phone.

Temple felt the first shiver of doubt and wondered if this was really as straightforward as the evidence seemed to indicate.

He got one of the uniforms to direct them towards the service entrance and fire exit. These were accessed via a door to the right of the reception desk that also led to the stairs. Temple clocked the security camera on the ceiling that covered the length of the corridor. It confirmed what the concierge had said about the doors being monitored.

They then checked out the car park which was almost full, and Vaughan told him that the uniforms had carried out a thorough search.

Back in the lobby, Temple said to Vaughan, 'It's time we got everyone together for a quick conflab. We need to make sure the uniforms are well organized and that they're making a detailed note of every conversation.'

Vaughan frowned. 'What's up, guv? You've got that look in your eyes that tells me something is bothering you.'

Temple shrugged. 'I'm beginning to think we shouldn't write this off as a simple suicide just yet. I know we have the note, but by all accounts Daniel Prince wasn't acting like a man about to do himself in.'

'That's often the case, guv. We both know that.'

'I agree, but his girlfriend is adamant that he wasn't depressed, even though in the note he said he'd been suffering for months.'

'Maybe she lied because she feels guilty about it.'

'I don't think so, but I could be wrong. We should check the flat for anti-depressants. And contact Prince's GP. Find out if he's been undergoing treatment.'

Sergeant Mackay and several other uniformed officers joined them at one end of the lobby. The residents who had been gathered there earlier had been told to go back to their flats.

Temple kicked off the briefing by telling them what was in the note that had been found in Prince's flat. He then said that

Beth Fletcher was claiming Prince wouldn't have written it.

'You all need to understand that this is a highly sensitive case,' he said. 'Daniel Prince was in the public eye. He was a hugely influential activist and blogger whose latest campaign has shaken up the government, and no doubt made him more than a few enemies.

'His sudden death could well provoke a backlash from his followers and from other activists. The rumour mill will go into overdrive, and a lot of people will probably try to stir up trouble. So we need to ascertain the facts as quickly as possible, but at the same time we must do a thorough job. We can't afford to ignore anything, even if at this stage it seems irrelevant.'

He said that nobody was to leave the building until they'd been spoken to.

'I don't suppose any of the residents saw or heard what happened on that tenth floor balcony,' he said. 'But that doesn't mean they won't have useful information to impart. Find out who knew Prince personally and who had visited his flat. Maybe one of his neighbours popped in to see him earlier, or perhaps he dropped in on one of them. Let's find out as much as we can about the man.'

Mackay updated them on progress and said about thirty people had so far been interviewed. None of them had witnessed anything and half had said they hadn't even known that Prince lived in the building.

'They're not a particularly neighbourly bunch,' Mackay said. 'There's a variety of nationalities including Polish, Indian, Russian, German and Spanish. Most appear to be professionals and there are only a handful of children.'

Temple said he wanted all conversations logged, and he didn't want anyone speaking to the media when the newspaper reporters and television crews started to arrive.

'I'll deal with Beth Fletcher myself,' he said. 'Dave here will liaise with forensics. So let's get to it and with luck it won't take us too long to find out exactly what happened here tonight.'

CHAPTER 10

HARI BASU ANSWERED the door in his dressing gown. He was a large, dark-skinned man with a thick upper body and dishevelled black hair. His eyes were bleary and bloodshot, and his mouth pinched and drawn in tight.

The first thing he did when Temple and Vaughan flashed their warrant cards was to complain that it was the second time he'd been woken up that night.

'I have to go to work at the crack of dawn,' he moaned. 'Why the fuck are you harassing me? I told the other plod I haven't seen or heard anything.'

'Did the officer tell you what's happened?' Temple asked him.

Basu dragged in a sharp breath. 'He did, and it's not nice. But it's got nothing to do with me if someone decides to throw themselves off a balcony.'

'Nevertheless we'd like to come in and have a word with you.'

'Can't it wait? It's not as if I can tell you anything.'

Temple gave him a belligerent look and suppressed the anger that flared inside him.

'You've got a choice, Mr Basu,' he said. 'You either let us in and cooperate, or we escort you down to the central police station and carry out a more formal interview there.'

Basu rolled his eyes and stepped back to let them in.

The flat had the same open plan layout as Daniel Prince's place, but it was far less impressive. The furniture looked old and worn, and nothing seemed to match. There were a few unsightly stains on the beige carpet, and the smell of stale sweat hung heavy in the air.

Basu sat on an armchair and begrudgingly invited the two detectives to park themselves on the sofa. He then crossed his legs to make sure he wasn't flashing his privates.

He looked to be in his early thirties, and there was an arrogance in his bearing that made Temple want to slap him.

'Do you live here alone, Mr Basu?' he said.

Basu stifled a yawn. 'My wife lives with me, but she's in India at present visiting her parents. She's due back next Friday.'

'And how long have you lived here?'

'Eighteen months in this place and seven years in this city.' He angled his head towards a wall clock above the breakfast bar. 'I have to be up at five, Inspector. So if I'm to get any sleep you need to get to the point.'

Temple mustered a half smile. 'Can you tell me where you were at ten this evening, Mr Basu?'

'I was in bed trying to get to sleep,' he said. 'The curtains were closed so I didn't see Daniel Prince fly past my window. First I knew of it was when your colleague in uniform came calling.'

'And were you alone at the time?'

'Of course.'

'Did you by any chance see Mr Prince today? He arrived back about six according to the concierge.'

He shook his head. 'I haven't been out since I went to get a paper this morning. Sundays are for chilling out in front of the television.'

'So you didn't pop up to see him and he didn't come here to see you?'

'You must be joking. We weren't friendly neighbours. I didn't like him and he didn't like me. But then you already know that, don't you?'

'We were told that you two had a fierce argument at a Hallowe'en party.'

'So what's that got to do with anything?'

'Almost certainly nothing,' Temple said. 'But whenever there's a suspicious death, we have to ask lots of questions that might seem irrelevant.'

'The other copper reckoned Prince killed himself. Are you saying he might not have?'

'I'm saying we still don't know exactly what happened and that's what we're trying to find out.'

'Well, I didn't push him if that's what you're thinking.'

'It's not, Mr Basu, but we do want to know why there was a degree of animosity between the pair of you. So tell me about the Hallowe'en party.'

Basu blew air out between pursed lips. 'Things kicked off and stuff was said. But it was over and done in a flash, and we haven't spoken since, not even on the few occasions when we got in the lift together.'

'Is it true that you made threats against him?'

He gave a mirthless grin. 'I told him I'd punch his lights out if he kept talking to me like I was some kind of idiot. But it never went that far.'

'So what was the problem?'

He shrugged. 'It was stupid, really. At the party everyone was fawning over him and saying what a great job he was doing. They were treating him like some highly respected statesman. I was drunk so I accused him of being a self-important activist who was trying to undermine the accepted order of things and in the process, doing more harm than good. He reckoned I didn't know what I was talking about, so I told him how he'd wrecked the lives of my family back in India.'

'How did he manage to do that?' Vaughan asked.

Basu brought his palms up to rub the sleep from his eyes and said, 'A year ago, he ran a campaign against a chain store that was buying clothes from a factory in Delhi. He caused such a fuss that the company stopped doing business with them and the factory closed down. My mother and two of my sisters lost their jobs and are now out of work and destitute. And my father left them because it all got too much for him.'

'I'm sorry to hear that, Mr Basu,' Temple said. 'But surely you can't blame Daniel Prince. A lot of individuals and organizations campaign against the exploitation of workers in sweatshops.'

Basu clenched his jaw. 'You don't need to tell me that. But millions of people wouldn't survive without them. And it pissed me off that Prince refused to recognize that. He acted like what happened to my family didn't matter, that everyone should be praising him for what he'd done. That's why I won't be shedding any tears for him, Inspector. And I don't give a toss if it makes me sound callous and insensitive.'

CHAPTER 11

TEMPLE'S PHONE RANG as Hari Basu closed his front door behind them.

It was the Chief Superintendent, letting Temple know that he was downstairs in the lobby.

'I need you to brief me, Jeff,' he said. 'I just arrived at the same time as the first TV satellite truck. And I'm told there are a couple of reporters outside as well, screaming for information.'

Temple didn't doubt that many more would descend on the Riverview apartment complex in the coming hours. This was, after all, a huge story regardless of whether Daniel Prince had jumped or was pushed from his balcony.

The media frenzy would pile on the pressure and likely as not last for days or even weeks. Temple knew that much from recent experience. MIT's last two investigations had been carried out in the glare of publicity.

The first had involved a sniper who was causing death and destruction on motorways by randomly shooting at traffic with a high-powered rifle. The second centred on the New Forest, where police uncovered a number of shallow graves containing victims who had been brutally tortured and murdered.

Those investigations had taken their toll both physically and mentally on his team of detectives. But for him the stress had been compounded because at the same time fate had been unkind to Angel.

She'd been one of the drivers seriously injured in the motorway carnage and had spent weeks in hospital. Then during the New Forest investigation she'd suffered the heartbreak of a miscarriage. In fact, she'd been back at work for only a matter of months and was still pretty fragile psychologically.

He wasn't sure how she and the rest of the team would cope if they were to find themselves back in the eye of another media storm.

Chief Superintendent Mike Beresford had a reputation for always being cool in a crisis. So Temple was surprised to see the burly Welshman looking uptight and anxious.

His cheeks were flushed, and there was a thin line of perspiration above his top lip. It was also unusual to see him dressed down in a casual sports jacket and open neck shirt.

Temple gestured through the window at the bunch of news hounds who had gathered in front of the building.

'You're just in time to take centre stage, boss,' he said. 'Looks like the media circus is about to begin.'

Beresford snorted. 'Are press liaison here yet? I'd rather let them handle this.'

Sergeant Mackay, who had joined them in the lobby, explained that they were still waiting for someone to turn up.

Beresford nodded. 'I feared as much. Well, I suppose I need to say something, if only to quell ill-informed speculation.' He turned to Temple. 'Give me an update, Jeff. Can I tell them we're certain that Daniel Prince took his own life?'

'It might be wise to hold off until forensics have wrapped up, sir. We don't want to jump the gun on this.'

Beresford's dark eyes crinkled at the corners. 'Are you saying that because you think it might not have been suicide?'

'At this stage I really don't know for sure, sir.'

'But what about the note? Surely that's proof enough that he jumped.'

'I'm sure it is, but I still think it's best to keep our options open until every scrap of evidence has been assessed and everyone in the block has been spoken to.'

The chief conceded that Temple was probably right. He then asked Sergeant Mackay if the body had been moved from outside on the forecourt.

'They took it away about fifteen minutes ago,' Mackay said.

'Good. In that case let's go and get this over with.'

The road in front of the block had been cordoned off and that's where the media pack had gathered. There were four reporters and a TV cameraman, and they started throwing questions before Beresford and Temple even reached them.

'Can you confirm the dead man is Daniel Prince, the blogger?'

'Did he jump or did he fall?'

'There are rumours that he was pushed from his balcony. Is that true?'

Beresford raised his hands to stop them and introduced himself. Temple recognized one of the reporters as a local hack. The others he didn't know.

'I can confirm that a 33-year-old man has died after a fall from a tenth floor balcony,' Beresford said. 'The flat in question is owned by Mr Daniel Prince, and although there's been no formal identification, we believe that's who the deceased is.

'A note was found in the flat, and we're not looking for anyone else in connection with the incident. However, we will keep an open mind until we've carried out all our inquiries.'

As soon as he stopped talking more questions were fired at him.

'Was Mr Prince alone at the time?'

'Where was his girlfriend? Has she been told?'

'Isn't it strange that this should happen on the very day that those four ministers resigned from the government?'

'What was in the note that was found?'

Beresford answered some of the questions and ignored others. He spoke slowly, measuring his words, and made a point of telling them that he himself had only just arrived on the scene and wasn't yet in possession of all the facts.

Temple's phone rang while he was listening, so he stepped back to answer it as the chief began winding up the impromptu press conference.

It was DS Vaughan on the line, and he was calling from inside Prince's flat.

'I suggest you get up here right away, guv,' Vaughan said. 'Forensics have found some stuff, and you need to see it.'

CHAPTER 12

LEE FINCH, THE chief forensics officer, was waiting for them upstairs. He was a tall, softly-spoken man with a stooped posture and rimless glasses that perched precariously on the end of a bulbous nose.

He insisted that Temple and Beresford put on white suits and shoe covers before entering the flat.

'I know this is not what you want to hear, gents,' he said. 'But I think it's time we started treating this place as a crime scene.'

Temple's chest tightened as he stepped over the threshold. Finch's team were going about their work in studious silence, dusting for prints and scouring every surface for clues as to what had happened.

Finch led them through to Prince's office where DS Vaughan was standing with his back to the desk. On top of it was a laptop and printer. One wall was covered with book-shelves and against another stood a large metal filing cabinet.

'OK, let's begin in here,' Finch said. 'On the face of it, this looks like a suicide, right? Daniel Prince threw himself over the balcony after typing up a short note to his girlfriend on his laptop.'

He pointed to the laptop and Vaughan stepped out of the way.

'The letter was on the screen when officers arrived,' he said. 'The data shows that it was actually typed up and printed off seven minutes before Prince hit the ground below. We've checked the note, and his prints are on it.'

He walked over to the desk and put his gloved hand on the mouse attached to the laptop.

'However, this is where things start to become less straightforward. You see, we also checked for prints on the mouse and on the keyboard and there aren't any.'

'How come?' Temple said.

Finch smiled thinly, opened the top drawer of the desk, and took out a small blue spray.

'It appears the mouse, the keyboard and the screen have been wiped using this cleaning fluid. It's a common product, and I actually use this same make on my computer at home. But the question it raises here is why would Prince have bothered to clean his computer just before killing himself? It seems highly unlikely to me.'

'So what are you suggesting?' Beresford asked.

Finch shrugged. 'Well, I think it's more likely that Prince wiped it clean earlier in the evening. Probably something he regularly did at the end of the day or after using it.'

'So you think he wore gloves when he wrote the note?' Temple said. 'Why would he have done that?'

'Well, I don't suppose for one second that he would have. So that means that someone else did. Someone who wouldn't have realized that there were none of Prince's prints on the mouse and keyboard because he'd wiped them clean.'

'But what about the note?' Temple said. 'You said his prints are on that.'

Finch nodded. 'They are. So either he removed it from the printer himself and placed it on the pillow in the bedroom. Or someone did it for him after pressing his fingers and thumb against the paper.'

Temple and Beresford exchanged anxious looks. They both knew that Finch was one of the best and most experienced forensic officers on the Hampshire force. Whenever he put forward a theory based on evidence he'd gathered, he was proved right ninety per cent of the time.

'But that's not all, gents,' Finch said. 'There's more. Follow me.'

CHAPTER 13

BACK IN THE living room, Finch pointed to an area of carpet leading up to the balcony door.

'If you look closely you can see two shallow track marks,' he said. 'They trail from about here to here, and if it wasn't for the fact that this is a fairly thick carpet, we wouldn't have noticed them.'

Temple had to kneel down and strain his eyes to see them.

'Unfortunately the scene has been contaminated to a degree,' Finch said. 'Too many people have walked on this spot.'

'Including me,' Temple said.

'Yeah, well it's made it more difficult to determine what's caused this, but it's quite possible they're scuff marks left by shoes being dragged across the floor.'

'Prince was wearing indoor slippers,' Temple said.

'They'd leave the same mark, Jeff. When we get his clothes back to the lab we'll check for carpet fibres.'

They were all silent for a moment as the ramifications of what Finch was saying sank in. A look of unease flashed across Beresford's features, and he slowly shook his head.

Temple stood there staring at the carpet, trying to work through a scenario that was altogether different from the one he had imagined.

'I've saved the best till last,' Finch said. 'We found it quite by chance while dusting for prints above and below the breakfast bar.'

He picked up a transparent evidence bag that had been placed on the coffee table next to him. It contained two black electronic devices the size of matchboxes and a short length of cable.

'It's a GSM room transmitter with power charger,' he said. 'In other words, a pretty sophisticated covert listening device. It was plugged into a wall socket beneath the breakfast bar. The socket is tucked in behind a wooden panel and was probably never used for anything else. We're checking other rooms now to see if there are any more.'

'So the flat's been bugged,' Temple said, unable to conceal his shock.

Finch nodded. 'That's right. It'll be up to you guys to find out if Prince knew about it and actually put it there himself. Or if someone else installed it to listen in on all the conversations.'

Finch handed him the bag and he examined the contents.

'It's tiny,' he said. 'How the hell does it work?'

'These things are fitted with SIM cards,' he said. 'All you have to do is dial a pay-as-you-go number in the unit from anywhere in the world. The device is silently activated and you can listen in to conversations that are taking place in the room. If you've got a charger attached to the mains then you don't have to worry about battery life.'

'So how easy are these to obtain?'

'Very easy,' Finch said. 'You can buy them from dozens of sites on the internet.'

Temple was about to speak when a noise outside in the hallway drew their attention. It sounded like someone was yelling. A second later the front door flew open and Beth Fletcher came charging in, trailed by a uniformed constable who was trying to stop her.

She was clearly distraught and angry at the same time. When she spotted Beresford standing in the centre of the room, she stabbed a forefinger at him and screamed, 'I just saw you on the television. Why did you give the impression that Daniel killed himself? He didn't. You're wrong, and I won't have you saying it.'

The officer caught up with her and grabbed her arm to stop her in her tracks.

'She just barged past me,' he exclaimed by way of an excuse.

Beth just stood there, her body rigid, her eyes filling with tears.

Temple rushed across the room and put a hand on her shoulder. He could feel her body shaking beneath it.

She screwed up her eyes and tried to focus on his face. He

smiled gently, hoping to take the wind out of her sails.

'It's not fair,' she mumbled, her lips quivering. 'Daniel loved me. He wouldn't have left me. I know it. Please believe me.'

Temple spoke straight from the heart and without taking into account the impact of his words.

'Look, we're really sorry, Miss Fletcher. We didn't know then what we know now. It seems you could well be right. We've just found evidence to suggest that your fiancé might not have taken his own life.'

CHAPTER 14

DAWN BROKE OVER Southampton, bringing with it the raucous cry of seabirds above the Riverview apartment complex.

A thin light bled through the curtains into William and Faye Connor's spare bedroom.

When Beth woke she felt a terrible sadness. She just lay there like a corpse and allowed the negative thoughts to engulf her.

Her mind was fuzzy, but she remembered how the detective had done his best to console her after she had burst into her own flat next door.

He'd brought her back here, and Faye had helped her get undressed and into bed. But she'd lain awake for what had seemed like hours before crying herself to sleep.

Now her eyes felt swollen and scratchy, and the grief was wrapped so tightly around her that she could barely breathe.

Her beloved Daniel was dead, and she knew in her heart that he'd been murdered. The detective had also said as much. Daniel was gone and she was alone. How was that possible? Why did it have to happen?

More questions spun round inside her head. Did he know his killer or killers? Did he let them into the flat? Was he conscious when he was hurled over the balcony?

She clamped her eyelids together, and her heart jolted into her throat.

Suddenly, involuntarily, a memory came back to her. It was one night in the summer and they were at a restaurant in the centre of town when he popped the question.

'Will you marry me, Beth?' he said. 'I love you more than you could possibly imagine.'

The echo of those words travelled through her head, causing her grief to plunge to a new depth.

The tears came then, trickling down her temples onto the pillow. She gave into it and cried for the best part of five minutes as more memories of their time together drifted through her mind, each one clamouring for attention.

It was the prosaic sound of the central heating kicking in that brought her back to the present. She wiped her eyes with the duvet and forced herself to resist the weakness that was taking her over.

She couldn't lie here all day in this strange bed. She had to get up and face the world, no matter how painful it was going to be.

She pushed back the duvet and got up. She was wearing the nightie she'd taken to Manchester. Jesus, she thought, it seemed like a lifetime ago that she was sitting with her father in the home he shared with his second wife, Lydia.

It was the third time she'd been up there since his stroke three months ago and she'd been pleased to see that he was making slow progress. He still couldn't walk, but he had gained the use of his left arm, much to the surprise of the doctors.

She would have to call him today to tell him what had happened, assuming he didn't already know.

Her father was going to be devastated. He had always liked Daniel and was full of admiration for the work he'd done.

'He must put the fear of God into those establishment arseholes whenever he posts something on that blog of his,' he'd said recently. 'You should be proud of him, Beth. I know I am.'

Was that why Daniel had been murdered, she wondered.

Had he pushed the powers-that-be too far?

Right now it seemed like the only plausible explanation. To her knowledge he'd had no enemies, apart from the faceless hordes who'd objected to what he wrote on his blog. They had made their feelings known through the various platforms of social media.

Daniel had never taken them seriously, describing them as venomous trolls who feared the old world order was in danger of disintegrating.

Governments and corporations he'd criticized had been more subtle in their condemnation of him, venting their anger through newspaper columns and broadcast interviews.

It hit her then with the force of a bullet that there were probably thousands, maybe even millions, of people who were relieved that Daniel's People-Power blog would now cease to exist.

They would be waking up this morning to the news that he was dead.

And for many of them it would be a cause for celebration.

CHAPTER 15

FAYE, BLESS HER, had draped a dressing gown across the bed for Beth to wear. As Beth slipped it on, she experienced a frisson of guilt for not having expressed more gratitude to the couple for taking her in.

She hadn't wanted to stay here, but she was glad that she had. Last night she'd been in too much of a state to go looking for alternative accommodation. She would probably have ended up in a hotel.

She stood and listened for sounds beyond the door. All was quiet, and she guessed they were still sleeping, having been in bed for only a few hours at most.

She shuffled barefoot into the en-suite bathroom to empty

her bladder. She didn't dare look at herself in the mirror for fear of losing it again. Instead she walked back into the bedroom and over to the window.

The sky above the city was grey and heavy. She could feel her heart twisting in her chest as she remembered how much Daniel had loved the view from up here. It was the main reason he'd been so keen to buy the flat.

She stifled a sob and turned away from the window. Her things had been placed on the chest of drawers. Watch, purse, mobile phone. She picked up her phone and saw that it had been switched off. Had she done that herself or had Faye done it so that she wouldn't be disturbed?

She switched it on and discovered she'd had five missed calls and four text messages. Four of the calls were from numbers she didn't recognize. The fifth was from their friend and neighbour Joseph Kessel. He'd also sent a text to say that he couldn't believe what had happened and would come and see her as soon as he returned to Southampton.

Tabitha Ferguson had also sent a text to express condolences, along with two of her friends from the gym who had seen the news on the television.

Beth put the phone back on the dresser and stepped out into the hall. She was gasping for a drink, and she was sure that Faye and William wouldn't mind if she made herself a cup of tea.

She walked through to the kitchen area of the open plan flat, filled the electric kettle and switched it on.

She purposely avoided looking across the room at the door leading to the balcony. She knew that if she did, she would visualize Daniel falling to his death.

She plucked a mug off a stand next to the sink and then got milk from the fridge. But when she opened the chrome teabag container on the worktop she found it was empty.

She started looking in the cupboards and quickly discovered that although the layout was the same as her own kitchen, things were stored differently.

The cupboard in which she and Daniel kept packets of

coffee, tea and biscuits, was filled with cookbooks, instruction leaflets and several cardboard box files.

Just as Beth was about to close the door, something caught her eye. On the spine of one of the files were the words DANIEL PRINCE.

She frowned and felt her face tighten. Behind her the kettle started to boil and squeal, but she ignored it and instinctively reached in the cupboard and took down the file.

Her curiosity was aroused to such a degree that she couldn't possibly have just left it there and carried on making the tea. She put the box down on the worktop and opened it up. When she saw what was inside, a jolt of unease made her shudder.

The box was filled with newspaper cuttings and photographs that featured Daniel. There were also sheets of A4 paper containing pasted-on passages from some of his blogs.

Beth hadn't realized that so much had been written about him and that so many newspapers and magazines had carried his photo during the past year or so.

But even more surprising was the fact that their neighbours had a secret file on him. It was more than a little odd. In fact, it struck her as downright creepy.

'I didn't realize you were up, Beth.'

Faye's voice behind her almost made her jump out of her skin. She spun round, dropping a pile of cuttings on the floor.

'Oh shit.'

Faye reached out and switched off the kettle. Then she looked at Beth and gestured towards the box file.

'I'm not sure it's a good idea for you to look through those,' she said. 'It will only upset you.'

Beth's confusion quickly turned to anger, and her eyebrows curled into a scowl.

'Never mind about that,' she said. 'Why the fuck have you been collecting all this stuff on Daniel? You've never mentioned it to us.'

'I can explain,' Faye said, her tone defensive. 'I assure you it's nothing sinister.'

'Really? Then you'd better put my mind at rest, Faye, because right now I'm really confused.'

CHAPTER 16

DANIEL PRINCE'S SUDDEN death was the lead story on every morning news programme and featured on most of the late-edition front pages.

Temple was taken aback by the sheer level of interest. He hadn't realized that Prince was such a high-profile figure. When, he wondered, did bloggers become A-list celebrities?

By 7 a.m., at least thirty reporters, photographers and TV camera operators had converged on the Riverview apartment complex. Some were reporting live from the scene via satellite links. Others were rushing around, getting sound bites and quotes from everyone who entered and left the building.

And this was all happening before the police had issued a statement confirming that there was now a reason to believe that Prince might have been murdered.

Temple was no longer at the Riverview complex. For the last couple of hours he'd been monitoring the coverage from the operations room of the Major Investigations Team. This happened to be only about a mile from all the action inside the city's central police headquarters overlooking the docks.

When he'd arrived the office had been empty. Now it was filling up with detectives responding to the message that had gone out, ordering them to attend a 7.30 a.m. briefing.

Angel was among them, of course, looking fresh, eager and as attractive as ever. The mere sight of her lifted Temple's spirits, reminding him yet again that fate had been kind to him for once by bringing her into his life.

After Erin he never thought he would love again, but he did love Angel with all his heart. And being her boss as well as her boyfriend made him feel lucky twice over.

This morning, she was wearing black pressed trousers and a smart beige blouse, which seemed to be the uniform of choice for most of the female detectives in the building. It suited Angel's slim figure and with her hair pulled back in a severe pony tail, she looked sexy and sophisticated.

He watched her walk across the room to her workstation. She acknowledged him with a quick smile and he smiled back. At work they had to maintain a respectful distance, and he couldn't show her any favouritism. When their affair began after she moved down from London to join MIT, it had been a bit awkward. For a time they kept it secret. But after a while it became easier, and since the rest of the team had a lot of respect for Angel, it was no longer an issue.

She was the only detective, apart from Dave Vaughan, who was up to speed on what had been happening during the night. That was because she'd called Temple on his mobile while he was still at the scene.

Now it was time for the rest of the team to be put in the picture and for the investigation into the strange death of Daniel Prince to begin in earnest.

The turnout was a hundred per cent. Even those detectives who were supposed to be on a day off had come in.

They were joined by a bunch of uniformed officers and several civilians from media liaison.

Chief Superintendent Beresford was there too, but unlike Temple he'd found the time to go home to shower and change. He was now looking refreshed and energized in a bespoke blue suit and red tie. Temple, on the other hand, was limp with fatigue and sporting a dark, five o'clock shadow.

He stood in front of the evidence board at one end of the room and raised a hand to get everyone's attention. When he had it, he cleared his throat and said, 'Welcome to morning prayers, everyone, and thank you for coming in at short notice. We have a lot to get through so I'll get straight on with it.'

He scratched his chin thoughtfully, then spoke in a tone that was even and controlled.

'At ten o'clock last night, 33-year-old Daniel Prince, the well-known blogger and activist, was killed when he plunged to the ground from his tenth floor balcony. A post-mortem will get underway soon, but it appears he died from the massive injuries he sustained.

'Initially we were convinced he'd jumped. He was apparently alone in the flat because his girlfriend, Beth Fletcher, was visiting her father in Manchester. We also found a suicide note to her which had been typed on his computer just before it happened and left on a pillow in their bedroom.

'However, during the forensic sweep of the flat, we came across evidence suggesting he may have been murdered.'

Temple pointed to a large, flat screen TV that had been wheeled into position next to the evidence board.

'Before we go into detail, I'd like to run this short video sequence from the security camera covering the front of the apartment building,' he said. 'It shows Prince hitting the ground. Be warned, it's quite shocking, so if you think it might cause you to bring up your breakfast, then turn away now.'

Temple had already seen the clip, but he forced himself to watch it again. And for the second time he felt his scalp tingle and his jaw stiffen.

Even without sound it was a horrifying spectacle. Daniel Prince's body flew into shot and slammed onto the concrete, throwing up a shower of blood. And then it just lay there, as more blood pooled around his head.

Forty-five seconds later, the concierge, George Reese, walked into frame, peered closely at the body and then hurried back inside the lobby.

Temple switched off the TV using the remote and paused for a moment before speaking so that everyone could collect their thoughts. Several people in the audience were shaking their heads and he noticed that Angel was sitting with a hand over her mouth.

'So that's what happens when a body hits the ground from ten floors up,' Temple said. Then he left it a beat before continuing. 'Dave is going to explain why it might not have been suicide. But first let me just state what is becoming increasingly obvious – that this is a highly sensitive investigation because of the identity of the deceased.

'There's a great deal of concern all the way up the chain of command to the Home Secretary and beyond. You're no doubt all aware that Prince was a successful online activist. He promoted causes through his People-Power blog. In the process he upset a lot of people in positions of power, including those four ministers who resigned yesterday from the government.

'Now because of that, some of his supporters have already taken to social media to claim that he must have been the victim of a government-backed conspiracy. I'm told that Twitter and Facebook are abuzz with wild accusations against everyone from the Prime Minster and the CIA to the Russian mafia and the Chinese government.

'And all this hysteria is going to present us with a serious problem. You see, not only are we going to have to tread carefully, but we also need to bear in mind that Prince would have had a ton of enemies – including those he targeted in his campaigns and those who've been worried that he was becoming too influential. I'm talking about individuals, organizations, governments and companies.

'It's clear that all of them would have had their own reasons for wanting to stop him stirring up trouble through his blogs. The thing is, did any of them decide to do something about it?'

CHAPTER 17

DAVE VAUGHAN BEGAN his presentation by referring to the evidence board. He'd spent the past hour getting it prepared.

On it was a photocopy of the suicide note and photographs of Prince while he was alive, his apartment block, the balcony, his body on the ground, and a close-up of the listening device found beneath the breakfast bar.

He had his own copy of the note, and he held it up and read it aloud for the benefit of those who weren't aware of the contents.

'When we showed this to his girlfriend, she claimed he couldn't possibly have written it,' he said. 'She insists he wasn't depressed, and when he spoke to her by phone early yesterday evening he was apparently in a buoyant mood. The concierge, who was the last person to see him when he got back about six, said much the same. We'll get a look at Prince's medical records today, but no anti-depressant tablets were found in the flat.'

Vaughan explained that Prince's fingerprints were on the note, but they weren't on his laptop's mouse and keyboard.

'This was because cleaning fluid had been applied to them,' he said. 'But it's hard to believe that he would have wiped the laptop clean himself after typing the note. There would have been absolutely no point if he intended to top himself. So it has to be possible that someone else typed the note while wearing gloves so as not to leave prints.'

Vaughan then went on to describe the tracks in the carpet and how they could have been made by shoes or carpet slippers being dragged across the floor towards the balcony. He said the pathologist had been asked to look for carpet fibres during the post-mortem.

'Which brings me to this,' he said, pointing to the picture of the covert listening device. 'This is a GSM audio bug and it was concealed beneath the breakfast bar. It's got a SIM card inside that can be dialled into from anywhere in the world. Once the device is activated the caller can listen to what's going on in the room. It's very high-tech and it's widely available online.'

'The significance of the device can't be underestimated,' Temple chipped in. 'It suggests he was under surveillance. Someone went to a lot of trouble to know what he was up to. I've asked for checks to be carried out on his phones and computer to see if they've also been bugged and hacked.'

'Maybe his girlfriend put it there to see if he was up to no good,' one of the uniformed officers said. 'Or perhaps he put it there himself to check on her.'

'That is possible, I suppose,' Temple conceded. 'However, I'm inclined to believe it was planted by a third party. Someone who needed to attach it to a charger because they couldn't get regular access to the flat to change the battery.'

There was silence for several seconds as everyone processed this information.

Then Vaughan carried on and said that the building had been in virtual lockdown since last night.

'According to the concierge, no one left the block in the brief period after Prince fell to his death and before the police arrived on the scene,' he said. 'He knows because he continued to man the reception desk until we arrived. We then secured the area, and I can confirm that nobody left during the rest of the night. The lockdown is still in place this morning. We're not allowing anyone to leave until we've recorded details of who they are and where they're going.'

It was Angel who put her hand up to ask the obvious question.

'Is that because you think the killer or killers are still in the building?' she said.

Vaughan nodded. 'Well, that's the assumption, unless they somehow managed to sneak out undetected. But the concierge says the fire escape and service entrance are locked, monitored and alarmed. So the only way in and out of the block is through the main entrance at the front.'

'So how many residents are there?' Angel asked.

'Sixty-five altogether,' Vaughan said. 'But ten of them were away last night for whatever reason. So we're talking about no less than fifty-five possible suspects.'

Vaughan handed back to Temple, who told the team about his conversation with Hari Basu.

'We need to have a closer look at the guy,' he said. 'He had a personal grudge against Prince, and he struck me as someone who might lose his rag and take things too far. He says he didn't see Prince yesterday, but there's no way of knowing if he's telling the truth.'

At this point the various assignments were handed out. Five detectives would go back to the Riverview complex to conduct interviews, two others would examine the footage from the cameras in and around the building. Vaughan volunteered to dig up everything he could on Daniel Prince, and Temple said he wanted Angel to go with him to the mortuary. The rest of the team were told to run checks on the residents.

Before the meeting broke up, Beresford declared that for the time being he still wanted this to be treated as a suspicious death inquiry and not a murder investigation.

'Before anyone asks me why, I need to tell you that this is an instruction that's just come from the Chief Constable himself,' he said. 'He in turn has been leaned on by someone high up in London. It seems they've gone into damage-limitation mode because they're worried about the public backlash if and when we confirm that Prince was murdered. So they want us to be a hundred per cent sure before we announce it.'

This was news to Temple, but he could understand the need for caution. He still wasn't entirely persuaded that Prince didn't commit suicide. Sure, the evidence uncovered by forensics was strange and compelling, but it was still only circumstantial.

'There's one other thing I need to mention,' Beresford said. 'The Met's Domestic Extremism Unit have decided to take an interest in this case because Prince was apparently a person of interest to them.'

Temple felt his hackles rise. 'What's that supposed to mean?'

Beresford shrugged. 'I can only assume he's one of the thousands of people in this country who are considered domestic extremists and are therefore on their watch list.'

A low murmur spread around the room. They were all familiar with the unit whose long-winded formal title was the National Domestic Extremism and Disorder Intelligence Unit, or NDEDIU.

It was a covert national police unit operated by the Met and it used surveillance techniques, undercover officers, paid informants and intercepts to monitor campaigners who were listed on its confidential database. The controversial unit was shrouded in secrecy and had attracted a huge amount of criticism from civil liberties groups.

Temple, like most other serving police officers in the UK, knew very little about it.

'You should also know that one of the unit's senior officers is winging her way to Southampton as we speak,' Beresford said. 'Her remit is to offer information and advice, whatever that means. So we can only hope she proves to be a help and not a hindrance.'

CHAPTER 18

'I TOLD YOU, Beth,' Faye Connor said. 'There's nothing sinister about it. William and I have followed Daniel's blog since we moved in and discovered he was living right next door.'

Beth shook her head. 'But that doesn't explain why you kept a box full of cuttings and photos hidden away in a cupboard.'

'What's to explain? Daniel was a celebrity of sorts, and we became big fans just like a huge number of other people who believed in what he was doing. We befriended him on Facebook and followed him on Twitter. Then a few months ago we decided to collect stuff to eventually put into a scrapbook.'

Beth was confused. Faye and William Connor just didn't seem the type to idolize someone in that way, especially not a man whose notoriety stemmed from whipping up public anger through an online blog. They were intelligent, well-educated people. He was a kind of business consultant and she was an event organizer. They weren't your typical celebrity groupies.

But then, why would Faye lie about it? What other possible

reason could there be for amassing a collection of photos and news stories about Daniel?

'Is everything OK?'

They both turned as Faye's husband appeared suddenly in his dressing gown, sleepy-eyed and unshaven.

'I didn't realize you were both up until I heard voices,' he said. Then he spotted the box file resting on the worktop and the cuttings that had fallen on the floor.

He leaned on the breakfast bar, his brow arched, and said, 'What's going on?'

Faye was quick to respond. 'Beth happened to come across our box of photos and cuttings. I was just explaining that we're collecting them to put in a scrapbook.'

A look passed between the couple that Beth wasn't able to interpret. Then William forced a smile and said, 'That's right. To us, Daniel was an unsung hero, Beth. We supported his campaigns and we're honoured to have known him. Those things are like mementoes.'

Beth breathed out a sigh and closed her eyes. She felt foolish suddenly for overreacting. She should have been pleased that the Connors had thought so much of Daniel that they wanted to keep a record of his rise to fame.

Faye put a hand on her arm. 'I'm sorry we've upset you, Beth. We really didn't think we were doing anything wrong.'

Beth opened her eyes, held back a sob. 'I'm the one who should apologize, Faye. My head's all over the place and it confused me for a second. That's all. It's good that you were so interested in Daniel. He would have been chuffed. I mean that.'

'Look, why don't you go back to bed?' Faye said. 'I'll bring you in a cup of tea.'

'I'd rather have a shower and get dressed. There are things I have to do. I need to call my dad and then find out what the police are doing now that they realize Daniel was murdered.'

'Are you sure that's what the detective told you?' William said. 'When they spoke to us they gave the impression that they believed it was suicide.'

'Well, that was before they found evidence that convinced them otherwise,' Beth said.

'What evidence?'

Beth shook her head. 'I don't know. I was in too much of a state to take it in. Before the detective brought me back here he said he would talk to me about it this morning.'

'Well, I'm sure that if Daniel was murdered then the police will soon find out who did it,' William said.

Beth felt a knot tighten in her throat. 'I won't rest until they do,' she said. 'No matter how long it takes them.'

Beth managed to hold back the tears while she took a shower in the en-suite bathroom. But it wasn't easy because she couldn't stop thinking about Daniel as the steaming jets battered her face and body.

The grief that engulfed her was all-consuming. It numbed her senses and made it hard for her to focus on anything other than the painful memories that flashed through her mind.

As she towelled herself dry, a sudden, intense flashback took her breath away. She remembered how on Saturday she and her father had watched Daniel as he stood with the other protestors outside Downing Street in London.

Oh my god, she thought. The last time she saw him alive was on television along with most other people. On the Friday when she went to Manchester, she left before he got up in order to catch an early train. She'd kissed his forehead in the dark, but he'd been half-asleep and had barely responded.

So she didn't even have a last intimate moment with him to remember and cherish. How cruel was that?

The thought of it brought a wave of emotion to the surface, but the ringing of her mobile phone gave her a reason to resist letting go. She rushed over to the chest of drawers to pick it up, thinking it might be her father.

'Is that you, Miss Fletcher? It's DCI Temple here. We spoke last night.'

'Have you found out who killed Daniel?' she said.

'I'm afraid that's not why I'm calling, Miss Fletcher. I

wondered if it would be possible for you or someone you care to nominate to come along and formally identify Mr Prince's body before the post-mortem is carried out. I know you saw him briefly last night, but—'

'I'll do it,' she broke in. 'I want to see him.'

'Are you sure you feel up to it?'

'Of course. I have to.'

The detective told her he would arrange for a patrol car to pick her up in an hour from in front of her building. He also said he'd update her on the investigation after the deed was done.

Beth hung up, tied her wet hair back in a ponytail and put on the same clothes she'd worn the night before. She was applying a layer of foundation to the inflamed redness around her eyes when Faye stepped into the room without knocking to see if she was all right, and to tell her that she had a visitor.

'It's Joseph from downstairs,' Faye said. 'He just got back and was told you were here.'

Beth composed herself as best she could and followed Faye into the living room. Joseph Kessel was sitting on the sofa next to William Connor, and they were having a muted conversation.

They both looked up when she entered, but Beth's attention was immediately drawn beyond them to the large television mounted on an Ikea unit.

It was showing a full-frame photograph of Daniel, and it sent a high-voltage shock though her body. A small cry escaped her lips and she felt the blood rush to her head.

'Turn that off, William,' Faye said.

Beth shook her head and held up a hand. 'No, please leave it on. It's all right. I want to hear what they have to say.'

As she moved further into the room, Joseph rose swiftly to his feet and came towards her. She found the sight of him oddly comforting because he had been Daniel's only real friend in the block since shortly after he'd moved in nine months ago. He was thirty-eight, with short, dark hair and sharp facial features. You could tell that beneath his tight black T-shirt and jeans, his body was tough and lean, stripped of every ounce of fat.

He gave her a hug and said, 'I don't think I can find the words to tell you how sorry I am, Beth.'

She closed her eyes, lost for a brief moment in the warmth of his embrace. If it hadn't been for what was happening on the television, she would probably have sobbed into his shoulder. But the newsreader's voice seized her attention again, prompting her to snap open her eyes and pull away from Joseph.

Daniel's picture had been replaced by footage from Saturday's demonstration in London against the four politicians. Then it cut to a live shot of their building with a reporter standing in front of a small crowd of people.

'Daniel Prince's death has come as a shock to his legion of online followers,' the reporter said. 'Since first light this morning, they've been gathering outside the building where he lived to show their respect and to make it known that they don't believe he committed suicide. Here are just a few of the views being expressed.'

The first vox pop was with a young woman in a woollen hat who described herself as devastated.

'Daniel Prince encouraged me and millions of others to realize that we could make a difference,' she said. 'In doing so he must have terrified the establishment. I'm absolutely sure that's why he was killed. And I'm not alone in thinking that.'

Next was an elderly man with grey hair who looked straight into the camera as he spoke.

'Unlike our pathetic, corrupt politicians, Daniel Prince managed to engage with the public through his wonderful blog. I followed him because he wrote about issues that were close to my heart. It's nothing short of a tragedy that he's gone.'

A black man in a high-vis jacket said, 'It's obvious to anyone with half a brain that Daniel Prince didn't kill himself. It's too much of a coincidence that it should happen just as he was causing massive problems for the government. This smacks of a diabolical conspiracy.'

And a young man in a smart business suit said, 'Daniel

Prince's inspiring blog made me believe that through people power, we could reverse unfair policies and decisions. If it hadn't been for him, those politicians would still be taking the piss, those Premier League soccer clubs would be ripping off their supporters with sky high ticket prices, Barclays Bank would be paying out obscene bonuses to staff who don't deserve them, and the country would still be forking out millions in foreign aid to a murderous dictatorship in Africa.'

After the sound bite sequence ended, the reporter handed back to the studio and the newsreader explained that Hampshire police would be holding a press conference later in the day, and a post-mortem would shortly be carried out on Mr Prince's body.

He then went on to say that in the last few minutes, the Prime Minister had issued a statement saying that what had happened was tragic and his thoughts were with Mr Prince's fiancée, Beth Fletcher. He also strongly denied that the government was somehow involved in a conspiracy to silence the young activist, describing the allegations as ridiculous.

'I hope he's telling the truth,' Beth said suddenly. 'Because if he isn't, there's no way that the investigation into Daniel's murder will be anything other than a whitewash and a sham.'

CHAPTER 19

TEMPLE KNEW THAT Angel hated visiting the mortuary, and normally he wouldn't have asked her to go with him.

But he also knew that she was good at dealing with grieving relatives. It was one of the strengths he had identified during those first few months when she came to work for him in Southampton.

She seemed to know instinctively how to respond to the needs of those whose worlds fall apart when they have to identify the corpse of a loved one.

And he had a feeling that Beth Fletcher was going to need all the support she could get, despite the fact that she had sounded quietly confident on the phone.

It was clear to him already that she and Daniel Prince had been very much in love. His death had shaken the very foundations of her existence.

He found himself hoping that for her sake they would be able to prove that he was murdered. He didn't like to think that she'd have to spend the rest of her life wondering why her fiancé had decided he'd rather die than be with her.

'What's your gut feeling on this one, Jeff?' Angel asked as they drove towards the mortuary in his car.

'It's a tough one,' he said. 'When I got there last night it seemed like an open and shut suicide, especially when we found the note. But now I'm not so sure. The involvement of the Domestic Extremism Unit makes it even more of a puzzler.'

'I don't know much about them.'

'Nobody does. They operate in secret and target anyone they believe has the potential to cause trouble. We're not talking about full-blown terror suspects. They leave those to MI5 and the Counter Terrorism Command. These guys focus on journalists, activists, bloggers and civil liberties campaigners.'

'I seem to remember they've been in the news for all the wrong reasons.'

Temple nodded. 'There was a big fuss when their undercover officers had affairs with animal rights activists. Then they were caught tapping the phones of newspaper journalists for no good reason.'

'So why were they interested in Daniel Prince?'

'That's obvious. Because through his blog, he was becoming far too popular for their liking. He was managing to influence public opinion on a range of topics he chose to pursue, including the scandal of those four politicians caught avoiding tax.'

'So do you think the unit planted the listening device in his flat?'

'I think it's a strong possibility,' Temple said.

They fell silent for a spell, and Temple knew that they were both thinking the unthinkable. It was Angel who put her thoughts into words.

'I suppose it's not beyond the realms of possibility that they also had a hand in his death then,' she said. 'If not directly, then through another clandestine branch of the security services.'

Temple rolled out his bottom lip and the muscles around his eyes tightened. The idea, as far-fetched as it sounded, had already burrowed its way into his head.

He let his breath escape in a low whistle and said, 'You and I both know that the security agencies carry out illegally sanctioned acts in this country on a fairly regular basis. And that includes ensuring that certain targeted individuals disappear in the interests of national security.'

Angel looked at him. 'So your answer to my question is yes then. You do think it's possible that Prince was murdered by one or more of our own esteemed colleagues.'

'Assuming he *was* murdered then I'm ashamed to say that we can't in all honesty rule it out,' he said.

The more Temple thought about the involvement of the Domestic Extremism Unit, the more uneasy he began to feel.

The unit's supposed remit was to gather information on extremist protestors so that the police could assess the threat they posed to public safety, and to investigate crimes linked to protests.

He'd seen an unofficial estimate claiming that it employed over a hundred officers, many of whom spent months and sometimes years working undercover across the UK.

But since it had been set up, the unit had been in the firing line. There was outrage that officers regularly monitored peaceful protests and photographed those taking part. There was disquiet too that detectives were infiltrating political groups and spying on people who had never committed a crime and probably never would. People such as bloggers, activists, journalists and even politicians. And there had been widespread condemnation because scores of officers had created false identities using documents relating to dead people, including children.

Not so long ago, a group of journalists had launched a legal action against Scotland Yard after discovering that the Met had been recording their professional activities on the unit's secret database – a database designed to monitor so-called domestic extremists.

One video journalist discovered that he was the subject of 130 entries detailing his movements, including what he wore when he attended demonstrations as a member of the media.

Other individuals had found they were on the secret database by submitting requests through the Freedom of Information Act. These included a pensioner who was targeted because he campaigned for peace and human rights. And a Green Party politician who learned that officers had been tracking her political movements for no less than ten years.

The controversy over covert operations and surveillance had been raging now for several years. There was growing concern among people generally that the police were overstepping their powers by invading the privacy of so many people. And that they were using the information they collected to stifle dissent, thus undermining the very fabric of democracy in the UK.

Intelligence gathering was a vital weapon in the fight against subversive groups and homegrown terrorists. But Temple wasn't alone in fearing that the police – and for that matter, the government – were fast losing the trust and support of a sceptical public.

A public that had become deeply suspicious of what was really going on around them – and were therefore only too willing to believe that a young online blogger could actually be murdered simply because his popular protest campaigns had captured the hearts and minds of so many people.

CHAPTER 20

TEMPLE HAD EXPECTED Beth Fletcher to arrive at the mortuary accompanied by her neighbours, Mr and Mrs Connor. Instead she was with a young, thirty-something man who had a mild accent and introduced himself as Joseph Kessel.

Temple recalled the concierge saying that he was the Israeli who lived on the fifth floor and occasionally went for drinks with Daniel Prince. He'd been away on a business trip last night so he had missed all the action.

He had his arm around Beth's waist as Temple introduced them to Angel and told them what was going to happen.

Beth listened, but he wasn't sure how much she was taking in. Her face was etched with grief and she looked exhausted, her eyes red-rimmed and vacant. She explained that she had just come off the phone to her father, who had taken the news badly.

'He can't believe it's happened,' she said. 'And neither can I.'

A moment later, Temple and Angel escorted her into the room where Dr Matherson had already prepared the body and laid it out on a stainless steel table. Sheets covered the injuries, but enough of Prince's face was visible under the harsh white light.

Beth walked up to the table and looked down at the man she had planned to spend the rest of her life with. The blood retreated from her face, and her breathing quickened until it wheezed out from between tight lips.

'Can you confirm that this is Daniel Prince?' Temple said gently.

She swallowed hard and nodded. 'It's him. It's my lovely Daniel.'

She started to cry silently, her chest rising and falling as she fought to suppress the sobs. Then she leaned over and kissed Prince on the mouth, whispering something to him that Temple didn't hear.

When she straightened up she took a tissue from her pocket

to wipe her eyes.

'Bye, bye, my love,' she said. 'I'm going to miss you so much.'

At that point she broke down completely, and Angel rushed forward to put an arm around her shoulders.

It was another five minutes before Beth allowed herself to be led back out of the room.

Angel stayed close to Beth until she stopped crying and regained her composure. Temple then explained that they wanted to talk to her about Daniel and she agreed to go along to the central police station.

To keep it informal they used Temple's office, and when Beth asked if Kessel could come in with her, Temple agreed.

It was Beth who asked the first question. She wanted to know when she could move back into her flat.

'Hopefully tomorrow,' Temple said. 'The forensic team are working there today and I'll let you know as soon as they've finished. In the meantime, DI Metcalfe here will arrange to pick up anything you need such as a change of clothes.'

'But after what you told me last night, I'm assuming they've found something that proves Daniel didn't kill himself,' she said.

Temple chose his words carefully. 'What they've found is not conclusive, but it does throw up some serious questions.'

'Such as?'

Temple asked them not to repeat what he was going to tell them and began with the lack of fingerprints on the mouse and keyboard.

'Daniel had a thing about cleaning his laptop,' Beth said. 'He wiped it with the fluid at the end of each day.'

'And I take it he didn't wear gloves when he typed.'

'Of course not. Why would he?'

'That's what I thought.'

'So that means somebody else must have typed the note,' she said. 'Just like I told you.'

'That's what we're trying to determine, Miss Fletcher.'

He then told her that there had been no sign of a struggle in the flat, but there were scuff marks on the carpet, which might have been caused by someone being dragged across the floor.

A choking sound rushed out of her on hearing this, and tears gleamed in her eyes. But she managed to hold it together and told him to continue.

'We also found a miniature listening device,' he said. 'It was concealed beneath the breakfast bar.'

The shock was evident in her expression. Her brow bunched up and her mouth dropped open.

'Are you saying that someone bugged their flat, Inspector?' Kessel said.

Temple nodded. 'It's a fairly sophisticated device and contains a SIM card. When the number on the card was called, the device was triggered and the person on the other end of the line was able to eavesdrop on conversations in the room.'

Beth suddenly looked as though she was going to be sick. 'My god,' she shrieked. 'That's horrible. I can't believe it.'

'But who the hell put it there?' Kessel said. 'And how did they get access to the flat?'

Temple asked Beth if she'd had any knowledge of it. She was taken aback.

'How dare you ask me that?' she steamed. 'What do you take me for?'

'The question had to be asked, Miss Fletcher,' he said. 'It's the kind of thing couples do when they don't trust each other.'

Her eyes flared. 'Jesus, is that what you think? That Daniel and I didn't trust each other?'

'Of course not.'

'Well, let me put you straight on that, Detective. There *were* no trust issues between us. We weren't spying on each other. We were in love and we were happy together. I know nothing about any bug. I swear.'

Temple apologized and left it a beat to get things back on track. Then he asked Beth if Daniel socialized with any other people in the building.

She drew a deep breath and said, 'No one, apart from

Joseph. But as a couple we had several friends, although we didn't go out much. We always seemed to be so busy. Me with my writing and Daniel with his blog.'

'Is that all he did – write the blog?'

'Yes, but there was more to it than you probably imagine. He updated it every day and had hundreds of messages and queries that he tried to respond to. He also wrote a monthly column for *The Guardian* and appeared as a guest on radio and television programmes. In fact, during this past year he's been very much in demand.'

'So why did his blog become so popular? There are millions of bloggers and activists out there gagging for attention.'

'It's a question he was asked many times,' Beth said. 'But he didn't really have an answer. He just put it down to the fact that what he wrote resonated with the British public. He wasn't a political activist in the sense that he was staunchly right or left. He just picked issues that were close to his heart and that most other people also felt strongly about.'

She dabbed at her eyes with a tissue and added, 'It also helped that he appeared on the scene at a time when trust in governments, politicians and everyone else in authority was at an all-time low. His People-Power slogan struck a chord. People started to think that perhaps they could make things better and fairer if they clubbed together.'

She paused to look beyond him at something that wasn't in the room. Temple watched as her eyes seemed to drift in and out of focus.

After a couple of seconds, he said, 'When you spoke to him on the phone yesterday, did he give any indication that he might have been expecting a visitor?'

'None at all,' she answered. 'He was busy watching the news and looking forward to me getting home.'

Temple sat forward and rested his elbows on the desk.

'What about enemies, Miss Fletcher? Do you know of anyone who might have wanted to hurt Daniel?'

'The only person he ever fell out with was Hari Basu who lives on the eighth floor. You should talk to him.'

'We have.'

'So is he a suspect?'

'Everyone is a suspect at this stage, Miss Fletcher. But you must remember that it's extremely rare for ill-feeling between neighbours to lead to murder. Is there anyone else you can think of, anyone at all?'

She suddenly blinked rapidly and her lips quivered. 'There are thousands of people out there who won't be sorry that Daniel is dead. He made enemies by fighting for the things he believed in. You should check his email and Twitter accounts. He's had hundreds of nasty messages, many of them threatening. And there were anonymous phone calls, too. He was warned more than once that if he didn't stop campaigning about certain issues bad things would happen to him.'

'Did he receive any death threats?'

She hunched her shoulders. 'A few. But he chose to ignore them. He told me that if he allowed them to bother him he wouldn't have been able to do what he did.'

'It must have worried you,' Temple said.

She nodded. 'It did, but I realize now that I wasn't as concerned as I should have been. That was a big mistake. As his girlfriend, I should have been more protective. I should have realized that what he was doing would eventually have serious consequences. For that, I'll never be able to forgive myself.'

A bout of trembling gripped her suddenly, and something close to panic filled her eyes. Then she slumped forward across Temple's desk and surrendered herself to another cry.

CHAPTER 21

'THERE'S SOMETHING YOU should know, Inspector,' Joseph Kessel said. 'I couldn't mention it in front of Beth.'

He spoke up as the two women left the room. At Temple's

suggestion, Angel had taken Beth to the toilets to calm her down and clean her up. Once she'd started crying, she hadn't been able to stop and had become quite distressed.

'What is it you think I should know, Mr Kessel?' Temple said.

Kessel shifted in his chair and coughed into his fist.

'It's something Daniel told me a couple of months ago,' he said. 'We were having a drink in the pub across the road as we often did on a Friday evening, usually when Beth was working away from home. On this occasion, Daniel had more than his usual two glasses of wine. So he was a little drunk and extremely talkative.'

'So what did he tell you?'

Kessel ran his tongue over his teeth and said, 'He confessed to me that an affair he'd been having with a married woman had ended that very day, and he was gutted about it. In fact, he even wept a little.'

Temple felt a ripple of unease. This was something he definitely hadn't expected.

'Is that all he told you or did he elaborate?'

Kessel shook his head. 'He wouldn't say any more than that, and the next day when he'd sobered up, he told me to forget he'd said it. And he made me promise never to tell Beth.'

'Do you know if she suspected that he'd been unfaithful?'

'I don't think so. Whenever he was with her he made it seem like she was the centre of his world.'

'Did he speak to you about it after that day?'

'No. I raised it once and he got annoyed so I didn't mention it again and neither did he.'

'So how did this affect him? Miss Fletcher says he wasn't depressed.'

Kessel shrugged. 'Well, I wasn't with him as often as she was. But I did notice that whenever we went for a drink after that night he was quieter than he'd been before. And maybe a little melancholy.'

Temple gave it some thought, said, 'Do you know if he might have confided in another friend or relative?'

'I very much doubt it. As far as I know he didn't have any close friends, and as you know, his parents are dead.'

More questions were piling up in Temple's mind, but he didn't get a chance to ask them because at that moment Angel and Beth returned from the toilets. Beth was still pretty upset so Temple told her to go and get some rest.

'We can talk again later, Miss Fletcher,' he said. 'Will you be going back to Mr and Mrs Connor's flat?'

'I suppose I'll have to.'

'In that case, DI Metcalfe will come along shortly and get whatever you need from your own flat. Will that be OK?'

Beth nodded. 'I'll make a list of things I need.'

Kessel got to his feet and took her arm. Before walking out of Temple's office, Beth turned and said, 'Please find out who did this to Daniel, Inspector. The future will be bad enough, but it'll be a thousand times worse if his killer or killers are not brought to justice.'

CHAPTER 22

AFTER BETH HAD gone, Temple briefed Angel on his conversation with Kessel. She was less surprised than he was that Daniel Prince had apparently been having an affair.

'So there might have been trust issues between them after all,' she said. 'In which case, Beth Fletcher could have planted the listening device to try to catch him out.'

'That's assuming she knew or suspected,' Temple said.

'Well, if she didn't, she's in for another nasty shock if and when it gets out.'

Temple made a *tch* sound through his teeth. He didn't believe that Beth had bugged her own flat. Her shocked reaction when he'd told her about the device had seemed totally genuine.

'Look, go over there now and get her things from the flat,'

he said. 'Then have another word with her, and see if you can get her to open up some more.'

'And what are you going to do?' Angel asked.

'I need to find out more about Daniel Prince and his blog. I'll also speak to the skipper about how we handle the media. He's under pressure to stage a press conference as soon as possible.'

'So will he announce that this is now a murder inquiry?'

'Good question,' Temple said. 'But I'm not sure I know the answer.'

Temple fired up his desktop computer and his Google home page appeared. He typed Daniel Prince's name in the search box and it became instantly clear that there were going to be thousands of hits. There were news stories from around the world, an entry in Wikipedia and a plethora of video clips of him giving interviews and standing with the protesters in London.

It took Temple a few seconds to locate the People-Power blog. He'd never visited it before. In fact, he couldn't think of a single blog he did visit on anything like a regular basis.

What struck him at first was how vibrant it was. It reminded him of the front page of a tabloid newspaper. The headline read: *We've done it – they've resigned!*

This was a reference, of course, to the four politicians who had stepped down as a result of the avoidance of tax scandal. The article had been posted at some time yesterday afternoon or early evening before Prince died.

In it, he explained what had happened and thanked his followers for turning out in such large numbers to protest.

'It shows that people power is a true force to be reckoned with,' he wrote. 'If we hadn't applied pressure then they would never have gone.'

Down one side of the main page were congratulatory messages from a list of celebrities, including pop stars, actors and a range of other high-profile activists from around the world.

There were also links to Prince's pages on Facebook, Twitter and other social networking sites.

At the bottom of the page was a menu of his other current and forthcoming campaigns. As soon as Temple started going through them he saw why Prince was making enemies of so many powerful people, governments and corporations. They would all have had a clear motive for wanting to shut him up.

One current campaign, which seemed to be gathering momentum judging by the online response, called on the government to stop a Chinese business tycoon from buying up so many of Britain's assets. Prince claimed that the level of investment had got out of hand. The billionaire's Asian corporation already had major stakes in Britain's ports, retail chains, railways and utility companies. Now it was bidding to buy a mobile phone company and five prime development sites in and around London. Prince contested, and so did his followers, that this was not in the interests of the UK.

Another campaign urged the public to demand that drunks who clogged up A & E departments at weekends be made to pay a fine of £300 to cover the cost of their treatment. This issue was gaining traction with over 200,000 people already signed up to an online petition which would soon be delivered to Downing Street.

Among the forthcoming campaigns was one that had already incurred the wrath of the Kremlin. Prince was about to add his weight to a call for people across the world to boycott Russian goods and services in protest at the country's continued aggression against the west. So far the campaign, originally launched in Ukraine, had failed to gain much traction. But with Prince's backing it was set to get a significant boost. The Russian President had accused Prince of being a rabble-rouser who needed to be locked up. And no doubt he would have been if he'd lived in Russia, Temple thought.

Out of curiosity, he moved his Google search on to bloggers around the world who had been persecuted and killed. He was surprised at how many there were.

There was the high-profile case of the blogger in Saudi

Arabia who was publicly lashed for criticizing the country's clerics.

In Mexico, a blogger who campaigned against the country's drug cartels was found beheaded with a note next to his body which read: *This happened to me for not understanding that I shouldn't report on social networks.*

In Bahrain, a blogger accused of inciting hatred against the government died after being beaten and tortured in police custody.

The list went on, and the more Temple learned about campaigning bloggers the more respect he had for them, especially those who knew they were risking their freedom, and even their lives, by pursuing worthy causes.

He would have gone on reading if Vaughan hadn't come into his office to tell him that Beth Fletcher was the subject of a breaking news story on the television.

Temple hurried into the operations room where the monitors were on pause.

'She walked into a media scrum when she went back to the flat,' Vaughan said. 'Then she surprised everyone by stopping to speak to the cameras. You need to see it, guv.'

'Press play then,' Temple said.

Beth was filmed getting out of Joseph Kessel's car in front of her apartment block. In the commentary the reporter said that she'd decided to face the media rather than drive into the building's car park.

Reporters, photographers and camera crews surrounded her as she stood on the forecourt. Behind them a crowd of people jostled with each other to catch sight of her.

Beth took a few seconds to compose herself. Then she began. 'I want you all to know that my fiancé Daniel Prince did not take his own life. I've just come from the police station where the investigating officer confirmed that Daniel was pushed from our balcony last night. He was murdered, and the suicide note that was found was written by someone else, probably the killer.'

Cameras flashed and questions were fired at her as she

paused to take a breath.

Then she continued. 'It's clear to me that my beloved Daniel was murdered because of what he campaigned for on his People-Power blog. Whoever killed him wanted to silence him – along with his followers.

'The police have uncovered evidence that Daniel was under surveillance. A listening device was discovered hidden in the flat. I have no idea who put it there or who is responsible for murdering the man I was going to marry. But I'm shocked that something like this could happen in a country where freedom of speech is supposed to be one of the basic tenets of our democracy.'

Beth choked up suddenly before she could say any more. She covered her mouth with her hand and forced her way through the crowd towards the building's entrance, where a uniformed police officer held the door open for her.

As she disappeared inside, Vaughan muted the TV output and turned to Temple.

'Did you have any idea she was going to say all that stuff, guv?' he said.

Temple issued a heavy sigh. 'I asked her not to, but I should have known she wouldn't listen.'

'So what now?'

'Now we brace ourselves because the media storm is about to turn into a full-blown raging hurricane.'

CHAPTER 23

TEMPLE STAYED IN the operations room and called the team together for a catch-up meeting. He kicked it off by confirming that Daniel Prince had been formally identified by his girlfriend.

He then let it be known what Joseph Kessel had said about Prince having an affair with a married woman.

'It makes this investigation even more complicated,' he said. 'We can't be sure that Beth Fletcher didn't know, so it's conceivable – though unlikely – that she planted the bug herself to spy on him. It also raises the question as to whether the end of his affair affected his state of mind.'

'I can tell you he wasn't being treated for depression,' Vaughan said. 'According to his GP, he hasn't been to the surgery for a couple of years.'

'That doesn't mean he wasn't suffering in silence,' Temple said. 'My guess is we'll never know for sure where he was psychologically. But if we're now working on the basis that he was murdered then it's irrelevant anyway. However, I still want to know how long he was playing away and who it was with. So we should check his phones and emails.'

'We're still trawling through those, guv,' Vaughan said. 'Quite a few of the numbers on his phones have yet to be identified and are probably media organizations. But so far we haven't come across anything that strikes us as suspicious.'

'Well, try to come up with a name for this married woman,' Temple said. 'It could be he had another mobile phone that he kept hidden. Or a confidential email account so he could stay in touch with her. I want to speak to this woman, whoever she is.'

The detectives then took it in turns to provide updates.

Temple was told that nothing useful had turned up during a history check on Prince's computer and tablet device. And he didn't appear to have had any financial problems. He and Beth had a joint bank account containing £45,000, much of which had no doubt been set aside for their wedding.

He was also informed that all the residents in the block had been interviewed and their names fed into the police database. So far none of them appeared to have links with any anarchist groups or foreign governments.

'There's a real mix of people,' Vaughan said. 'Doctors, lawyers, nurses, teachers, IT consultants. Plus a whole range of nationalities – German, Spanish, Russian, Chinese, Asian. Four of the residents have got previous.' He looked at Temple. 'And you and I actually spoke to two of those in the early hours of this morning.'

It turned out that Hari Basu had a police record for grievous bodily harm after a fight with a man outside a pub. Given his aggressive nature, this came as no surprise to Temple.

But he was surprised to learn that the concierge, George Reese, had spent a year in prison and was on the sex offenders register for an attack on a schoolgirl.

The two other residents with form were a man who ten years ago had been convicted of a knife attack outside a pub, and a woman who at one time fraudulently claimed welfare benefits.

'But so far, Hari Basu appears to be the only person in the block who had any kind of personal grudge against Prince,' Vaughan said.

'Anything more from forensics?' Temple asked.

Vaughan shrugged. 'They've found a bunch of fingerprints in the flat, but none of them belong to Basu or Reese and the other two whose prints are on file. We still haven't got prints from all the other residents yet.'

'What about the CCTV footage?' Temple said. 'Have we turned up anything there?'

This was the cue for a young, fresh-faced DC named Tony Wallis to put in his penny's worth. He'd been monitoring the footage from the security cameras covering the outside of the building and inside the lobby.

'I've spotted something that's at odds with what we've been told,' he said. 'According to the concierge, the only people to enter and leave the building yesterday afternoon and evening were residents. But that doesn't appear to be strictly true. Someone in the block did have a visitor.'

Temple felt his interest peak. 'Go on,' he said.

'Well, at just before eight o'clock, a young woman entered the building and was greeted in the lobby by the concierge,' Wallis said. 'She then got into one of the lifts, but I don't know which floor she went to. However, two hours later, at eight minutes past ten, she's captured on the cameras exiting the building while the concierge was outside next to Mr Prince's body. He was standing alongside several other people who'd gathered by that time.'

'Did the concierge speak to the woman?' Temple asked.

'He didn't even notice her, sir. She simply walked out and headed in the other direction without bothering to see what was going on.'

'So what makes you so sure that she was visiting someone in the block? How do you know she doesn't actually live there?'

'It's probably best if I show you, sir,' he said.

The team gathered around DC Wallis's workstation as he brought up the various clips of video footage on his computer.

The first showed the woman entering the building from the outside. She was wearing a short, dark overcoat and had bouncy, shoulder-length fair hair.

But they saw her more clearly on the lobby camera as she approached the desk and smiled at George Reese, who was standing behind the desk and seemed to recognize her.

She looked to be in her mid-to-late twenties and had a slim figure and attractive face.

Reese smiled at her and they exchanged words. He then picked up the desk phone and made a call, presumably to one of the residents. He said something into the phone, nodded, replaced the receiver, and then appeared to tell the woman that she could go up.

She walked to one of the two lifts and pressed the button. The doors slid open immediately and she stepped inside.

Wallis then ran the sequence where she appeared on the same camera as she stepped out of the lift two hours later, and less than ten minutes after Daniel Prince hit the ground.

She walked across the lobby and through the doors. One of the outside cameras picked her up as she threw a glance at the small group of people standing around Prince's body. Then she turned away from them and walked in the opposite direction.

'I was curious to see where she was going so I then checked the footage from several street cameras around the complex,' Wallis said. 'And I got a result.'

He clicked on another clip showing the woman walking through the apartment complex to where several cars were parked at the roadside. She opened the driver's door of a red VW, got in, and then drove off.

By zooming in on the car, Wallis was able to get a clear image of the number plate.

'I ran a check and just got back the details of who owns the vehicle,' he said. 'Her name is Clare Brennan. She's aged twenty eight and lives in Regents Park Road, Shirley.'

'That's good work, Tony,' Temple said.

Wallis grinned. 'But it's not all, sir. I ran the name and Miss Brennan is a known prostitute with a record. A year ago, she was done for assaulting a client whom she claimed refused to pay her. She was given a community service order. Then six months ago, she was fined for drugs possession.'

Temple felt his heart rate go up a notch. He turned to Vaughan and said, 'So we have our first real lead. Terrific. Let's bring Clare Brennan in along with George Reese. I want to know why our little bald friend lied to us.'

CHAPTER 24

BETH STOOD INSIDE the lobby for what seemed a long time. Her heart was thudding hard in her chest and the adrenaline was pounding through her veins at a rate of knots.

She had acted impulsively by speaking to the press. She hadn't been able to resist the opportunity to let the world know that her fiancé hadn't killed himself.

But talking about Daniel had shaken her to the core and filled her head with graphic images of him lying on the ground, his body shattered and drenched in blood.

'Are you all right, Miss Fletcher?'

It was the concierge, speaking from behind his desk. Not bald-headed George, but one of the others whose name escaped her.

'I'm OK,' she said, but it wasn't true because she was having to fight back another avalanche of tears.

One of the uniformed police officers in the lobby came across and asked her if she needed help. She shook her head and looked beyond him at the media pack gawping at her through the window.

It scared her to think that this was how it was going to be for weeks to come; another facet of the unbearable nightmare that her life had become.

She felt someone take hold of her hand and she turned. It was Joseph, who had just emerged from the car park.

'Come on, Beth,' he said. 'Let's get you upstairs.'

On the tenth floor, the door to her flat stood open and she saw a white-suited forensics officer kneeling on the floor in the hallway. She drew a sharp breath and felt her ribs smart.

'Don't look,' Joseph said as he nudged her towards where Faye Connor was standing in the open doorway to the flat next door.

As she stepped inside, Beth was hit by a sharp wave of nausea. She ran to the bathroom where she retched into the sink until her throat was raw.

When she came back out, Joseph said he had to go because he had an appointment.

'It's with a potential client,' he said. 'So I'm reluctant to cry off.'

As a freelance IT consultant, Joseph had to work hard to attract business. It was the same for writers who didn't have a staff job, so Beth quite understood. She thanked him for going with her to the mortuary and police station, and he said he would see her later.

As he was walking out the door, he almost bumped into DI Metcalfe.

Beth introduced her to Faye.

'DI Metcalfe has come to collect some things from the flat,' she said. 'They're not going to let me back in at least until tomorrow.'

'Don't you worry about it,' Faye said. 'You can stay here as long as you need to.'

Faye gestured for them to follow her through to the living room and invited them to make themselves comfortable while she put the kettle on.

Beth went into the spare room and rummaged in her case for a pen and pad. Then she and Angel sat at the dining table while Beth composed a list of what she needed, including a change of clothes, shoes, clean underwear and some toiletries.

'Thank you for doing this for me, Detective Metcalfe,' she said.

'Call me Angel, please. It's short for Angelica.'

Beth looked at the detective properly for the first time. Her face was pleasantly proportioned, not a feature standing out as wrong. She had pale, translucent skin, with high cheek bones and full lips. Her make-up was discreet, but flawless, and she had a pleasant demeanour.

Beth gave her the note and Angel went straight next door.

'I just saw you on the television,' Faye said, as she placed a mug of tea on the table in front of Beth.

'I didn't want people to think that Daniel had committed suicide,' Beth said.

Faye pulled out a chair and sat down. 'If there's anything I can do then you only have to ask.'

Beth managed a small smile. 'You've done more than enough by letting me stay here.'

She remembered that she'd switched her phone off earlier because she was being inundated with calls. So she took it from her pocket and turned it on. Fifteen missed calls and eight text messages. She couldn't face responding to any of them at that moment so she turned it off again.

The room seemed suddenly smaller, as if the walls were closing in. She sat there staring across at the balcony door, her eyes haunted and still.

Then her heart contracted as the memories once again started to cascade through her mind.

Daniel making love to her that last time in their bed and telling her that he loved her.

The pair of them checking out their wedding venue at the hotel in the New Forest.

Daniel blowing out the candles on the cake she made for him for his last birthday.

Daniel on the BBC Newsnight programme talking about his blog and looking oh so handsome.

She remembered too how passionate he'd been about the blog he'd created, and how he'd put his heart and soul into it.

'I know it sounds corny,' he once said to her. 'But I really want it to be a force for good.'

Beth had been with him when he started blogging seven years ago. But he only began to attract attention after his mother, a dementia sufferer, died from a stroke in the care home where she was supposedly being looked after.

The post-mortem revealed that she was severely malnourished, and her body was covered in unexplained bruises. A subsequent investigation concluded that she'd been neglected and abused along with other residents, but no order was made to shut the home down. And it would have remained open if Daniel hadn't launched an online campaign calling for it to be closed.

From then on, Daniel's blog had gone from strength to strength, and his reputation had spread far and wide.

Beth couldn't bear the thought that the blog would now die with him. It was such a crying shame that there was no way to keep his legacy alive. And not just for him, but for the millions of people who had been supporting his campaigns, especially those who had responded to his call to take to the streets.

But Daniel had produced the blog by himself and not with the help of other journalists and activists. In fact, the only person other than him to have written anything on it was Beth herself. She'd also acted as his sounding board and checked his copy before it was posted. She'd never held back from telling him when she thought he was wrong, or from praising him to the hilt when she liked what he'd written.

'It's a team effort, Beth,' he'd said more than once. She had never really taken him seriously, but now, suddenly, those words sent a shiver skittering down her spine.

She wondered if he had truly believed that they were a team and that she'd been partly responsible for everything that had been achieved.

She knew she could never be sure. But she also knew that if she chose to believe it then she had a moral obligation to carry on where Daniel had left off.

Even if that meant putting her own life on the line.

CHAPTER 25

THE REAPPEARANCE OF DI Metcalfe – or Angel – jerked Beth out of her reverie. But not before the idea of taking on Daniel's People-Power blog had become rooted in her mind.

It would be a way of keeping him close, she reasoned, and she felt sure that if he could have spoken to her from beyond the grave, he would have told her to do it.

But even if she eventually decided not to, it would at least give her something positive to think about as she struggled to cope with the grief.

'I picked up everything you asked for,' Angel said.

Beth took the stuff into the spare bedroom and then came back to finish her tea. The three of them sat at the table and Angel made it known that DCI Temple had just called to tell her what Beth had said to the reporters outside.

Beth managed a sheepish smile. 'I know that what Mr Temple told me was in confidence, but I just couldn't hold back,' she said.

Angel's expression was sympathetic. 'Don't worry about it. It would have come out soon enough anyway.'

'Well, please apologize to him for me, would you? He seems a nice man and I'm sure he's good at his job.'

'He'll appreciate that,' Angel said. 'And you're right. He is a nice man.'

There was something in the tenor of her voice that made Beth wonder if the two detectives were involved in more than just an on-the-job relationship.

Angel asked Beth if she wanted her to arrange for a family liaison officer to come over, but Beth declined.

'It won't help,' she said. 'Besides, Faye's here for me so I'll be OK.'

Angel then got Beth to describe Daniel and their life together. It hurt to talk about him, but in a way it was also cathartic. She told the detective how they'd met and how he'd proposed. She spoke about his kindness and generosity and how his commitment to promoting various causes was perhaps his most endearing quality.

She even asked Faye if she could show Angel the photographs and cuttings in the box file.

Faye appeared reluctant, but after a moment's hesitation she got the box down from the cupboard and placed it on the table.

'Can you believe this?' Beth said. 'Faye and William have been collecting all this stuff about Daniel and I didn't even know. Imagine my surprise when I found it this morning hidden in a cupboard. And it makes me feel so proud.'

She expected the detective to be impressed. Instead, a look of suspicion came over Angel's face.

'So why would you want to keep all these photos and cuttings?' Angel said, directing her words at Faye.

Beth looked at her neighbour and noticed that she seemed suddenly uncomfortable. She cleared her throat and said, 'We were going to put it all into a scrapbook. We wanted to remember the good things that Daniel had done.'

Angel pursed her lips and raised her brow, and Beth got the clear impression that the detective – for some reason – didn't believe what Faye had said.

CHAPTER 26

Beth Fletcher's brief appearance in front of the cameras was pumped around the world by the news organizations. Her comments electrified the media coverage of the story and went viral on the internet.

So it came as something of a relief to Temple when Dr Matherson rang through with his initial post-mortem findings.

There were no defensive wounds on Prince's body and although toxicology showed a significant amount of wine in his blood, there probably wasn't enough to have rendered him paralytic.

'However, I found some carpet fibres on his face and in his hair,' Matherson said. 'There was also a severe swelling and bruise to the left side of his forehead, which is still just visible despite the damage caused to the rest of his head when he hit the ground. This wound is consistent with a blow from a hard object, but at this stage I'm not sure what it could have been.'

'So what does this mean?' Temple said.

'Well, there's no question that he died as a result of the injuries sustained in the fall,' Matherson said. 'But I believe he was struck before he fell. Whoever was responsible probably assumed that his body would be in such a mess that the wound wouldn't be noticed. The carpet fibres must have been picked up while he was lying face-down on the floor.'

'So you reckon he was murdered?' Temple said.

'That's correct. I believe that Daniel Prince was knocked out in his flat and then dragged across the floor to the balcony. One or more people then hurled him over the balustrade. I'd say he was unconscious but alive at the time.'

Her name was Jennifer Locke and she held the rank of detective chief inspector within the Domestic Extremism Unit. She struck Temple as a formidable figure as soon as he set eyes on her.

She was somewhere in her late forties, well-groomed and

expensively-dressed. Her dark hair was cut into a layered bob and her features were hard, but not unattractive. She wore a black suit that hung fashionably loose on her trim frame.

Temple had been summoned to Beresford's office and when he walked in, she was sitting across the desk from the chief. Beresford performed the introductions, and when Temple shook her hand she smiled just enough to expose her teeth.

'It's a pleasure to meet you,' she said as he sat in the chair next to her. 'The Chief Superintendent has been telling me about you and your team.'

'Then perhaps you can tell me about you and *your* team,' Temple said. 'I know very little about the unit, except what I've gleaned from gossip and from newspapers.'

He felt her sizing him up, her expression cool and calculating.

'I'll be happy to brief you on our activities,' she said. 'But first I'd like you to update me on Daniel Prince. I've just learned that you're now treating his death as a murder and not a suicide.'

'We are. Does that give you a problem?'

'It gives us all a problem,' she said. 'Which is why we were hoping you wouldn't come to that conclusion.'

'Well, I'm sorry to disappoint you. But the evidence leaves me in no doubt that he was pushed from his balcony.'

'It's a shame, but it's not as though we didn't anticipate it after we heard that he'd died suddenly.'

Temple frowned. 'When you say *we*, who are you actually referring to?'

'I'm referring to everyone in authority right up to the PM,' Locke said. 'Prince's sudden death is already causing shock-waves, and not just here in the UK. When the news spreads that the police now believe he was murdered, we're likely to see a strong, even violent reaction.'

'Are you sure you're not overreacting?'

'I wish we were. But my people have already got wind of at least three demonstrations that are being planned by people who want to use Prince's death as an excuse to attack the police and the government.'

'So where has this intelligence come from?' Temple asked.

Locke shrugged. 'Surveillance, of course. It's what we do. And it's how we know there's a shit-storm brewing. Daniel Prince has been the subject of most of the phone and web chatter that we've monitored since late last night when the news broke. Every anti-establishment group and high-profile activist is jumping on the bandwagon. They all want to believe that Prince was the victim of a government-sponsored conspiracy.'

'And was he?'

Her eyes lit up with a touch of fury. 'Don't be ridiculous. In this country, the police and security agencies don't go around assassinating people for writing blogs and organizing protests.'

'Well, it looks as though someone did,' Temple said.

Locke pressed her lips into a thin line and took a deep breath through her nose.

'The fact is Daniel Prince made himself a target,' she said. 'His growing popularity and influence turned him into one of the most formidable bloggers so far to emerge from the cyber world. He was in a league of his own when it came to being able to sway public opinion. The media loved him and he had eight million followers on Twitter alone. He therefore posed a serious threat to any individual or organization he chose to pick on.'

'Surely that's a bit of an exaggeration?'

'Not at all. Bloggers like Prince are becoming increasingly influential. A short time ago I was given access to a report commissioned by the Intelligence and Security Committee. It laid bare the threat posed by the growth in online activism and it's given our government a good deal to worry about. Just look at how Prince was able to get the public behind him on the issue of those politicians.'

'Did you expect that to happen?' Temple said.

She shook her head. 'We monitored that campaign closely and thought it would fizzle out. But then Prince surprised us by urging people to take to the streets. We got an even bigger shock when so many people responded. Faced with such a public display of disapproval, those ministers had no choice but to step down.'

'Serves 'em bloody right,' Temple said. 'But coming back to the surveillance on Prince. Just how extensive was it?'

'We had intercepts on his phones and email accounts,' she said, as though it was no big deal. 'And with the help of our friends at GCHQ, we sat across most of his online activities. That's the reason I've been sent here. I've been asked to share with you the information we gathered, which should save you a lot of time and trouble.'

Temple leaned forward. 'Well then, you can start by telling me if you planted the listening device in his flat. I assume the chief has told you about it.'

'He has, and I can assure you that we didn't put it there. But I'm not surprised that someone else did. We've long suspected that we weren't the only ones who were keeping a close eye on Daniel Prince.'

CHAPTER 27

DCI LOCKE AND the Chief Superintendent listened intently as Temple brought them up to speed with the investigation. Much of it they already knew, but not in any great detail.

He told them about the head wound and carpet fibres found by Matherson during the post-mortem. He mentioned what Joseph Kessel had said about Prince confessing to an affair. And he ran through the forensic evidence from the flat, including the lack of prints on the laptop and the marks in the carpet.

But he saved the best until last.

'There's been a significant development in the past hour,' he said. 'We've now got a credible suspect in the frame. She's a prostitute named Clare Brennan who was caught on the security cameras leaving the apartment block just minutes after Prince landed in front of it.'

He explained how Brennan wasn't a resident in the block and must have gone there to visit someone.

'She was in the building for about two hours,' he said. 'So there's a good chance she was servicing a client.'

'And could that client have been Daniel Prince?' Locke asked.

Temple said he wasn't sure. 'We haven't spoken to her yet, but I've asked my team to bring her in.'

'So if she went to his flat then it's conceivable that she attacked and killed him.'

'I suppose so,' he said. 'But I can't imagine that she would have been able to lift him over the balcony by herself.'

'She might have had an accomplice,' Beresford offered up.

Temple shrugged. 'Hopefully we'll know soon enough.'

He then added that the building's concierge also had some serious questions to answer.

'He lied to us. He told us that none of the residents had visitors yesterday afternoon and evening. Yet on the security footage, he's seen speaking to the woman as though he knows her and then phoning to tell whoever was expecting her that she'd arrived. We're bringing him in for questioning as well.'

Temple went on to say that no one else left the block after Prince's death plunge.

'That means there are fifty-five possible suspects in addition to Clare Brennan,' he said. 'All of them have been questioned, and they're all pleading ignorance. It's a daunting task, to be honest. We've come across only one fellow resident who had a personal grudge against Prince. His name is Hari Basu.'

Temple went through his conversation with Basu and explained why the man disapproved of what Prince had been doing with his blog.

'Well, I can tell you that Basu's name doesn't show up in Prince's surveillance file,' Locke said. 'But then I suppose he could be one of the hundreds of trolls who sent Prince anonymous emails and text messages containing threats.'

'We need to see that file,' Temple said.

Locke nodded. 'I'm arranging for a copy to be sent to you. But be aware that not every phone conversation or online exchange he had was logged. Only those deemed to be interesting.'

'And have you been through the file yourself?'

'I had it emailed to me on the train from London.'

'Does he allude at any time to an affair? It apparently ended a couple of months ago. I'm anxious to trace the woman he got involved with.'

She shook her head. 'No mention at all. And there's nothing that points to him being a regular user of prossies, either.'

'Well, if Clare Brennan didn't go there to see Prince then we need to find out who she was visiting,' Temple said. 'And of course it might simply have been a coincidence that she left the building minutes after Prince was killed.'

'If she does turn out to be the killer, it'll be a result for us,' Locke said. 'It'll deter a lot of people from getting involved in any protests if Prince has been shagging whores behind his girlfriend's back.'

'But if she's not the killer then who else might it be?' Temple said. 'You got any ideas?'

She jammed her tongue to the side of her mouth and thought about it.

After a few moments, she said, 'My money is on someone living in the block who's acting on behalf of an individual or organization that Prince was targeting or planning to target. That person could have been keeping tabs on Prince until it was deemed necessary to silence him.'

'Jesus Christ,' Temple said. 'That's all a bit James Bondish, isn't it?'

'Not when you consider that he was pissing off the likes of the Chinese and Russian governments,' she said. 'Think about it. He was calling for a worldwide boycott of Russian goods and services, and he was even urging people not to go to that country on holiday. This had alarmed the government there, along with Russian corporations. They understandably feared that if enough people responded, it would further damage their economy, which has already been hit hard by western sanctions. So I should imagine that his death has been greeted with a huge sigh of relief in the Kremlin.'

'Who knows?' Temple said. 'They might even be congratulating themselves on a job well done.'

CHAPTER 28

BETH WAS ALONE in the spare room and her mind was spinning in circles. There was just too much going on, too many thoughts to process.

She still didn't know what to make of DI Metcalfe's reaction to the contents of Faye and William's box file. Had she mistaken the detective's surprise for suspicion? Beth hadn't been able to ask her because Faye had been at the table with them up until the time Angel left.

Now Faye was in the living room talking on the phone to someone and Beth was lying on the bed, trying to unscramble her brain.

She knew that in the scheme of things, the photos and newspaper cuttings were irrelevant, and it annoyed her that she had allowed them to become a distraction for no good reason.

So she tried to refocus her thoughts on what was actually important. Such as how was she going to manage without Daniel? When should she start thinking about the funeral? And would Daniel want to be buried or cremated?

She was pretty sure that this last point had been discussed at some time in the past, but she couldn't dredge up the memory.

Daniel's parents had been cremated, so that was probably what he would want. But getting her head around it was not going to be easy. Just thinking about making funeral arrangements was causing her stomach to twist and drop.

Daniel didn't have any family alive to help her cope. He'd been an only child. So Beth knew it was going to be the most distressing thing she would ever have to do.

Beth felt a sudden need to talk to her father. He was the only person who really knew what she was going through because in his own way, he too had loved Daniel.

She got up and turned on her phone. Ignoring all the missed calls and text messages, she rang his number, and when he answered she told him she would call him on Skype so he should switch his computer on.

A minute later, her father appeared on her iPad screen, his face looking gaunt and hollow. And the moment she saw him she succumbed to another crying fit and could barely speak. He started sobbing at the same time.

'I just needed to speak to you, Dad,' Beth said. 'I didn't mean to upset you.'

He begged her to come straight up to Manchester to stay with them.

'If I was able to travel I'd come to you,' he said.

Beth said she couldn't leave Southampton just yet as there were things to do and arrangements to make. She updated him on the police investigation, and he said he'd been stunned by the outpouring of grief and anger that Daniel's death had generated.

'I tried calling you after I saw you on telly,' he said. 'But I couldn't get through.'

She explained why she'd turned her phone off and then gave him William and Faye's home number. But after that it was difficult to sustain a conversation because they were both too emotional. Beth said she would call him again later and severed the connection.

She decided that having powered up her iPad, she might as well check her emails. There were over a hundred unread messages in her inbox, many from people whose names she recognized.

She didn't bother to open them and instead went into Daniel's Twitter account. She had all his online passwords and he'd had hers.

The tweets were still pouring in from people who had followed him.

You were a voice of integrity in a corrupt world. RIP.

You've paid a heavy price for taking on the establishment. God bless you.

I reckon you were done in by those Russian bastards.

Those scumbag politicians you forced to resign must have taken out a contract on you.

I followed your campaigns and they always made sense. Here's to people power.

You gave up your life for what you believed in. We'll all miss you.

Beth then signed into Facebook and checked out Daniel's People-Power page. His friends and fans had been posting messages continuously and Beth was touched beyond words.

The response to what had happened filled the gnawing emptiness inside her with an overwhelming sense of pride. And it made her realize that for Daniel's sake she couldn't let this be the end of everything he had worked – and died – for.

She felt her chest expand as she took a deep breath. Then she turned her mind to how she would tell the world that she intended to keep Daniel's blog alive. Her mind was now made up, and as soon as she knew what she was going to say she would post the message on Twitter and Facebook.

She had no idea how it would be received by his legion of followers, but she knew in her heart that she had to do it, regardless of the consequences.

CHAPTER 29

IT WAS 3 p.m. when Temple left the chief super's office, after it was agreed that a formal press conference would be held an hour later.

'It's time we confirmed what the press already knows,' Beresford said. 'That this is now a murder inquiry.'

As he walked back to the operations room, Temple turned over in his head what DCI Locke had said about the monitoring of Daniel Prince's phone calls and emails.

Not so long ago, that level of activity would only have been authorized for suspected terrorists, not bloggers and activists who did not pose an imminent threat.

But DCI Locke and her team could spy on just about anyone under their remit of gathering intelligence on so-called 'domestic extremists'. It reminded Temple of the famous quote from Edward Snowden, the whistleblower who revealed that the US was spying on hundreds of millions of people.

'Everyone is under surveillance,' he said. 'They monitor phone calls, emails, texts, search history, what you buy, who your friends are, where you go, who you love.'.

Snowden, who was a contractor for America's National Security Agency, also said that the UK's surveillance capabilities showed it to be an 'intelligence superpower' that rivalled even the US.

Temple had always felt uneasy about the scale of surveillance and the fact that people's privacy could be violated without suspicion of wrongdoing.

Daniel Prince was a case in point. He wasn't a suspected terrorist or a known criminal. He was just someone who harnessed the power of the internet and social media to campaign on certain contentious issues. But his every move had been monitored because too many people were actually listening to what he had to say and agreeing with him.

DCI Locke had admitted that her own unit had intercepted his phone calls and emails. But she'd denied planting the listening device in his flat and Temple couldn't see why she would lie about it. So it meant that someone else had put it there, possibly someone who worked for a foreign intelligence agency. If so, then did that same agency have him killed?

Temple rolled this idea around inside his head and let it rest. It was yet another question that he needed to find the answer to. But he wasn't sure that he ever would. This was not a straightforward murder inquiry. That much was already blatantly obvious. There were threads going off in all kinds of directions.

And there were enough suspects to give any detective palpitations.

Temple grabbed a coffee and sandwich from the canteen before stepping back into the operations room.

He was dog-tired having missed a night's sleep. His eyelids were heavy and his limbs ached. He was also conscious of his appearance; he was in need of a shower and shave.

In fact, he was toying with the idea of popping home to freshen up when DS Vaughan collared him to say that George Reese, the concierge at the Riverview apartment building, was being brought in to be interviewed.

'What about Clare Brennan?' Temple said.

'Baines and Scott just called at her house, but there's no answer,' Vaughan said. 'A neighbour has told them she went out earlier and hasn't returned. I've put a call into Vice to see what they have on her.'

'Well, if there's no sign of her in the next hour, I want us to get a warrant and gain entry to the house to see what we can find.'

'I'll put a team on stand-by, guv.'

'Good. Meantime, give me a shout when Reese is in. I want to take the lead on that particular conversation.'

He retreated to his office to finish his coffee and sandwich and check his emails. While on his computer, he pulled up the BBC news and saw that the public furore over Prince's death was showing no sign of abating. The crowd outside his apartment block had apparently grown, and police had been called to maintain order.

Prominent activists were also lining up to allege that Prince was the victim of an establishment conspiracy. And the video clip of Beth Fletcher talking to reporters was being widely circulated and mentioned.

Temple could see now why there was concern at the top that things could get really nasty. Known troublemakers were already exploiting the situation by calling on people to organize street protests.

One MP was even quoted as saying that if the tension continued to mount, he feared a repeat of the August 2011 riots. That was when thousands of people rioted across London and other cities and towns after a man was shot dead by police in Tottenham. Over five days, the UK saw the biggest display of civil unrest for thirty years. More than 3,000 people were arrested and parts of the country were awash with arson, looting and violence.

Temple didn't want to believe that the death of a blogger could spark a similar situation. But he knew it was possible.

If enough people could be whipped into a frenzy then just about anything could happen.

CHAPTER 30

GEORGE REESE WAS clearly nervous. His bald head was shiny with sweat, and his chubby face was bleached almost white.

Temple and Dave Vaughan faced him across the table in the interview room. He had waived his right to have a solicitor present after being told he was not under arrest.

'We're just hoping that you can help us clarify a few points,' Temple told him. 'It shouldn't take very long.'

'Well, I will if I can,' Reese said. 'Is it true that you now think Mr Prince was murdered?'

'Indeed we do,' Temple said.

Reese shook his head. 'I can't believe it. Why would anyone want to kill him? He was such a good person, for heaven's sake.'

'He was also a very controversial figure,' Temple said. 'And as such he attracted enemies.'

Reese pulled at the neck of the heavy woollen sweater he was wearing. He shifted his gaze between the two detectives and kept licking his lips. It looked as though he was getting ready to run at a moment's notice.

'What time did you get away from there last night?' Temple asked him.

He swallowed. 'Not until two a.m. That's when the relief concierge arrived.'

'Have you managed to get some sleep?'

'You've got to be joking. Every time I close my eyes I see his body on the forecourt. I can't get it out of my mind.'

There was a leather folder on the table. Temple flipped over the cover to reveal a sheet of paper with typewritten notes on it. Under that was a large brown envelope.

He picked up the notes and said, 'I'd like to go through what you told us last night. It seems that you weren't entirely honest with us.'

Panic washed over the concierge's face like a rogue wave.

'I don't know what you mean,' he said.

Temple knotted his forehead. 'Oh, I think you do. And I suggest it would be very much in your interest to come clean before you find yourself in serious trouble.'

'I don't understand,' Reese said. 'What am I supposed to have lied about?'

Temple released a small sigh. 'You told us there were no visitors to the apartment building yesterday evening. I asked you if you were sure and you said you were positive because all visitors have to go past you.'

Reese nodded. 'That's right. I don't remember any visitors. I'd have told you if there were any.'

'But you're lying.'

Temple picked up the envelope and took three large photographs from it, placing one of them on the table in front of Reese.

'So are you saying that you have no recollection of this woman?' he said. 'Her name is Clare Brennan and in that picture she can be seen entering the building at about eight o'clock.'

Reese's eyes came out on stalks as he stared at the picture.

Temple then placed another photo on top of it. 'In that one, she's talking to you before she gets in the lift to go upstairs.'

Reese continued to stare, his breath becoming short and erratic.

Temple put down the third photo. 'That shows her leaving the building just a few minutes after Daniel Prince hit the ground. You were outside watching over the body. She slipped out and walked to where she had parked her car, then drove off.'

Temple paused and waited for Reese to react. It was several beats before he raised his eyes from the table and said, 'I honestly forgot. I'm really sorry. It was stupid of me.'

'I don't believe for one minute that you forgot,' Temple said. 'I think you deliberately withheld the information.'

'No, Inspector. In all the excitement it slipped my mind.'

Temple's voice was soured with scepticism. 'Stop bullshitting me, Mr Reese. We know that Clare Brennan is a prostitute who probably describes herself as an escort. And it obviously wasn't the first time she'd been there.'

Reese held up his hands. 'OK, look, this is stupid. I did know but I didn't mention it because Miss Brennan has a client in the building and I've been sworn to secrecy. So I didn't want to betray a confidence, partly because I'm tipped well to keep quiet.'

'But you must have known we'd spot her on the videos,' Temple said.

Reese shrugged. 'I just assumed you'd think she was a resident. I didn't realize the visiting thing would become such a big deal.'

'And am I right in saying that the man she was visiting was Daniel Prince?' Temple said. 'And that's why you lied to us. You were trying to cover up for Clare Brennan.'

Reese suddenly sat bolt upright and the words imploded out of him.

'My God, no. It wasn't Mr Prince. He would never have entertained other women in his flat.'

'Really?' Temple said. 'Then who was it?'

Reese rubbed a hand across his face before answering.

'It was Mr Basu,' he said. 'Hari Basu. He's the man I talked to you about. He often has Miss Brennan over when his wife is away or at work.'

They questioned George Reese for another forty-five minutes because Temple suspected he was holding something back. It was based on nothing more than experience and the amount of sweat that was seeping out of the man's pores.

But Temple also wanted to make him suffer a bit for wasting police time by withholding information. So before the interview ended, he decided to bring up the little matter of Reese's previous conviction for a sex attack on a 16-year-old girl.

'If you've checked it out then you'll know that I pleaded not guilty,' Reese said. 'The girl lied when she claimed that I assaulted her.'

'Well, she managed to convince a court that you pulled her behind some bushes to molest her.'

'It was a lie. She was walking home, drunk and lost. I offered to help her, and she came on to me.'

'So she pulled *you* into the bushes, did she?'

'That's more or less what happened, yeah.'

Temple gave him a withering look. 'Seems to me you're a prolific liar as well as a pervert. Now I'll ask you one last time. Is there anything you're still not telling me?'

'Absolutely not.'

'So you didn't have any more contact with Mr Prince after he arrived back yesterday? And nothing happened last night in the building that aroused your suspicion?'

'I've told you. There's nothing else. I accept I should have mentioned Clare Brennan, but it was a mistake. That's all.'

Temple still wasn't satisfied, but Reese said he wouldn't answer any more questions without a lawyer present.

'You can get representation if and when we have to talk to you again,' Temple said. 'But that's all for now so you can go.'

CHAPTER 31

ON THE WAY back to the operations room, Temple told Vaughan to dig up whatever information he could on George Reese.

'Do a number on his bank account and phone records,' he said.

'What about Hari Basu?' Vaughan asked.

'We need to confront him as soon as possible. He claimed he was alone yesterday. No mention of entertaining a working girl. So it looks as though he's another one who's fond of fibbing.'

'I'll locate him, guv,' Vaughan said. 'Do you want him brought here or shall we go to see him?'

'If he's at home we'll go there. Before the day is out, I want to pay another visit to the Riverview apartments.'

When he got back to the operations room, Temple was disappointed to learn that Clare Brennan still hadn't turned up, but a team had broken into her house with a warrant.

'There's no sign of her,' he was told by DC Doug Wells. 'So far they've found nothing to indicate where she might be. But they have found a stash of class B drugs in the house.'

'Do we know if she lives alone?'

'The neighbours say she does. It's a rented two-bedroom house and she occasionally entertains her clients there apparently. Different men have been seen going in and out.'

'What about a boyfriend?'

'One neighbour who's on speaking terms with her says she

has one, and his name's Barry. But that's all she knows.'

'Any luck with her mobile?' he asked.

'We've got a trace on it, sir, but it seems it has been switched off. I've put in a request for her phone records.'

It turned out that Vice did have a file on her, though, and the salient facts had been sent over. She apparently operated independently of any of the city's escort agencies and had a website on which she advertised her services.

According to a detective who knew her she was a 'gobby cow' with a fierce temper. Her conviction for assault came about after a client refused to pay the fee she demanded for an hour of her time. She responded by smashing him over the head with a half-empty wine bottle.

Temple wondered if she held the answer to the mystery of Daniel Prince's death. Surely the timing of her exit from the building couldn't just be down to coincidence. She had slipped out only minutes after he'd plunged to the ground.

For that reason she was at the top of his list of suspects. Along with Hari Basu.

Temple had been hoping that he wouldn't have to attend the press conference. But Beresford called down to say he wanted him there and to hurry because it was about to start.

At the same time Dave Vaughan confirmed that Hari Basu had left work for the day.

'I got one of our officers at the building to check with the concierge on duty,' Vaughan said. 'Basu arrived back about fifteen minutes ago and is in his flat.'

'Then tell them to stop him if he tries to leave. You and I will go over there as soon as I'm out of the presser.'

Temple then bumped into Angel in the corridor, and she said she wanted to talk to him.

'It'll have to wait,' he said. 'The press conference is about to start and I've been summoned.'

She seemed a little anxious so he stopped and asked her if she was all right.

'It's just that something is bothering me about Prince's next door neighbours,' she said. 'I'd like to know what you think.'

'Do you mean the Connors?'

She nodded. 'I was over there earlier as you know, and I was shown something that I thought was a bit odd.'

'What was it?'

'A box file filled with cuttings and photographs of Daniel Prince. Plus print-outs from his blog. The couple have apparently been collecting them.'

'Why?'

'Good question. According to Faye Connor, it's to eventually put them into a scrapbook. She reckons that she and her husband were big fans of Prince. But to me that just doesn't ring true. I mean, it's not like the guy was a famous actor or pop star. And I got the distinct impression that she was reluctant to talk about it.'

Temple squinted. 'So are you wondering if they had another reason for collecting information on him?'

'I suppose I am. But I'm not sure if I'm reading too much into it.'

'No, you're right to be suspicious. It sounds to me like a weird thing for them to do.'

'Exactly. Either they're obsessed with Prince or they had an ulterior motive for building up a file on him.'

'Did Beth Fletcher know about it?'

'Not until this morning apparently. She came across it hidden in a cupboard.'

'Then have a closer look at the couple,' Temple said. 'We'll talk again later.'

'Will do. By the way, I got Beth to open up about Prince and her relationship with him. She clearly adored the guy and I'm pretty sure from the way she spoke that she didn't suspect him of having an affair.'

'Did you ask her?'

'I didn't get a chance because Faye Connor was with us the whole time.'

'Sooner or later we'll need to put the question to her,' he said.

'Well, I'd rather that was you and not me, boss.'

Temple couldn't help but smile. 'You're far too soft-hearted, Detective. Do you know that?'

She laughed and her face lit up. 'Isn't that one of the reasons you love me?'

He felt a strong urge to kiss her, which was never a good idea while they were both on duty.

'I'd better go before I do something I'll regret,' he said.

CHAPTER 32

THE PRESS CONFERENCE kicked off as soon as Temple arrived. He sat at a long table with Chief Superintendent Beresford and Mark Ramsay, the head of media liaison.

The room was packed with journalists, photographers and TV crews. The turnout reflected the news value of the story. It was big and about to get even bigger.

DCI Locke stood to one side of the room with her back to the wall and her arms folded. Temple had been told that she was staying in Southampton overnight and would be around for most of the next day to assist with inquiries.

He made a mental note to ask her a few more questions about the Domestic Extremism Unit – including whether she had been entirely upfront about its activities leading up to the death of Daniel Prince. Temple's gut told him that he shouldn't just accept what she'd said. After all, it was entirely possible – given the clandestine remit of the unit – that her team had overstepped the mark and she was here to make sure it was covered up.

Ramsay started the ball rolling by introducing himself and then Beresford and Temple. He had a loud, booming voice that immediately seized everyone's attention.

Beresford then read out a pre-prepared statement confirming that they were now treating Prince's death as murder.

'Forensic evidence indicates that Mr Prince was pushed from his balcony, probably after being rendered unconscious in the flat,' he said. 'His assailant, or assailants, then tried to make it appear as though it was suicide. We're following up several lines of inquiry but at this stage we don't know whether the motive for the killing was linked in any way to Mr Prince's online campaigns.'

Beresford then dismissed rumours of a government conspiracy. He described them as absurd and said that some individuals and anarchic groups were attempting to stir up trouble.

As soon as he paused for breath, he faced a barrage of questions. Some of them related to forensic evidence found at the flat, and Temple answered these by saying that they couldn't disclose details for fear of compromising the investigation.

'What about the listening device?' someone said. 'Do you know who put it in the flat?'

'No, we don't,' Temple answered. 'But we're carrying out exhaustive inquiries to try to find out.'

'Can you tell us if you have any suspects?' asked a reporter from the Press Association.

Temple nodded. 'I can confirm that we've identified a number of people who might be able to help us and we'll be talking to them in due course.'

'Do they include other residents in the Riverview complex?'

'I'm afraid I can't be more specific on that point.'

A woman who identified herself as a BBC journalist said, 'There have been claims online that a multi-national corporation or even a foreign power might have been behind the killing. What do you say to that, Inspector?'

'I'd say it was nothing but wild speculation,' Temple said. 'It has no basis in fact.'

The questions kept on coming, and Temple struggled not to let his frustration show. He was eager to get on with the job, and as always he resented having to take time out to feed the media beast.

So he was glad when the hacks started running out of

things to ask, and Ramsay announced there was time for only two more questions. That was when a Sky News reporter dropped a bombshell.

'Are you aware that Prince's girlfriend has – in the last few minutes – posted an online message announcing that she's going to take over his blog?' he said.

Temple and Beresford looked at each other. It was Beresford who admitted that it was news to them.

The Sky reporter then read out the message Beth had posted on Facebook and Twitter. *I'm Beth, Daniel's fiancée. We were a team and now I intend to keep his blog alive in his memory. And in defiance of whoever killed him.*

The reporter looked up and said, 'Do you think that what she's done is wise, Superintendent, in view of what happened to Mr Prince?'

Beresford's expression tensed. 'That's really a question you should put to Miss Fletcher.'

The reporter turned to Temple. 'What about you, Inspector? Do you think Miss Fletcher is being brave or foolish?'

'What Miss Fletcher does is her business,' Temple said. 'If she's going to carry on where her fiancé left off then I'm sure she's taken into consideration the risks.'

Beth Fletcher's decision to take over her boyfriend's blog pro-voked a fierce reaction, and not just among the febrile media pack.

'This is not good news,' DCI Locke said when they were back in Temple's office. 'With passions and sentiment running so high she's likely to become a cause célèbre. The grieving girlfriend keeping the murdered man's legacy alive. She'll not only rally those who were already following Daniel Prince. She'll attract a whole new audience. Those who think she's a hero. Those who feel sorry for her. And those who will see an opportunity to make mischief on a grand scale.'

'So how does that give us a problem?' Temple said.

'Because it'll turn the heat up to boiling point on the inves-tigation. And it'll make Beth Fletcher a potential target just like her boyfriend. She too could wind up dead, and if she does then the flak will really be flying.'

'You think that could happen?'

'Of course. If Daniel Prince was murdered by someone because of his campaigns, then whoever was behind it will be monumentally pissed off to hear what Beth plans to do.'

Temple wondered if Beth really knew what she was letting herself in for. Or if the sudden loss of her partner had prompted her to act without thinking. Her reaction was under-standable, but almost certainly ill-advised. DCI Locke was right to warn that Beth might now become a target herself.

'You should try to get her to change her mind,' Locke said. 'And if you can't then it might be wise to provide her with some level of protection.'

CHAPTER 33

BETH HAD WATCHED the televised press conference while sitting with Faye and William Connor in their living room. The couple were clearly shocked to learn that she was going to take over Daniel's blog.

'I really don't think it's a good idea,' Faye said. 'You'll have enough to cope with as it is. It'll be too much.'

'It will also be dangerous, Beth,' William said. 'Why take the risk? It doesn't make sense.'

'It does to me,' Beth replied. 'Daniel's blog was a big part of our lives. He'd want me to keep it going.'

'Not if it means exposing you to the same people who killed him.'

'We don't know who killed him,' Beth said. 'But even if it was because of his campaigns then it still won't stop me.'

'But you're in shock,' William said. 'You shouldn't be making such big decisions. Give yourself time to grieve first.'

'I don't need time,' she said. 'I know what I'm doing.'

She wanted to tell them that she wasn't worried about the risks because she didn't care if she lived or died. But she knew they wouldn't understand. They still had lives that were worth living. She felt like hers was over.

Even Joseph joined the chorus of disapproval when he came up to the Connors' flat after returning from his business meeting.

'When I read the tweet I couldn't believe you were serious,' he said.

'Well, I am,' she told him. 'So please don't try to make me change my mind. It won't happen.'

'But it's insane. Do you even know how to go about it?'

'Of course. I was involved from the start and I helped him put it together. We were a team.'

Red dots of rage appeared in front of her eyes suddenly. She knew that if she didn't leave the room she would either burst into tears or blurt out something she'd regret.

So she jumped to her feet and rushed out of the room without another word. Thankfully the others had the good sense not to follow her. She slammed the door of the spare room behind her and threw herself onto the bed.

She lay without moving for several minutes, listening to the patter of rain against the window. Her head felt fuzzy, clotted with too many thoughts and distressing images. Among them, Daniel's battered body lying in a pool of blood.

Had nineteen hours already elapsed since he had died? Soon it would be a full day and night. Then a week. A month. A year.

She feared the future more than anything. She couldn't see how she would fill the time without Daniel. Or how she would cope with the aching loneliness, the endless nights, and the painful memories. At least managing the blog would give her something to focus on, a reason to get up in the mornings.

And if she too ended up dead like Daniel, then maybe that would be a blessed release.

CHAPTER 34

IT WAS 6 p.m. when Temple and Vaughan returned to the Riverview complex. By then a few heavy showers had driven away the crowd that had gathered to pay tribute to Daniel Prince. But a few TV crews remained, huddled under brollies and inside large satellite trucks.

Hari Basu wasn't expecting them, and he was none too pleased when he opened his front door.

'You've got to be kidding me,' he said. 'What do you want now?'

'We need to talk to you again, Mr Basu,' Temple said.

'What for? I've already been interviewed twice.'

'That's right. And you told us you spent yesterday evening by yourself.'

'So?'

'Well, that wasn't true, was it? There was a woman with you. A prostitute named Clare Brennan.'

Basu's eyes sparked with fury. 'Was it that bald-headed prick who told you?'

'It doesn't matter who told us, Mr Basu. We just need to know why you lied to us.'

'Surely that's fucking obvious.'

Temple's expression showed his irritation. 'I suggest we have this conversation inside if you don't want the neighbours to know what you've been up to.'

Basu shook his head and mouthed an obscenity. Then he led them into the living room where he invited them to be seated on the sofa. He then sat in the armchair facing them, a grim, tight expression on his face.

'Let me start by reminding you that this is now a murder investigation,' Temple said. 'Lying to us could land you in serious trouble, so be sensible and tell us the truth. At the same time drop the attitude. It's getting on my nerves.'

An artery throbbed at the side of Basu's head, and his eyes danced in their sockets. His shoulders sagged, and the arrogance appeared to vanish in an instant from his posture.

A gush of breath, then, 'Look, I didn't want you or anyone else to know about the girl. I'm married, for God's sake. It's hard enough trying to making sure the neighbours don't see them coming and going. But so far I've managed it. I don't want my wife to know I see other women.'

'You mean prostitutes?' Temple said.

Basu bit his lip and passed a hand over his face. 'What difference does it make? Paying for it means it doesn't get complicated. I can have a bit of fun on the side and my wife doesn't get hurt.'

'Providing she doesn't find out.'

'That's exactly right, which is why I'm pissed off that George Reese went and blabbed. I paid him to keep his trap shut.'

'Well, it's irrelevant anyway,' Temple said. 'What I need you to tell me is exactly what happened yesterday.'

He shrugged. 'What's to tell? Clare came here and I had sex with her. It cost me a hundred and fifty quid.'

'I gather it wasn't the first time,' Temple said.

Basu nodded. 'She's been here on a few occasions, and I've been to her place a couple of times.'

'What's so special about her?' Vaughan asked him.

Basu flashed a thin, nervous smile. 'She's attractive and good at what she does. And I like her, which helps.'

'So what time did she arrive here?' Temple asked.

'I'm sure you already know that from Reese.'

'Tell us anyway.'

He heaved a sigh. 'It was about eight o'clock. She stayed for an hour and then left.'

Temple pursed his lips. 'So are you saying she left here at nine o'clock?'

'Dead on. She said she had another appointment to go to.'

'But she was captured on the security cameras leaving the building at a few minutes past ten. Just after Daniel Prince fell to his death.'

Basu's eyes jumped. 'That can't be right. I swear she didn't stay beyond nine. She never does because I always have an early start the next morning.'

Temple studied his features, but he found it impossible to tell whether or not he was lying.

'So how do you explain it?' Temple said. 'If what you're saying is true then it took her a good hour to get from this flat to the lobby.'

'I can't explain it,' Basu said. 'It doesn't make sense. But I'm telling the truth.'

'So what did you do when she left?'

'I had a shower and went to bed. A couple of hours later, one of your officers rang the bell.'

'Do you have any idea where Clare Brennan went when she left the building?'

'None whatsoever. She didn't tell me.'

'Do you know where she is now?'

'At home, I suppose. Or at work. I don't keep tabs on her.'

'So how do you get in contact with her?' Vaughan asked.

'Mobile phone.'

'Then let us have the number.'

Basu retrieved his phone from the kitchen and read out the number, which was the one they already had.

Temple then asked to see the phone to check when the number was last called.

'It would have been yesterday morning,' Basu said. 'That was when I rang to arrange for her to come over.'

Temple glanced through the phone's call log and confirmed it for himself. He then speed-dialled the number but it went to a recorded message.

Temple wasn't sure what to make of it. If Clare Brennan had indeed left Basu's flat at nine then where the hell did she spend the following hour before departing the building?

They went through it with Basu again, but he stuck resolutely to his story.

'Did Clare Brennan know Daniel Prince?' Temple asked.

Basu shrugged. 'I doubt it. His name was never mentioned when I was with her.'

'So the pair of you didn't go up to his flat last night and kill him?'

Basu's breath left him with a gasp. 'No way. That's ridiculous. But if it's what you think then I won't say another word until I see a solicitor.'

'I don't blame you,' Temple said. 'But there's no need to call one just yet. I think we can leave it at that for now. It shouldn't be long before we track down Miss Brennan and find out what she's got to say for herself. You'd better hope she backs up your story, because if not, we'll be straight back.'

CHAPTER 35

WHEN THEY LEFT Hari Basu, the two detectives split up. Vaughan went back downstairs to the lobby to get an update from the officers who had spent the day wrapping up the second round of interviews with residents.

Temple, meanwhile, went up to the tenth floor to check with the forensic team in Prince's flat and to have another chat with Beth Fletcher.

The flat had offered up no further clues, according to Lee Finch, the chief forensic officer, although the analysis of collected fibres was still ongoing. He said they hadn't found any blood on the carpet or on any of the surfaces. And there were no more concealed listening devices. The glass and half-empty wine bottle left on the breakfast bar contained only Daniel Prince's fingerprints. Plus, there was no evidence to suggest that he had entertained anyone else in the flat in the hours before he was killed. The bed hadn't been slept in and there was only one used coffee mug in the dishwasher.

'I think it's safe to assume that the killer – or killers – didn't hang around for long,' Finch said. 'I reckon Prince would have been attacked soon after opening his door. There's a peephole in the door so he probably knew who he was letting in.'

'How easy would it have been for one person to drag the body out onto the balcony and then lift it over the balustrade?' Temple asked.

Finch shrugged. 'Difficult, but certainly not impossible. Prince was of average build so you and I could probably have done it without tearing a muscle.'

'How hard would it be for a woman, do you think?'

'Depends how strong she is. And how determined, of course. You'd be surprised what physical feats people are capable of when they put their minds to it.'

Temple left Finch and went next door to the Connors' flat. The door was answered by William Connor, who was wearing a navy shirt and denim jeans. He was several inches taller than Temple and about ten years younger. He had dark, thin hair and a strong jaw.

Temple was suddenly reminded of what Angel had said about the couple and their box of cuttings on Prince. But he decided not to raise it during this visit and instead wait to see what Angel came up with.

'Hello, Mr Connor,' he said. 'I've come to see Miss Fletcher. Is she in?'

He nodded. 'She is, but I'm afraid she's had another upset and has asked to be left alone.'

'What's happened?'

'A newspaper reporter rang here to speak to her,' he said. 'She wouldn't come to the phone so the reporter asked me to pass her a message. He said there was a story on the internet claiming that Daniel had been having an affair. The reporter wanted to know if Beth was aware of it.'

'Shit. What did she say?'

'She was furious. She said it wasn't true. Then she broke down and said she wanted to be alone.'

'I still need to talk to her.'

He gestured for Temple to step inside. 'You're welcome to try, Inspector.'

A few seconds later, Temple was tapping lightly on the door to the spare room.

'It's DCI Temple here, Miss Fletcher. Would you mind if I come in?'

Much to his surprise she responded straightaway.

'The door isn't locked.'

He pushed it open and went in. The light was on and Beth was sitting up on the bed with her iPad on her lap. She was still wearing the clothes she'd had on earlier. Her eyes were dark and rimmed with shadow, and she looked at him with an air of mild apprehension.

'I thought I'd check to see how you were holding up,' he said.

She waved at the chair next to the bed. 'So you haven't come to tell me that you've caught the killer?'

He sat down. 'Sadly, no. But we are making progress.'

She regarded him warily. 'I suppose you've heard about the vicious rumour that's being spread around on the internet.'

'You mean about an affair?'

She nodded. 'I can't believe people can be so nasty.'

'Could there be any truth in it?'

Her lips creased into a wry smile. 'I might have known you would ask that question, Inspector. Well, the answer is no. Daniel was never involved with another woman. He was faithful to me.'

'How can you be so sure?'

'Because I knew Daniel as well as I know myself.'

'Most women who've been cheated on have probably thought the same thing.'

'Well, I'm not most women. Daniel would never have put our relationship in jeopardy just to get his leg over someone else.'

Temple resisted the temptation to tell her what Daniel had told Joseph Kessel. Right now the Israeli was one of the few people she seemed able to lean on for support, and he didn't want to drive a wedge between them.

But he did want to trace the married woman who Prince was seeing.

'Have you any idea where the story came from?' he asked.

She shook her head, brown eyes creasing at the edges.

'I suspect some anonymous troll posted it on a social media site, knowing it would go viral.'

'Why would someone do that?'

'To upset me, I suppose. I can't think of any other reason.'

'It happens,' Temple said. 'And you can expect a lot more of that kind of thing if you take over Daniel's blog.'

She lifted her brow. 'That's why you're here, isn't it? To tell me how stupid I am.'

'I do think it's a bad idea. You said yourself that Daniel received death threats before yesterday, and we know that someone – or some organization – was spying on him. Do you really want to put yourself in a similar situation?'

'It's hard to explain,' she said. 'But I feel it's something I have to do. His blog meant a great deal to a lot of people. I feel I'd be letting him and them down if I don't keep it going.'

She looked away for a long moment, as if her mind was suddenly elsewhere. Temple could see the pain and sorrow in her eyes, and he decided it would be best if he left her to her thoughts. He could talk to her about the blog and about her boyfriend's alleged affair another time.

'We're almost finished next door,' he said. 'Hopefully you can move back in soon.'

She turned to look at him. 'That would be good. Faye and William have been kind to me, but I don't feel comfortable here. I need to be in my own home.'

'I can understand that,' Temple said. 'Don't hesitate to call me or DI Metcalfe if you have any questions or if you want to discuss something.'

'Thank you, Inspector. I will.'

She closed her eyes then and withdrew into herself. Temple took it as his cue to get up and leave the room.

CHAPTER 36

TEMPLE WAS DEAD on his feet by the time he got home. Even a long, hot shower failed to fully revive him.

Angel arrived with an Indian takeaway while he was drying himself.

'Missing a night's sleep is never a good thing,' she said. 'You've done well to stay awake this long.'

'I've had no time to think about it,' he said. 'It's been a shockingly busy day.'

And Temple was glad it was coming to an end. He needed to relax and recharge his batteries. He was no longer young enough to function on adrenaline alone. He needed his sleep.

The living room of his modest semi-detached house on the outskirts of Southampton was small but cosy. As usual, they settled in front of the TV and spread the cartons of food out on the coffee table.

While they ate, Temple filled Angel in on his conversation with Beth Fletcher.

'I'm convinced she didn't know about any affair,' he said. 'She's absolutely sure that Prince was faithful to her. If we do eventually trace the married woman he told Joseph Kessel about, then she's going to be devastated.'

He also filled Angel in on what Hari Basu had said about Clare Brennan.

'Do you think he's telling the truth about when she left his flat?' Angel said.

Temple shrugged. 'I don't know. But if he is, then it's conceivable that she spent the time between nine and ten in Prince's flat.'

'But surely she wouldn't have been able to toss him over the balcony.'

'She may have had help.'

'But then why would she have done it? She's a sex worker, not an assassin.'

'Well, I suppose the escort thing could be just a front.

Maybe she really works for a foreign power or even one of our own intelligence agencies.'

'Are you serious?'

'Of course. After my conversation with DCI Locke, I'm prepared to accept that any wild scenario is possible.'

Daniel Prince's murder continued to dominate the news, along with Beth's decision to keep his blog going.

Hundreds of thousands of people had reportedly taken to social media to offer her their support. One expert was even predicting that the People-Power blog would now attract millions of additional followers.

'We're seeing something quite extraordinary develop,' he said. 'If Beth Fletcher can keep the momentum going by producing blogs that trigger public outrage, then who knows how big it will get? It's quite possible – given the level of awareness and support – that she could become far more powerful than Daniel Prince.'

Another interviewee described what was happening as an unprecedented backlash against the establishment.

'This has been a long time coming,' she said. 'People who for years have felt betrayed by politicians, the police and big business have found a way to assert themselves and vent their anger. Daniel Prince created a channel through which they believe they can actually alter the balance of power. Inevitably, his death has served to compound their resentment and strengthen their resolve.'

There was extensive coverage of the press conference, which prompted Angel to tell Temple that he needed a haircut.

'But I must say you do look as though you've lost a bit of weight,' she said.

The coverage continued with footage of the crowd that had formed earlier outside Prince's apartment block. And there were various sound bites from his followers.

A couple of high-profile activists also appeared. One of them said he believed that Prince was murdered on the orders of the British government to stop him whipping up more dissent.

The other accused the Russians of being responsible because they feared Prince's call for a boycott of Russian goods would hit their economy hard.

'The Russians have form when it comes to murdering people on British soil,' he said. 'We shouldn't forget how assassins poisoned Alexander Litvinenko in London on the orders of the Kremlin. And I don't doubt there have been other killings that have been covered up.'

What he was hearing increased Temple's sense of unease. He knew it would bring more pressure to bear on the government and his own superiors. And in turn on him and his team.

'You need to stop thinking about it for a while,' Angel said as she got up to switch off the television. 'Go to bed and I'll clear up. I'll put the alarm on for six.'

Temple thanked her and dragged himself into the bedroom. He cleaned his teeth and slipped beneath the duvet.

He was fast asleep before Angel joined him.

CHAPTER 37

BETH DIDN'T BOTHER trying to go to sleep. A stream of tortured thoughts tore through her mind, and her tired body was rigid with tension.

Grief was now just one of the emotions she had to contend with. Anger was stalking around inside her like a tiger, and she was aware too of a growing sense of anxiety.

She had made it worse for herself by deciding to wade through her emails, tweets and phone messages. Dozens of people she knew had sent their condolences. Hundreds of people she didn't know had written to say they were backing her decision to run the People-Power blog.

There were even heartfelt pleas from a number of celebrities who wanted her to carry on Daniel's good work as an activist.

But there were also inflammatory posts from some trolls who were accusing Daniel of being unfaithful.

He was a two-timing bastard, one wrote. *Good job he's dead.*

And another: *If it's true then you're better off without him.*

Thankfully those voices were drowned out by those that were overwhelmingly positive and supportive. Beth was both surprised and moved by the response to her announcement. But she also began to realize that it was going to change her life. And impose on her an immense responsibility.

She hoped to God she would be able to live up to the expectations of Daniel's followers. He was going to be a tough act to follow. His posts had been infused with unbridled passion and commitment. He'd been able to articulate his arguments in a way that was balanced and uncompromising. And his integrity had shone through in everything he had written, which was why his campaigns had been so successful.

At least she'd been in tune with his beliefs and concerns, and she still had access to all his notes and the blogs he'd filed away that were ready to be posted.

In fact, it was she who'd kept those files in order, along with his diary and financial records. As good as Daniel had been at writing and motivating his audience, he'd been crap at organizing the blizzard of paperwork that his blogging generated. So that had been her job as his silent partner.

Eventually her reddened eyes were struggling to find focus. She blinked away the fresh tears that started to gather and fought against the sudden crushing despair that swept through her.

She hadn't moved from the same spot for several hours and she wondered now if she'd feel any better if she had a shower.

She wanted a drink, but she knew that Faye and William were still up and she couldn't face another lecture from them. So she decided to take a pill and make a conscious effort to get to sleep.

She put down her iPad and phone and shuffled into the en-suite bathroom. Ten minutes later she emerged and slipped on her nightie. Then she crawled into bed and tried to take comfort in the weight of her duvet.

But no sooner had she closed her eyes than her iPad pinged with an incoming email. She cursed aloud for not switching the damn thing off.

Before she did so, she opened it up to see who the email was from. But the sender's address was actually anon@ at-home.com, which was obviously a fake. But that was hardly surprisingly given the nature of the message.

It read:

Miss Fletcher, by midday tomorrow you will announce to the world that you have changed your mind and will not take on the People-Power blog after all. If you don't, you will suffer the consequences. Please do not treat this as an idle threat. I was the person who threw your boyfriend from the balcony and wrote his suicide note. And I'll be the one to ensure that something just as unpleasant happens to you.

Temple woke up in a cold sweat after three hours. The bedroom was in darkness and Angel was sleeping fitfully beside him, her breath soft and audible.

He'd had another bad dream, and he could remember it vividly. In it, Angel fell to her death from a ten-storey building.

It was a variation on a familiar theme that played into his fear of being alone again. Sometimes she died and sometimes she left him. The outcome was always the same. He was back to being by himself and facing a bleak future.

The dreams, he knew, were born of a deep-rooted insecurity. After Erin died he'd found it hard to cope. He had wallowed in self-pity and buried himself in work. But the loneliness had been painful and debilitating. Sometimes he would go home to his empty house and spend the evening crying.

His daughter, Tanya, who lived in London, tried to persuade him to get counselling. But he'd resisted. As the tough and unflappable old-school copper, he didn't want to admit he was struggling, not even to himself.

Angel had come into his life at just the right time, pulling him back from the brink of despair.

And now the thought of losing her weighed heavily on his mind, prompted by two recent scares.

She'd almost died during the pile-up caused by the sniper on the motorway. It had been touch and go for a time. And then she'd miscarried their baby after a mad dash to the hospital.

So was it any wonder that he felt insecure? And that he dreamed of losing the one person who gave meaning to his life?

'Are you all right, Jeff?' Angel whispered.

He rolled on his side to face her and told her to go back to sleep.

'Why are you awake?' she said.

'I was just thinking about the case,' he lied.

'Well, you shouldn't be. You've got another long day ahead of you tomorrow.'

He grinned. 'I know, and I'll soon drop off again so don't worry.'

She pushed herself up on her elbow, leaned over, and kissed him on the forehead.

'Sweet dreams then, hon,' she said. 'See you in a few hours.'

He closed his eyes and forced his thoughts away from the dream and his irrational fears. He decided he had to focus on other things, and it wasn't long before he was mulling over every nuance of the investigation he was now working on.

The longer he dwelt on it, the more convinced he became that it was going to be a hard one to crack. It kept him awake for another two hours as he churned over in his mind the various facts and theories.

He eventually went back to sleep at 5 a.m. An hour before his alarm went off.

CHAPTER 38

THE TEAM GATHERED for an 8 a.m. briefing. It was slightly later than planned because Temple had to attend a pre-meeting with Beresford in his office.

The chief super had asked to be updated before explaining that they were under intense pressure to get a result.

'I've been told that if we don't start making progress they'll consider putting someone else in charge,' he said.

'That's a bit much,' Temple reacted. 'We've been at it for less than forty bloody hours.'

'I know, Jeff. But they're in a panic so they're expecting a frigging miracle as usual.'

It was the kind of threat that invariably came down from on high when an investigation was in the spotlight. And this one was right up there with some of the most high-profile cases that the team had dealt with.

Beresford's desk had been covered with the morning news-papers and every front page was splashed with the story. The inside pages were filled with various side-bars, including Beth's decision to take over the blog and the wild theories about who had murdered Prince.

Several actually revealed that the police were convinced that the killer was among the fifty-odd residents who were in the building at the time.

Temple started the briefing by referring to the coverage and warning his detectives not to talk to the press.

'They seem to know a lot more than we've released through official channels,' he said. 'So I want to remind everyone that this is a hugely sensitive investigation, and I don't want it derailed by unauthorized leaks.'

Having made his point, he cracked on with the business of the day. Top of the agenda was Clare Brennan.

'Her whereabouts are still unknown,' DC Doug Wells said. 'We've been at her house with forensics throughout the night. There are no pointers so far to her location and her mobile phone remains switched off so we can't track it.'

Temple felt rattled by a profound fear that something had happened to her. He wondered if her sudden disappearance had anything to do with her visit to the Riverview apartments.

'There was a laptop at the property and a drawer full of utility bills,' Wells said. 'We're sifting through 'em now.'

'Then keep me informed,' Temple said. 'That woman is our prime suspect. We need to know what she did after leaving Hari Basu's flat at nine.'

'*If* she left when he claims she did,' Angel said from the front. 'We still can't be certain he's telling us the truth about that.'

Temple nodded. 'Precisely. So what more have we found out about the guy?'

Vaughan provided the update. Reading from his notes, he said, 'We've checked his phone records and there's nothing suspicious there. He made only two calls on Sunday. As you already know, guv, there was one in the morning to Clare Brennan's number, which is presumably when he arranged for her to visit him. The other was a long-distance call to his wife's mobile in India. We've also been across his email account and again, it hasn't thrown up anything of interest.'

A young DC named Felicity Munroe had been assigned to the task of going through the surveillance file on Daniel Prince that DCI Locke had arranged to be sent over from the Domestic Extremism Unit.

She confirmed that Basu's name hadn't cropped up in any of Prince's recorded conversations over the past year.

'The most interesting stuff from our point of view are the anonymous death threats that were made against him,' she said. 'Most were via email from fake addresses and some were texts and calls to his phone from untraceable numbers. There are about twenty in all and we're still working through them.'

'Anything else of interest?' Temple asked.

'Well, I suppose it's significant that there's nothing to suggest that he was having an affair with a married woman. If he was, then he must have communicated with her through other devices that hadn't been bugged by the unit.'

The conversation then moved to the other residents in the building, and none of them stood out as likely suspects.

'We haven't been able to establish a link between any of them and the individuals and organizations that were targeted by Prince in his blogs,' Vaughan said. 'But it's a time-consuming process because there are so many of them. So there's a lot more work to be done.'

'What about George Reese?' Temple said.

'We've checked with the company that employs him as a concierge,' Vaughan said. 'They didn't know he'd served time in prison for a scx assault. He didn't declare it before he was taken on and they neglected to carry out a check.'

'Anything suspicious arise from his phone records?'

Vaughan shook his head. 'No, but his bank account shows some large cash deposits over the past few months. The first was in June when £2000 was put into his account. Then he deposited £2000 in August and again in October.'

'And we don't know where the money came from?'

'It wasn't from his employers. But according to them, Reese does have a gambling problem, which is why in the past he was always overdrawn and in debt.'

'So the cash could have come from winnings?'

'It's possible,' Vaughan said. 'But then why would it be the exact same amount each time? I reckon that's a bit odd.'

'I agree,' Temple said. 'I want to have another chat with him so I'll raise it then.'

Finally Temple updated them on his conversation with Beth Fletcher in respect of the People-Power blog.

'She's determined to take it on,' he said. 'And that will mean another headache for us because she's setting herself up as a target.'

Less than half an hour after he spoke those words, Beth called to tell him about the death threat she'd received during the night.

CHAPTER 39

'WHY ON EARTH didn't you tell me sooner?' Temple asked Beth over the phone.

'Because I'm not going to take it seriously,' she said, her voice brittle. 'It was Faye who insisted I tell you. I wish now that I hadn't mentioned it to her.'

'She was right to insist, Miss Fletcher. You can't just ignore it.'

'Well, Daniel received many such threats, Inspector.'

'True. And look what happened.'

Silence stretched between them for a few seconds and he could hear the stress in her breathing.

'Would you please forward the email to my phone?' he asked. 'The address is on the card I gave you.'

'Very well. But I want you to know that it doesn't change anything. I won't be doing what this person wants me to do.'

'Then I hope you won't mind if I arrange some protection for you, just as a precaution.'

'I don't want to be followed around by a team of police heavies if that's what you mean. I'm sure this threat is only the first of many.'

'It's better to be safe than sorry, Miss Fletcher.'

'I feel I'm as safe as I need to be, Inspector. Whoever sent the email is almost certainly some nut job who wants a reaction.'

'Let's hope you're right, but in the circumstances I have to treat this as a credible threat.'

'But I don't think it is.'

Temple let out a breath. 'Look, I'll ask one of my officers to keep a close eye on you for a couple of days. It won't be intrusive, I promise. We can review the situation beyond that.'

She left it a couple of beats before responding.

'OK, but that's all. Not an army of men in bullet-proof vests.'

'You have my word. I'll get back to you asap. Meanwhile, I suggest you don't go out until we can determine whether or not this is a serious threat.'

After ending the call, Temple waited for the email to come through. It did a minute later, and after reading it twice, he felt a shudder run up his spine. To him it sounded genuine, and that was scary. But he was willing to bet that the email would not be traceable.

He contacted the technical team anyway in the hope that they'd prove him wrong. They said they'd give it a shot so he forwarded it to them.

Then he called Angel into his office and showed it to her.

'Blimey,' she said. 'That's disturbing.'

'Beth isn't taking it seriously, though. But I am so I want you to arrange for a team to watch her, discreetly and at a distance. I also want you to go over there and stay with her, at least for today.'

'Why me?'

'Two reasons. You've met her a couple of times already, and in the state she's in, she won't want a stranger hanging around. And secondly, you can use the time to keep an eye on William and Faye Connor. See if you can pick up anything else about them that's suspicious.'

'I've already put their names into the system,' she said. 'I should get feedback today on their work and financial status. I've also requested access to their bank accounts.'

'If you have any problems getting what you want, then let me know.'

Temple went up to Beresford's office to brief him on the latest development. DCI Locke was already there, providing him with her own update.

'Beth Fletcher received an anonymous death threat last night,' Temple said without preamble. 'It was in an email from someone claiming to be the person who killed Daniel Prince.'

Beresford nodded. 'I already know about it, Jeff. DCI Locke just told me.'

Temple fought down a sudden rush of anger and turned to Locke. She gave a small, apologetic smile without showing any teeth.

'I was only informed about it a little while ago during a

conference call with London,' she said. 'I came straight in to pass on the information.'

'So you lot now have Beth Fletcher under surveillance as well,' Temple said.

Her jaw tensed. 'It shouldn't come as a surprise to know that she's been on our watch list as long as her boyfriend was. She's helped him with his blogging from the start. Now that she's taking over, it's even more important that we know what she's up to.'

'Well, what's important to me is finding out who sent that email.'

'You won't be able to.'

'How can you be so sure?'

'Because we've tried. One of the death threats against Daniel Prince came from the same anonymous email address. It's among those in the file we sent you.'

'So maybe we should provide Beth Fletcher with some protection,' Beresford said.

'It's in hand, sir,' Temple said. 'But you should know that she's not happy about it. She had to be persuaded and she wants it kept low key.'

Beresford frowned. 'So she isn't taking it seriously then.'

Temple shrugged. 'She's convinced that the sender is just trying to scare her and that there'll be other threats before long.'

'There already have been,' Locke said. 'We're monitoring her Twitter account too. During the night, she received two tweets with threats to kill her. She probably hasn't seen them yet, and I expect they'll soon be taken down by the administrators.'

'Do you reckon they're from the same person?'

Locke shook her head. 'I doubt it. I've spoken to our people in London who are liaising with GCHQ. They believe the tweets are part of a coordinated campaign aimed at trying to persuade Beth not to keep the People-Power blog alive. Thousands of posts attacking her decision have already been uploaded to forums and social media sites.'

'So who the fuck is behind it?' Temple said.

'That's what I was just getting to with the Chief Superintendent when you arrived,' Locke said. 'The considered view among the experts is that the campaign was launched within an hour of Beth making her announcement and is being coordinated by the Russians.'

Temple laughed out loud. 'This just keeps getting better. How the hell would they organize something like this, for Christ's sake?'

'With very little difficulty,' Locke said. 'Have you heard of the Troll Factory?'

Temple had no idea what she was talking about and said so.

'The Troll Factory first came to our notice when one of its foot soldiers broke ranks and exposed the operation a few years ago,' Locke said. 'Ironically, the whistleblower is now a well-known blogger who campaigns against Russian aggression.'

'So what exactly is this Troll Factory?' Temple said. 'It sounds like something out of fantasy novel.'

Locke grinned. 'Its official title is the Internet Research Centre. It's run from a four-storey building in St Petersburg, and the set-up is somewhat Orwellian. Over a thousand state-sponsored employees work around the clock. Their job is to bombard the internet with pro-Kremlin propaganda and attack anyone who is critical, or poses a threat to Russia.

'The operation targets sites across the world, including CNN and the BBC, and it posts messages on hundreds of fake Twitter and Facebook accounts. It also sends out emails, and these include death threats against various individuals. So it's quite possible the one sent to Beth Fletcher came from the factory.'

'But if that's the case, then doesn't it give credence to the theory that the Russians were behind Prince's murder because of his upcoming campaign urging people to boycott Russian goods?' Temple said.

Locke nodded. 'Absolutely. And what better time to strike than while Prince is causing major problems for the

British government, who would be bound to suffer from any backlash.'

'So why not just kill him? Why try to make it look like suicide?'

'Well, I suppose they'd have taken the view that with a suicide there wouldn't be a major inquiry, just a load of flak. And suicide would have made Prince less popular among his blog followers.'

'But instead they made mistakes and we realized it was murder.'

'Exactly. So might I suggest you see if any of the residents in the block are from Russia or have links, however tenuous, with the Kremlin?'

CHAPTER 40

As TEMPLE STRODE back to the operations room, he could feel the frustration growing inside him. This case was like no other he had ever dealt with and it was proving extremely challenging.

The Russians, for pity's sake. How the hell was he supposed to explore that line of inquiry?

Beresford and DCI Locke had agreed to seek help from the intelligence agencies, including MI5 and MI6. They'd ask them if they had any information linking the Russians with Prince's death and the threats against Beth.

Temple, meanwhile, would press ahead with trying to identify the person, or persons, who had actually carried out the killing, perhaps on behalf of the Kremlin, or more specifically the country's notorious Federal Security Service.

He would never have put it past them, of course. In recent years, the escalating tensions between Russia and western countries had plunged the world into a new cold war. This time round, the battlegrounds were less extensive and the battle-lines less clear. But it was nonetheless a serious situation because Russia was feeling threatened like never before.

Capital was fleeing the country, its credit markets were shrinking, and its economy had entered a deep recession, partly due to western sanctions.

It was therefore highly plausible that the Kremlin would seek to put a stop to campaigns by an influential blogger that threatened to impose further economic hardship on the country.

Daniel Prince would have been regarded as an enemy of the state. There was no doubt about that. The Russians, like the Brits, would have been monitoring his blog and probably intercepting all his communications as well. They would have known that his popularity was growing and that he was about to target them.

Indeed, the Russian president had publicly slammed Prince as a rabble-rouser for proposing a goods boycott.

It was highly unlikely they'd be able to prove that the Russians – or any other foreign power for that matter – had given the order to have Prince eliminated and to make it look like suicide.

But mistakes had been made so there was a strong possibility that whoever committed the murder was still in Southampton, and perhaps living in the Riverview apartment complex.

It was up to Temple and his team to find out who it was.

Every nerve in Temple's body was jumping when he entered the operations room. He had to force calm into his voice as he started barking out orders.

'I know there's a real mix of nationalities in the Riverview building, including one or more Russians,' he said. 'Have a closer look at them, and at any other residents who might have links with that country.'

He told the team about the threat contained in the email sent to Beth Fletcher and how they were responding. He also gave them a rundown of his conversation with DCI Locke about the so-called Troll Factory.

Then he asked for an update on Clare Brennan. He was told they had just been sent a copy of her mobile phone record for the past two months.

'I was just about to go through it,' DC Doug Wells said.

'Bring it into my office and we'll look at it together,' Temple instructed him.

As expected, Clare Brennan made and received a lot of calls. Many of those she'd made began with the 02380 code for Southampton and were probably her clients. But most were mobile numbers and they were invariably short, lasting no more than a minute on average.

There was also a long list of text messages and these proved more illuminating. Some were quite explicit, especially those she'd received from punters.

Can I book you for two hours tonight? I'm feeling really horny.

I'm desperately in need of a fuck. Can you come over in the next hour? The wife's at her mum's.

Have to say the BJ you gave me last night was the best I've ever had. Worth every penny. X until next time.

A series of messages stood out, though. They were less crude and suggested a different kind of familiarity between Brennan and the sender, who signed them off with the initial B.

Call me when you're done, babe. We should go out ... B x

Bumped into Fran today. She sent her regards ... B x

The last recorded text exchange was actually at 11 p.m. on Sunday evening, an hour after Daniel Prince was pushed from his balcony.

Finished for the night, hon. Shall I come over?

You'd better. Got plenty of booze and shit so we're gonna have a real bender ... B x

It didn't take them long to run a trace on the other mobile phone number. It belonged to a man named Barry Woodwood, who had an address in the Portswood area of the city.

Temple felt his heart jump. 'He must be the boyfriend the neighbour mentioned. We need to get over there pronto.'

CHAPTER 41

BARRY WOODWOOD LIVED in a rundown street where the terraced houses were drenched in the same dull shade of grey. Overflowing wheelie bins lined the pavements and bits of rubbish were strewn across the small front gardens.

Even the sun that had at last penetrated the cloud cover couldn't eradicate the grimness. There were similar streets all over the city, infested with lost hope and people struggling on benefits.

They arrived mob-handed. Two police patrol cars, a rapid response vehicle, and an unmarked pool car containing Temple, Dave Vaughan and two other detectives.

The vehicles screeched to a halt in front of Barry Woodwood's house, blocking the road and causing alarm among the few people out walking.

'That's Clare Brennan's car on the driveway,' Vaughan said, pointing to the red VW they'd seen on the security video. 'Looks like we've found her.'

The softy-softly approach had been discounted in favour of a forced entry. Clare Brennan was, after all, the prime suspect in a major murder investigation, and Temple and his team had no idea what to expect or what she was capable of.

An officer wearing a visored helmet used a steel tubular battering ram to shatter the door locks. Then four more officers in body armour stormed in, yelling at the tops of their voices.

It was a textbook entry and in less than a minute, the all-clear was given.

The heavy, cloying stench of drugs hit Temple as soon as he stepped into the hallway. It hung in the air like an invisible cloud and made him feel nauseous.

The downstairs looked as unpleasant as it smelled. The hall carpet was threadbare and wallpaper was peeling in places.

In the living room, clothes and discarded cigarette packets were strewn across the floor. The beige sofa was covered in unsightly stains and Temple spotted at least two ashtrays filled with the remains of soggy cannabis joints.

The kitchen was even messier. The sink was filled with dirty crockery and the worktops cluttered with fast-food cartons half-filled with leftovers.

'This is what I call a classy joint,' Vaughan commented as he followed Temple up the stairs.

In the main bedroom, a uniformed officer was standing over a double bed on which two people were lying.

They both appeared to be naked beneath a duvet that barely covered their bodies. And they remained unconscious despite the fact that the curtains had been opened, flooding the room with bright, winter sunshine.

The woman was face up and Temple recognized her as the same woman who had walked out of the apartment block shortly after Prince tumbled to his death. She looked pale and dehydrated, not anywhere near as glamorous as she'd seemed on the video.

She had dark crescents under her eyes, and her hair was damp and matted.

The man next to her was lying on his side and snoring. He was thin and unhealthy looking, with a shaved head and a short, gingery beard.

'I'm assuming the beefcake is Barry Woodwood and he's her boyfriend,' Temple said. 'Looks like they're sleeping off one hell of a bender.'

The response to a criminal records check had come through

while they were in the car. It revealed that Barry Woodwood, aged twenty-nine, had three convictions for minor drug offences and one for shoplifting. He was an unsavoury character all right, and Temple wouldn't have been surprised if he was pimping out his girlfriend.

Vaughan prodded them both awake, but although they opened their eyes and protested, it was obvious they were in the throes of a drug-induced hangover.

'We won't get any sense out of them in this state,' Temple said. 'Let's call an ambulance and get them checked over. Then we'll bring them round and see what they've got to say. Meanwhile, call out forensics. I want this place turned over.'

The couple were hauled out of bed and told to get dressed. It was a farcical sight because they were still spaced out and couldn't find their clothes. But they did wake up enough to confirm who they were.

'So who the fuck are you lot?' Barry Woodwood mumbled.

Temple backed away from him because the guy's breath stank.

'We're the police,' he said. 'An ambulance will be here shortly and you'll be examined to make sure that you're OK. Then you're coming to the station to be questioned.'

Woodwood stared at Temple through eyes that struggled to focus.

'What are we supposed to have done?'

Temple ignored the question and asked him what they'd been bingeing on.

Woodwood smiled broadly. 'A batch of mind-blowing shit, man. Once we got started we couldn't stop. What a night!'

Temple tried but failed to get any sense out of Clare Brennan. She managed to pull on a black velour tracksuit as she moved around the bedroom, as though sleep-walking.

Up close, she wasn't exactly a stunner. Her eyes were set too close together, her teeth were slightly off colour, and her skin bore the pallor of excessive smoking and drinking.

Temple left her to the paramedics as soon as the ambulance arrived and then went back downstairs with Vaughan.

'If those guys tell us the pair are OK, then we'll let them sleep it off in a cell,' he said.

In the event, the paramedics decided it was best if they took Brennan and Woodwood to the general hospital to be given the once over by a doctor.

It was just as well because as they were being led out of the house, Temple took a call that threw up a new problem he needed to react to.

'It's about Beth,' Angel said. 'I'm at her neighbours' flat and she's not here.'

'So where is she?'

'That's just it. She went out about fifteen minutes ago and no one can contact her.'

Temple gave a sharp intake of breath. 'Christ. Didn't the Connors try to stop her?'

'They say she ignored them and said she had things to do.'

CHAPTER 42

BETH'S PULSE HAMMERED against her skull as she walked and her stomach was churning. But she was relieved to be outside at last, drawing the cold air into her lungs.

Faye and William's flat had started to feel small and oppressive, and she hadn't been able to stand it any longer. She wanted to be alone to get her head straight.

She didn't care about the fuss she'd cause or about threats from anonymous trolls. She needed to take care of herself and start the fight back against grief. She couldn't do either if she felt imprisoned in a flat that wasn't her own.

Beneath her coat, she wore thick black tights, one of Faye's woollen sweaters, and a knee-length skirt. Her hair was fastened tightly back and her leather handbag hung from her shoulder.

She made her way through the streets with a slow gait, in

no hurry to get anywhere. She had turned her phone off so that no one, not even the police, could contact her. That way she wouldn't come under any pressure or have to explain herself.

As she walked the memories pulled at her. She passed Daniel's favourite coffee shop next to the marina development called Ocean Village. It was where he went to write many of his blogs.

Then she paused outside the restaurant in Oxford Street where they'd had their last meal out together. A sob exploded in her throat as her mind conjured up an image of the two of them sitting at the table next to the window.

Her mind drifted through other memories as she approached the city centre, but she tried not to let them over-whelm her. She knew that this would only be a short respite before she was forced back into the spotlight. The baying media would be waiting and so too would the thousands of people who were already hailing her as Daniel's successor.

But she wasn't ready to lose total control of her life just yet. Not until she at least began to emerge from the black hole of bereavement.

Assuming that she ever would.

'So what exactly did Beth say?' Temple asked William and Faye Connor when he got to their flat on the Riverview apartment complex.

It was the husband who replied. 'She just said she needed to go out because she had things to do. We told her we didn't think she should because of the death threat, but she didn't seem worried about it. When we offered to go with her she told us she wanted to be alone.'

'And did she give a clue as to what she needed to do and where she might go?'

'None at all. She suddenly appeared wearing her coat and it looked as though she'd been crying again.'

They were standing in the living room – Temple, Mr and Mrs Connor, Angel and Joseph Kessel, who had popped up to

145

see Beth, only to discover that she had gone walkabout.

'She must have switched her phone off,' Kessel said. 'I've been trying to call her.'

'We all have,' William said.

Kessel shook his head. 'I wish I'd known about the email earlier. I would have come straight up. Maybe I could have made her see sense.'

'I doubt it,' Faye said. 'She was determined to go out. I think she felt she needed space. This isn't her home and she hasn't been entirely comfortable here.'

'Do you think she's in danger?' Kessel asked Temple. 'I mean, are the police concerned about the email threat?'

Temple chose not to tell him that it was one of several death threats.

'We have to take it seriously,' he said. 'That's why Detective Metcalfe came over here to be with her.'

'So are you able to find out who sent it?'

'We're working on it, but in all honesty it's highly unlikely. Anyone can send an email anonymously and not leave a trace.'

Temple noted down a description of what Beth was wearing and relayed it to Control so that an alert could be put out.

A dark unease had pushed its way into his mind. He wanted to believe that Beth wasn't in imminent danger if she had simply gone for a walk into town. But it would soon be midday and there was always the chance that the emailer would follow through with the threat to kill her if she didn't announce that she'd changed her mind about running the People-Power blog.

He would probably have been less worried if it hadn't been for what DCI Locke had told him about the Russians. If they were behind it, then it was reasonable to assume that they were monitoring her movements and could therefore swoop at any time.

Faye offered to make everyone tea and while she set about it, Temple asked Kessel if Beth had any friends in the city she might have decided to visit.

'I know she had a few,' he said. 'But I've never seen any or heard her talk about them.'

As William Connor turned away to help his wife, Temple lowered his voice and said, 'Have you told anyone else about Daniel Prince's affair since we discussed it, Mr Kessel?'

'Of course not. And it wasn't me who spread it all over social media. I assumed that you must have told someone.'

'I can assure you, we didn't make it public.'

'Then perhaps it was the woman he got involved with,' Kessel said. 'Do you know who she is yet?'

Temple shook his head. 'We haven't actually come across any evidence of an affair. All we have to go on is your conversation with Prince.'

'Well, I don't know what to say, except that I didn't make it up.'

'I'm not suggesting for one minute that you did, Mr Kessel. But whatever your friend was up to, he did a bloody good job keeping it under wraps.'

A phone went off suddenly and they all looked at each other to see whose it was.

'It's mine,' Angel said as she pulled it from her pocket.

Kessel chose that moment to announce that he was going to take a walk into the city centre to see if he could spot Beth.

'If I do, I'll call you straightaway,' he told Temple.

As he left the flat, Angel came off the phone and said to Temple that she needed to have a quiet word with him. They went out on the landing from where Temple could see that SOCOs were still at work inside Prince's flat next door.

'So what's up?' he said.

'I told you I was waiting for answers to my questions about William and Faye Connor,' she said. 'They've just come through and it turns out my suspicions were justified.'

'How so?'

'Well, we put in motion all the usual checks. Inland Revenue, DVLA, passport office. But we've been denied access to all of them. We've been told we can't even get our eyes on the tenancy agreement to this flat.'

'I don't understand,' Temple said. 'Who's shutting us out?'

Angel raised her brow. 'Believe it or not, it's the Home Office. They've apparently attached a red flag to the names.'

'But why?'

'That's the question we're going to have to put to the couple. And there's no time like the present.'

CHAPTER 43

WHEN BETH ARRIVED at her first destination, she was almost too upset to go in.

Her heart was beating high up in her chest and her legs felt weak. But she told herself it had to be done and the sooner she confronted it, the better.

It was the only funeral directors office she knew of in Southampton because she'd walked past it many times.

As she stepped through the doorway, she was hit by a wave of sadness that left her reeling. She stood for several seconds in the unmanned reception area, doing all she could to stop herself crying. Then a woman appeared and Beth took a deep breath, as though preparing her lungs for a long underwater siege.

'Can I help you, madam?' the woman said in a pleasant voice.

She was middle-aged, plump and wearing a black trouser suit. Dark freckles dotted the bridge of her pointed nose.

Beth managed a limp smile. 'I need to arrange a funeral for my fiancé.'

She was there for almost an hour. The woman, who recognized Beth as soon as she gave Daniel's name, took down all the relevant details. She said she would enquire on Beth's behalf as to when the body would be released and she read out a list of costs.

Beth selected a mahogany coffin from a brochure and said

she wanted Daniel to be cremated.

Somehow she managed to get through it without breaking down, but her jaw ached from where she'd been grinding her teeth so much.

Her next stop was a nearby pub where she sat in a corner and downed two gin and tonics. A flush of red crept back into her cheeks, but the drink didn't make her feel any better.

As she left the pub, she checked her watch and realized that the deadline of midday set by her anonymous emailer had come and gone. It was now two o'clock and she was still very much alive.

She found herself in the little park just off the high street in the city centre. It was virtually empty. Clouds were gathering overhead and a breeze set the trees swaying.

She sat on a bench and contemplated contacting DCI Temple to assure him that she was OK, but then decided not to. She wasn't ready to face the world again just yet. There were other places she wanted to visit, including St Peter's Church where she was going to light a candle and immerse herself in prayer for a while. She wasn't a religious person, but she did believe in God and she was hoping to find comfort by being close to him.

A voice jerked her out of her reverie. It belonged to one of two men who were suddenly standing in front of her. She hadn't noticed them approaching along the path and her first thought was that they were a homeless pair who wanted money.

But then she registered the fact that their clothes looked clean and expensive. One was wearing a long, dark overcoat and the other a smart, black leather jacket. Both appeared to be in their mid-thirties.

'I'm sorry, I didn't catch that,' Beth said. 'What did you say?'

'We just wondered if we might sit next to you,' the one in the overcoat said.

But before she could respond, they quickly sat either side of her, causing a twist of panic to wrench in her gut.

She was given no time to react. The overcoat man flung his

arm behind her and grabbed her hair, pulling back her head.

'If you scream, I'll break your neck,' he warned, and she noticed this time that he had a slight Slavic accent.

At the same time, his mate produced a hypodermic syringe from his pocket, which she caught a glimpse of before he plunged the needle into the side of her neck.

She let out a small cry, but she knew there was no one close enough to hear it and raise the alarm or come to her aid.

'It's just to make you more compliant,' Overcoat Man said. 'In a second, we're all going to take a short walk and we want to make sure you don't try to run away.'

Whatever it was that had been injected into her blood-stream started to work immediately. She felt dizzy suddenly and her vision blurred.

She realized with sickening clarity that there was nothing she could do. She was at their mercy.

She could feel the muscles knotting in her stomach and along her arms. Her mouth flooded with saliva and she thought she would vomit.

But instead she was overcome by a sense of weightlessness as her senses were swamped by the drug. She tried to speak but the words wouldn't form in her mouth. It was as though a lump had reared up in her throat.

'Time to go,' a voice said.

She felt herself being lifted off the bench. Her legs were as fragile as twigs but the men stood either side of her to keep her upright.

She was conscious of walking between them and she was vaguely aware of her surroundings, which were grey and out of focus.

Sludge was running through her veins and in the deeper folds of her mind, she was angry with herself for being so stupidly complacent. She should have listened to the detective and taken the death threat seriously.

Now it was too late.

'It's just a short walk to the car,' the voice said. 'You're doing well, Miss Fletcher.'

She could just make out the shape of a car as they approached it. She heard the click of the central locking system and her brain told her to try to run for it. But her body wouldn't – or couldn't – respond.

As she was pushed onto the back seat, she wondered who these men were.

And if they were the same bastards who had pushed Daniel to his death.

CHAPTER 44

TEMPLE SPENT A couple of minutes studying Beth's neighbours when he and Angel went back into their flat.

He watched Faye Connor as she poured the teas, and he watched her husband as he placed the mugs on the table in front of them.

They looked and behaved like any ordinary couple. He'd been told that she was an event organizer and he was a business consultant. They did not have any children and had lived in the block for six months.

But Temple wondered now if they were actually who they said they were. And he wondered too what was so special about the pair.

It was very rare to come across individuals who had red flag alerts attached to their names by a government department, security agency or even the police. It usually meant one of three things - they were wanted by the authorities, they were being watched, or they were being protected.

Whatever the case was with the Connors, their presence in the building raised some alarming possibilities. As did the fact that they were renting the flat next door to Daniel Prince.

Was it possible they had dropped in on him on Sunday evening? Prince would no doubt have opened the front door to them. And together, the couple could have dragged him out onto the balcony and hauled him over the balustrade. The thought of it sent a cold blast through Temple's body.

Were they working for the Russians? he wondered. Had they been installed in the block so that they could spy on Prince? Was that why they had been collecting cuttings and files on him and storing them in a box file? And were they ordered to kill him just as his blogging campaign against Russia was about to get off the ground?

Neither of them seemed ill at ease playing host to the two detectives. William Connor sat with an easy composure facing Temple and Angel across the dining table. He had piercing brown eyes and came across as self-assured without being arrogant.

His wife, who stood with her back to the sink while sipping tea, had a posture that was straight and confident. There was nothing in her manner to suggest that she was anything other than a respectable, law-abiding British citizen.

Temple was still trying to decide how to approach the situation when Faye Connor cleared her throat and said, 'So how is the investigation coming along, Inspector? Are you close to finding out who killed Daniel?'

Temple leaned forward across the table and allowed a frown to form on his forehead.

'Actually there's a question I'd like you to answer first, Mrs Connor,' he said. 'And I'm hoping you'll be totally honest with me.'

He saw a slight shift in her eyes and her voice wavered a little when she replied.

'That's an odd thing to say, Inspector. I wouldn't dream of lying to you about anything.'

He held her gaze and noticed how her face suddenly filled with colour.

'I'm glad to hear it, Mrs Connor. So perhaps you can tell me why you and your husband have really been collecting newspaper photos and cuttings featuring Mr Prince. And don't insult my intelligence by saying it's because you were his biggest fans and you wanted to put them in a scrapbook. That just doesn't fly. In fact, it's got to be complete bullshit, if you'll excuse the language.'

She swallowed hard and looked at her husband, whose expression didn't change and remained unreadable.

Then she moistened her lips and said, 'I suggest you finish your tea and leave, Inspector. I'm not prepared to respond to your slanderous allegations. You have no right to speak to me like that.'

Temple shifted his gaze to her husband. 'What about you, Mr Connor? Are you prepared to tell me what the pair of you are really up to?'

The man's composure faltered and he suddenly seemed keen not to make eye contact.

'I don't know what you're talking about,' he said. 'But my wife is right. You're out of order.'

'And you're mistaken if you think I can just drop this,' Temple said. 'You see, the box file isn't the only thing that doesn't make sense. We've been trying to find out more about you and your wife and we've been coming up against an unusual amount of resistance.'

'That's probably because you have no business prying into our private lives. We've done nothing wrong, and I'm sure you can't believe we were involved in Daniel's death.'

'That's where you're wrong, Mr Connor. This is a murder investigation so we have a right to delve into your background. But for some reason we're not being allowed access. And let me make it clear that you *are* suspects, just like everyone else living in this building. In fact, you've shot right to the top of the list. So you need to tell me who you really are and why our own government has put a red flag alert against your names.'

'What's a red flag alert?'

'Don't pretend you don't know what I'm talking about,' Temple said. 'You're either being monitored because you're dangerous and pose a threat, or you're involved in some clandestine activity. So what is it?'

William Connor pulled in a long breath and looked at his wife, who surprised Temple by shrugging her shoulders.

'You might as well tell him,' she said with a heavy sigh. 'I don't want it coming back on us.'

Her husband then turned back to Temple and said, 'For your information, Inspector, we wanted them to tell you yesterday. But they thought it best if we kept quiet in the hope that you wouldn't find out. They were keen for us to stay put with our assumed identities intact so that we could continue the close monitoring of Beth Fletcher, especially after she told the world she was going to take over Daniel's blog.'

Temple's mouth went dry, his tongue sticking to the palate. He suddenly knew the answers to his next two questions, but he asked them anyway.

'So who is it the pair of you work for, Mr Connor? And who should I be bollocking for keeping me in the dark?'

After a pause, William Connor said, 'We work undercover for the Domestic Extremism Unit. The officer we report to is DCI Jennifer Locke. I believe you've made her acquaintance.'

CHAPTER 45

ON THE WAY back to the station, Angel warned Temple not to lose his temper when he confronted DCI Locke.

'I know what you're like,' she said. 'You'll go over the top and say something you'll later regret.'

As he drove, his eyes glittered with repressed anger. One of the things he hated about the modern police force was the lack of trust and respect between department heads. It was as though playing politics and keeping secrets was expected of them. It happened on a scale that should have been unacceptable, but for some reason was tolerated.

Too many senior officers ran their divisions and departments as if they were their own little fiefdoms. They failed to cooperate, they adopted a defensive stance, and they seemed to relish territorial disputes.

DCI Locke should not have withheld the information about her two undercover detectives, and Temple was going to tell her that in no uncertain terms.

'Why don't we go and have some lunch and a drink?' Angel said. 'Give yourself time to calm down.'

'I'm not hungry,' he said. 'And besides, I need to sort this out so that I can move on to the other stuff. With any luck, we'll shortly be able to talk to Clare Brennan.'

'What about Beth? How long do we give it before we start to worry?'

'I'm already worried,' Temple said. 'If we don't hear from her soon, I might even start to panic.'

'Chances are she's just having a walk through town to clear her head. And I can understand it. She's upset and stressed out. Who wouldn't be considering what she's going through?'

'You're probably right. I'm just praying she doesn't come to any harm while she's doing that.'

Temple had called ahead, asking for an urgent meeting with DCI Locke and the chief super. Locke was waiting in Beresford's office when he arrived, and before he even opened his mouth to speak, she said, 'I know what this is about because William Connor just rang me.'

He gave her a cold, implacable stare. 'So why don't you call him by his real name, whatever the fuck that is?'

She stood up to face him, a defiant glint in her eyes. 'I've explained to the Chief Superintendent why I felt it necessary to maintain their covers. A lot of time and effort went into creating and then establishing their fake identities. I didn't want to see them blown if it could be avoided. That was one of the reasons I came to Southampton. I needed to monitor the situation in respect of my detectives.'

Temple felt the blood move to his face, warming it.

'Is that because you knew they were suspects and you wanted to protect them?'

'They don't need my protection. They didn't kill Prince and you know it. I can vouch for them and what happened shocked them more than anyone. They were the ones who called to tell me what had happened.'

'You should have told me about them,' Temple said. 'You shouldn't have let us waste our time.'

'And you should have told me they were in the frame. But you didn't mention them so I didn't think I needed to worry.'

He let loose a snort of derision. 'But you knew we were looking at every resident in the building. And you must have known that DI Metcalfe was carrying out background checks on the Connors.'

'I was only made aware of that when it was flagged up a short time ago,' she said, her voice soft and solicitous. 'And for what it's worth, I'm sorry you found out the way you did. I wish now I'd been open with you from the start. I've already apologized to the chief here.'

Temple was in no way placated, and the blood continued to thunder through his veins. He was about to say something he would probably have regretted, but Beresford got in first with a timely intervention.

'Look, this is an issue for me to deal with, Jeff,' he said. 'I don't want you to get worked up about it. You've already got enough on your plate. So please just take a breath and accept the apology. Then get on with the job. I hear you're about to question our prime suspect.'

Temple bit his tongue and counted to ten, by which time he had his anger under control. Then he turned his attention back to Locke.

'I just hope you're not holding anything more back from me,' he said, softening his words with a smile. 'Only I've had my fill of nasty surprises.'

'There are no more to come,' she said. 'And please believe me when I say that I'm here to assist you in any way I can.'

'Then tell me you weren't lying about having no knowledge of the listening device in Prince's flat,' he said.

She shook head. 'I wasn't. We had his phones and internet covered. Plus we had our people next door whose job it was to stay close to him and keep us informed of what he was up to.

They were also tasked with building up a dossier. The box file Beth found was part of that process. She was never meant to see it.'

She crossed the room and held out her hand for him to shake.

'No hard feelings then?' she said.

He took her hand and squeezed it slightly harder than was necessary. Then he told her that he accepted her apology and there were no hard feelings.

But he didn't tell her that he still wouldn't trust her as far as he could spit.

CHAPTER 46

BETH WOKE SLOWLY through a haze of fog that felt cold and claustrophobic. Her head was heavy and her chest was pumping for oxygen.

It wasn't until the fog had lifted that she realized that she wasn't surfacing from a horrible nightmare. And she wasn't in her own bed.

She remembered the park, the two men, the hypodermic syringe. And before that, the walk through the city and her visit to the funeral directors.

She took a large breath, struggling to keep the panic in. But a raw terror rushed through her body, freezing the blood in her veins. Her eyes took a while to focus, and when they did, her breathing became even more laboured and frantic.

She was lying on a bare mattress in a small, drab room. An insipid light came from an exposed light bulb suspended from the ceiling. It revealed scores of dust motes floating in the air.

There was no bed, and no sheets, pillows or blankets. But thankfully she was still fully-clothed, except for her coat which was lying on the hardwood floor next to the mattress. There was no sign of her handbag, though, which contained her phone and purse.

She hauled herself to a sitting position and saw that she was alone. At once questions crowded her mind.

Where am I? What the hell did they inject me with to render me helpless so quickly and for so long? How long was I unconscious?

She checked her watch and found the answer to that last question. It was 5.30 p.m. So she had been out for over three hours. Jesus.

She looked around, scared and disoriented, the panic clouding her thoughts.

There was no furniture and in that respect it was like being in a cell. The mattress lay on the floor in the centre of the room, which was about ten feet square, and had a single door and a window with a curtain pulled across it.

She held her breath to listen for any sounds, but the silence had a texture to it. She felt she could almost touch it.

An image of her two captors flashed unbidden into her mind. Their faces were indistinct but they were tall and smartly dressed. An overcoat and a leather jacket.

They must have been following me, she thought. How else would they have known I'd be sitting on a park bench at that time? And they knew her name. She distinctly remembered one of them referring to her as Miss Fletcher.

So who were they and why had they brought her here?

A sharp spike of dread worked its way under her ribs, and she fought down the urge to cry. She knew that her situation was dire and that she was intensely vulnerable. They had her bag and her phone. Nobody else knew where she was, and she wouldn't be able to stop them doing whatever they wanted to do with her.

There was little doubt in her mind that they would eventually kill her. She was certain too that her captors must have been behind the death threat email.

Please do not treat this as an idle threat. I was the person who threw your boyfriend from the balcony and wrote his suicide note. And I'll be the one to ensure that something just as unpleasant happens to you.

She had convinced herself it wasn't a credible threat. After all, Daniel had received lots of them.

And she'd also told herself that she didn't care if she died. But of course that was before she was faced with the gruesome prospect. Now she recoiled at the thought that she probably didn't have very long to live.

In fact, all the muscles and sinews in her body were taut with fear, and she could feel her heart pounding high up in her throat.

She waited for her head to stop spinning and got to her feet. But it was a struggle because it felt like her limbs had been infused with cement.

She shuffled across the room and grabbed the door handle. She wasn't at all surprised when she discovered that the door was locked.

She turned and went over to the window, pulling back the thin cotton curtain. There was nothing much to see beyond the grimy glass. It was dark outside, but she could just make out the black shapes of trees set against an inky canvas sky.

A cold chill crept over her shoulders and down her neck. She clenched her fists to stop her hands from shaking and placed her back against the wall. Then she slid to the floor and sat with her knees raised.

Tears filled her eyes and she quickly wiped them away because she didn't want to cry. Instead, she was going to get her breath back to a steady rhythm and wait to see what fate had in store for her.

CHAPTER 47

CLARE BRENNAN LOOKED a right mess when she was escorted into the interview room just after five. Her face was ashen, drained of any blood, and she looked wide-eyed and detached.

She and her boyfriend Barry Woodwood had been

checked over at the hospital and given the all-clear by a doctor. According to him, they had binged on cannabis joints and legal highs. But they didn't actually overdose and were described as seasoned drug takers, not hardcore addicts.

They'd been brought to the station in separate cars, and Woodwood was being questioned in another room. They hadn't yet been told why the house had been raided and they'd been arrested.

That was the first thing Clare demanded to know when she sat down opposite Temple and Vaughan.

'It's fucking outrageous,' she said, her bottom lip quivering. 'I haven't done anything wrong and neither has Barry.'

Temple switched on the recording machine and went through the routine of stating the date, time and names of those present.

As he spoke, Clare's nostrils flared and she started to shiver even though it was warm in the room.

'You're wasting your time if this is because of the drugs,' she said, and for the first time Temple detected a faint trace of an Irish lilt in her voice. 'They were legal. We're not into the hard stuff.'

She was clearly agitated, but still too wasted to go into a full-blown rant. She kept blinking, and her eyes seemed to lose focus every few seconds.

Temple suspected that she still wasn't in a proper state of mind to be formally interviewed, but he wasn't prepared to wait any longer given the seriousness of the situation.

'I'll get straight to the point, Miss Brennan,' he said. 'This is not about the drugs. We want to ask you some questions about your visit to the Riverview apartment complex on Sunday evening.'

A deep frown scored her forehead.

'How do you know I was there?' she said.

'We've spoken to your client, Hari Basu. And we saw you on security cameras arriving and leaving.'

She leaned forward. 'So what's the problem? Hari is a friend and we're consenting adults. No money changed hands if that's what he's told you.'

It was Vaughan who responded. 'Look, don't waste our time, love. We know you're a whore and that you have previous. But right now we don't give a monkey's about that. What we want to know is what else you got up to on Sunday apart from shagging Hari Basu.'

Her body stiffened and her voice became more strident.

'Hey, what's going on here? Am I missing something? Do I need a lawyer?'

'Just keep calm and answer the questions,' Temple said, his tone more conciliatory. 'If you've done nothing wrong then you won't need a lawyer.'

'But you're making this sound like it's serious shit.'

'Murder *is* serious, Miss Brennan. That's why I'd advise you to be completely truthful with us.'

'Murder!' The word came out of her mouth with a loud gasp. 'Who the fucking hell has been murdered?'

Her reaction appeared genuine and prompted the two detectives to exchange glances.

'You're really scaring me now,' Clare said. 'I ain't no murderer.'

'We're not saying you are,' Temple said.

'Then what are you on about?'

Temple narrowed his eyes. 'Can you confirm that Barry Woodwood is your boyfriend?'

She nodded. 'He is, but so what?'

'And have you been at his house since Sunday evening?'

She nodded again. 'You know I have. I told the doctor.'

'So what time did you arrive there?' Temple asked.

She shrugged. 'I'm not sure. Around midnight, I suppose. I've been there ever since.'

'So you haven't seen the news?'

She looked even more confused. 'We didn't switch the telly on. We were too busy having a good time and sleeping.'

'You're not aware then that Daniel Prince was thrown from his balcony at the Riverview apartments while you were there?'

'Who's Daniel Prince?'

'Are you saying you don't know him?'

'I'm saying I've never frigging heard of him.'

'Are you sure about that?'

'Of course I'm bloody sure.' The muscles in her face appeared to seize up. 'Look, is this some kind of joke, because if it is then it's not fucking funny. I don't know anyone named Prince and I certainly didn't push him from his balcony.'

'So what time did you leave Hari Basu's flat?' Vaughan asked her.

'Nine o'clock,' she said. 'I was with him for an hour.'

'So how come you didn't leave the building until ten?'

Her confusion grew, and she had to think about it.

'Well, there's no mystery to that,' she said. 'I went to see another client. Viktor Lorak. He lives on the fourth floor. I was with him for an hour, too.'

Now we're getting somewhere, Temple thought and made a note of the name.

'So you left Mr Lorak at ten,' he said. 'Then where did you go?'

'I went straight home. When I got there, I sent a text to Barry, asking him if he wanted me to come over.'

'When you left the building, did you see anything happening out front?'

She screwed up her brow and said, 'I saw George. He's the concierge. He was standing around with a group of people on the forecourt, but I didn't pay them any attention because I was in a hurry to get away.'

Temple made her go through it again and she didn't change her story. She said that Viktor Lorak was a regular client who was single and lived alone. He was a Ukrainian and worked for an insurance company in the city centre.

She insisted she had never met anyone named Daniel Prince and she had no other clients in the Riverview building.

She also told them that Barry Woodwood was not her pimp, but he was aware of what she did for a living.

'He loves me despite that,' she said.

Temple felt deflated. If what she was saying was true – and it sounded to him like it was – then they were no further forward.

'I don't know why you think I had anything to do with that man's murder,' Clare said. 'I've never heard of him and I didn't go to his flat. Why am I even a suspect? That block of flats must have been full of people when I was there.'

'But you walked out of the building only a few minutes after Mr Prince was pushed from his balcony on the tenth floor,' Temple said.

She shrugged. 'But that must have been a coincidence. Viktor will vouch for me. He'll tell you I was with him until ten.'

'And what about after you left his flat? Did you see anyone or anything suspicious then?'

She tightened her face in concentration for a few moments and said, 'Well, there was no one around except for the bloke in the lift. But he totally ignored me when I said hi.'

Temple felt his stomach muscles contract. 'Why didn't you mention this man before?'

'Because you didn't ask me if I'd seen anyone else.'

'So what more can you tell us about him?'

She pursed her lips. 'Nothing much really. He was wearing jeans and a blue cardy with a hood, so I only got a glimpse of his face because he turned away from me.'

'Was he young or old? Black or white?'

'White and not very old.' Her hand flew to her mouth. 'Jesus. Do you think he could have been the killer?'

'It's possible,' Temple said. 'On what floor did he get into the lift?'

'I don't know. He was in it already when it stopped for me on the fourth.'

'And what happened then?'

'Nothing. We went down together and he kept his body turned slightly away from me. You know, like he wanted to avoid eye contact so he didn't have to make conversation.'

Temple frowned. 'But that can't be right. On the security

footage, you were the only person who stepped out of the lift when it reached the lobby.'

She nodded. 'That was because he got out on the first floor.'

CHAPTER 48

CLARE BRENNAN WAS told that she'd be kept at the station while her story was checked out. She didn't object, and was clearly relieved rather than annoyed.

Temple and Vaughan hurried back to the operations room and called the troops together. Temple told them what Clare Brennan had said and then invited DC Doug Wells to brief them on his interview with Barry Woodwood.

'He confirmed what Brennan said about them being together at his house since Sunday night,' he said. 'They've been off their heads on drugs and booze the whole time apparently. He claims he knows nothing about what happened to Prince and that Brennan never tells him about her clients.'

'Do you believe him?'

'Actually I do, guv. He's a low-life waste of space, but I don't think he's a killer.'

'That mirrors my impression of Clare Brennan,' Temple said. 'But I want to know if either of them have any links with the Russians or any other foreign power.'

'They don't strike me as the type to operate in the big league,' Wells said.

Temple shrugged. 'That might be the very reason they were recruited.'

They moved swiftly on to Clare Brennan's claim that she saw another client after Hari Basu on Sunday night.

Vaughan, reading from a computer screen, confirmed that a 48-year-old Ukrainian named Viktor Lorak lived on the fourth floor. He was interviewed by both a uniformed PC and DC Joan Topper, the team's newest recruit. She wasn't in the office, but Vaughan accessed her statement and notes that had been uploaded to the system.

'Surprise, surprise,' Vaughan said. 'Lorak claimed he was by himself all Sunday evening. No mention of getting his leg over a prossy. He reckoned he met Daniel Prince a few times and knew who he was. But he'd never been up to Prince's flat and didn't know what had happened until the police called on him.'

'Did Joan run a background check?'

'She did and it came up clean. He's an insurance broker who moved here from Ukraine seven years ago. Divorced with two kids who live with their mother in Portsmouth.'

'Let's flag him up to the security agencies,' Temple said. 'With a name like Viktor Lorak, it wouldn't be such a shock if he was involved in some way with the Russians.'

Before the briefing began, Angel had been asked to check who lived on the first floor of Prince's building.

She got Temple's attention now by waving a sheet of paper on which was printed the information.

'As with all the floors there are four flats,' she said. 'One is unoccupied and has been for three months while the owner tries to sell it. The second flat is being rented by a single woman from South Africa named Helen Pederson. The third is owned by a couple in their late sixties named John and Val Creasy.

'A Latvian guy named Jans Migla lives in the fourth flat. He's aged fifty-three, but he went away on business last Friday and so he wasn't in the building on Sunday. He's not due back for another week. Pederson and Mr and Mrs Creasy were at home and gave statements. Neither of them knew Daniel Prince.'

'So none of the residents on the first floor matches the description of the hooded man in the lift,' Temple said. 'So perhaps he was just another resident from one of the upper floors who, in all innocence, decided to visit someone on the first. According to Clare, when she got in the lift, the first floor button had already been pressed. She remembers it being lit up on the panel.'

165

'What about the empty flat?' someone said. 'Could the man have gone in there?'

'That's unlikely,' Angel said. 'All the empty flats in the block have been accessed and searched.'

Temple pointed to DC Tony Wallis and asked him if he could remember seeing a man in a blue cardigan on any of the security camera footage.

'He might have been among those residents who gathered in the lobby,' Temple said.

Wallis said he didn't think so but would pull up the video and have another look.

'It's possible we've missed something,' Temple said. 'If the hooded guy entered any of the public areas then he must have been captured on camera. If he didn't, we need to find out where he went when he got out of the lift.'

Temple made it clear that the hooded man was now their number one suspect. They would work on the assumption that he had entered the lift on the tenth floor after hurling Daniel Prince from the balcony. Then he'd decided to go down to the first floor.

'So we need to find the answers to two questions,' he said. 'Why did he go to that floor and where did he go after alighting the lift?'

CHAPTER 49

TEMPLE WENT BACK to the Riverview complex with a small team of detectives, including Angel and Vaughan.

It was after six when they got there, and the rain had started up again, keeping the onlookers away. But a couple of TV crews were still hanging around, waiting for another break in the story. He wondered how long it would be before they discovered there had been two major developments in the last couple of hours.

Clare Brennan's revelations had galvanized the team and thrown open the investigation. And Beth Fletcher's vanishing act had given them all something else to worry about.

She still hadn't turned up, and Temple was becoming increasingly concerned. He wasn't sure what to make of it, and was wondering now if the death threat in the email had freaked her out and she'd decided to go into hiding.

He could only imagine what she was going through. First, the tragic death of her boyfriend. Then being told that her own life was in danger.

He still believed that it had been a bad move on her part to announce that she was taking over Prince's blog. Sure, it was guaranteed to attract attention and win her support. But it was also bound to make her a target, along with every other activist, social justice blogger, independent journalist and maverick politician who was able to have a significant impact on public opinion.

Temple was beginning to realize, perhaps for the first time, that these were the people who would shape the future, not elected politicians or mega corporations.

The world's political and economic structures were in a fragile state, and powerful voices that secured a large, attentive audience presented as much of a threat as wars and natural disasters.

Temple could see why Beth Fletcher would scare the powers-that-be by taking on Prince's blog. As his courageous and grieving girlfriend, she'd attract plaudits and publicity on a mind-blowing scale. Her campaigns would almost certainly attract a huge following, no matter what they were in support of or against.

It was the nature of celebrity that people idolized the person, regardless of what he or she stood for. It was why film stars wielded so much influence over large sections of society. They could persuade millions of people to buy crappy brands of perfume, and they could destroy fashion companies with derogatory tweets about their latest designs.

And that was why Beth Fletcher – the girl who had lived

for so long in her boyfriend's shadow – was now a force to be reckoned with.

She became an instant celebrity – as well as a target – the moment she appeared before the cameras and told the world what she was going to do in the wake of his murder.

CHAPTER 50

VIKTOR LORAK HAD just got out of the shower when they called on him. He was wearing a grey bathrobe and carpet slippers.

His face was rough with a day's stubble, and he had watchful eyes behind rimless glasses.

He invited Temple and Vaughan in when they told him what it was about. And he found it hard to conceal his embarrassment when asked why he'd lied about being alone on Sunday.

'We know you entertained a local call girl named Clare Brennan because she's told us,' Temple said.

Lorak gave them the standard excuse: that he didn't need to tell anyone what he got up to in the privacy of his own home. But Temple advised him that he had committed a serious offence by withholding information from the police.

'Look, I was caught off guard,' he said, in a heavily-accented voice. 'Once I'd said it I knew I couldn't go back on it. I'm sorry.'

Lorak went on to confirm what Clare had said – that she'd arrived at his flat at nine and left around ten.

'She's been here a few times,' he said. 'It suits me because I don't have the time for a relationship these days. It's just a bit of fun.'

He went on to say that he had been a fan of Daniel Prince and had actually followed his blog.

'What happened to him is a great shame,' he said. 'The man knew exactly how to get people on his side with his campaigns. He was more appealing and convincing than any of the current crop of politicians.'

Lorak said he had also met Beth Fletcher in passing and described her as a pretty girl who was obviously highly intelligent.

'I sent her a tweet yesterday,' he said. 'She's got my full support if she picks up where Daniel left off.'

Lorak had added nothing to what Clare had already told them, and Temple came away disappointed.

'I can't imagine him and the prossy as a pair of assassins,' Vaughan said.

Temple nodded. 'Me neither. I'm sure they were both telling the truth. Let's go find out what Angel has come up with.'

Angel and Doug Wells had gone directly to the first floor to speak to Helen Pederson and Mr and Mrs Creasy, the residents in two of the flats.

When Temple and Vaughan arrived they were just emerging from the vacant flat on the same floor.

'It's empty,' Angel said. 'And there's no sign that anyone has been in there for weeks. As for Miss Pederson and Mr and Mrs Creasy, well, they insist they did not have a visit on Sunday night from a man in a cardigan. And I don't get the impression they're hiding anything.'

Temple looked around. In addition to the front doors, there was the lift and the door leading to the stairs.

'So if they're telling the truth, then the mystery guy must have gone either up or down the stairs,' Temple said. 'My guess is he would have gone down them.'

Temple pushed open the door to the stairs and the others followed him through. He spoke as he descended towards the ground floor.

'By coming this way he would have avoided coming out of the lift into the lobby,' he said.

Angel shook her head, confused. 'But if his aim was to avoid appearing on the security cameras out front, then he couldn't have known there were more down here covering the emergency exit and service entrance.'

'Or if he did know, he might have been able to bypass them.'

'I don't see how,' Vaughan said, pointing up at the cameras above the doors. 'The output from those is monitored by the concierge at the front desk and recorded on the system.'

Temple had a thought and took out his mobile. He called DC Wallis, who answered on the second ring.

'Any luck with the security footage, Tony?' he asked.

'Not so far, guv. I haven't spotted anyone wearing a blue cardigan or a hood.'

'What about the cameras covering the emergency and service doors at the back?'

'We haven't checked them yet. The concierge said nobody entered or left through those doors so we didn't consider them a priority.'

'Well, he might have been lying so check them now. Focus on the time period between nine and ten.'

'Will do, guv.'

Temple hung up and the three detectives went through to the lobby from where Temple called Beresford to bring him up to date.

'What are we doing to find Beth Fletcher?' the chief super said.

'Every copper in the county is on the lookout for her, sir. But it's not going to be easy if she doesn't want to be found. She's switched off her phone.'

Beresford had more questions, but Temple cut him short because he had an incoming call from DC Wallis.

'Have you found something?' he asked the DC.

Wallis sounded excited. 'Indeed I have, guv.'

'So don't keep me in suspense, Detective.'

'Well, I've just been through the footage from the cameras covering the fire exit and service entrance, and I spotted a time code,' Wallis said. 'It's easy to miss unless you're really paying attention.'

'Go on,' Temple prompted him.

'Well, it turns out there's a gap on the recording from both cameras between 8.30 and 10.30 on Sunday evening.'

'You mean they were switched off for two hours?' Temple said.

'They must have been, guv.'

Temple disconnected the call before Wallis could say any more.

To Angel and Vaughan, he said, 'Those cameras out back were switched off between 8.30 and 10.30. That would have enabled the man from the lift to walk out of the building undetected.'

'And the person who was in control of those cameras was our shady little concierge, George Reese,' Vaughan said.

Temple nodded, his heart racing. 'The bastard has been lying to us all along. He must have done it deliberately.'

'We can be at his place in ten minutes,' Vaughan said.

They were hurrying across the building's forecourt to their car when Temple received another call on his mobile.

It was Joseph Kessel, and he sounded anxious.

'I just had a text from Beth,' he said. 'I thought you should know straight away, Inspector.'

'Where is she?'

'I don't know. I'm still in town looking for her. I was just about to head home when the text came through.'

'Send it to me straight away, Mr Kessel. I need to see it.'

'Consider it done,' Kessel said.

Seconds later Temple's phone pinged and he opened up Beth's text. It read:

Joseph. Got your voicemail. Don't worry. Am OK. You and everyone else will hear from me soon. There's something I have to do.

CHAPTER 51

NOTHING HAPPENED FOR over two hours, and no one responded to her cries for help.

She was still sitting on the floor with her back to the wall when suddenly she heard footsteps beyond the door. They grew louder as they came closer.

She held her breath as alarm shivered behind her eyes. After a few agonizing seconds the door was wrenched open.

The man who stepped through it she recognized immediately. In the park he'd been wearing the overcoat. Now he was dressed in a thick woollen jumper and jeans.

'It's time to get down to business,' he said. 'But first I've been told to tell you that you brought this on yourself. He warned you that something unpleasant would happen to you if you didn't make the announcement. And he wasn't bluffing.'

The house wasn't derelict, but it was empty of furniture and clearly hadn't been lived in for some time. The power was still on, however, which was why the lights worked and the radiators gave off heat.

Beth had been ordered out of the little room with the mattress, and told that she could use the toilet to empty her bladder or her bowels. There was a bathroom beyond the first door she came to along the corridor. The man insisted it be left open, but he stood back so that he couldn't see her sitting on the pan.

She had to force herself to pee even though she was bursting to go. She was terrified beyond rational thought and it was as though it had robbed her of her ability to function properly.

She didn't bother to wash her hands. She just stepped out of the bathroom after pulling up her tights and rolling down her skirt.

The man was leaning against the wall with his arms folded. Her vision had cleared by now so she looked at him carefully for the first time. He had fair hair that was thin and wispy, and a face lightly cratered with the fading remains of acne.

'What do you want with me?' she said.

His eyes were like black dots in their sockets and they assessed her from head to foot.

'You're about to find out,' he replied, and she was pretty sure that his accent was Eastern European, possibly Russian or Polish.

'Who are you?' she asked him.

'There's no need for you to know that.'

'Are you going to kill me?'

He wet his upper lip with his tongue and grinned.

'We will if you refuse to cooperate. But I'm confident that you will, which is why I don't feel it's necessary to restrain you. So get moving, Miss Fletcher. You're wanted in the living room.'

She took nervous steps along the corridor to a square-shaped hall. Through the glass panel on the front door she could see the dark outside. But that was all she could see.

Just inside the door, a For Sale sign had been placed on the floor up against the wall.

'That's right,' the man said. 'Nobody lives here at present and there are no close neighbours. So there's no one around to hear you scream and shout.'

Beth felt a cold stab of fear in her chest and she found it hard to swallow.

For a fleeting moment, she wondered how she would fare if she attacked her captor. But just as quickly she dismissed the idea. She was no match for him, not unless she had a weapon.

'There's no need to stop,' he said. 'Go through the door right in front of you.'

The living room was large, with bare floorboards and closed curtains. The light bulbs in there were much brighter and that somehow made it even more terrifying.

The man's partner was sitting on a fold-up chair in the centre of the room, still wearing the leather jacket he'd had on in the park. He had one leg crossed over the other and was smoking a cigarette.

There was nothing else in the room except for a small video camera perched on a tripod. The sight of it caused an upsurge of bile into Beth's throat.

'Hello again, Miss Fletcher,' the seated man said. 'I'm sorry you've been ignored for so long.'

He was a brute of a man, she now realized. He had a large, bullet-shaped head, and was heavily muscled with a

Neanderthal forehead. His nose was broken, and his eyes were little more than slits. The intensity of his gaze unnerved her.

'My name is Anton,' he said. 'My friend there is Yuri. We've been instructed to look after you until the person we report to gets here, which shouldn't be too long.' He paused to draw on his cigarette, letting the smoke jet from his nostrils.

'Here are the things you need to know,' he continued. 'The first is that if you do exactly as you are told, you will survive this. But if you make things difficult for us, you won't. You should also know that the police won't be desperately looking for you. We sent a text from your phone in which we made it clear that you are OK. So you shouldn't expect the cavalry to arrive.'

Beth stood there, her hands bunched into fists at her sides. She could feel the sweat gathering on her forehead, even though the air in the room felt cold and heavy.

'Why have you brought me here?' she said, and her voice came out as a whisper.

It was the other man, Yuri, who answered the question.

'Surely that's obvious,' he said. 'You were given a warning which you chose to ignore. As soon as the deadline passed and we realized that you had no intention of making the announcement about the People-Power blog, we were told to pick you up.'

'How did you know where to find me?'

He shrugged. 'There's a bug in your handbag. We've been monitoring your every move.'

She closed her eyes. It felt like her mind was coming apart. She had got involved in something she simply could not comprehend.

'We're going to give you a chance to put things right,' he said. 'You're going to give a little performance for the camera.'

'What do you mean?'

Yuri took a folded sheet of paper from the back pocket of his jeans.

'You will memorize the words written on here and then we'll record you reading them into the camera. You'll make every effort to sound sincere and you won't give the impression that you were forced to say it. We'll do as many takes as necessary until we've got it right.'

'And what happens after that?'

'Then the video will be uploaded to the internet and we're confident it will go viral within minutes.'

His words seemed to suck the air out of the room and Beth's rapid heartbeat suddenly filled her head.

'And what will happen to me?' she said.

'You will go free, of course. But we'll expect you to keep your mouth shut about us and to never again entertain the idea of becoming a blogger.'

She looked from Yuri to his accomplice and her body froze in breathless panic.

They were going to kill her. She was sure of it. But she was also sure that they would make her suffer if she didn't do what they wanted.

CHAPTER 52

THERE WERE NO lights on in George Reese's terraced house when the police pool car pulled into the kerb in front of it. It was followed by a patrol car with its neon lights flashing.

The street was in the Portswood area of the city, just a couple of miles from the Riverview apartments. It was lined with trees, and most of the front gardens were small and untidy.

Temple's heart was thumping as he and Angel walked up the short path to the front door. Vaughan and one of the officers from the patrol car made their way around the back.

Angel rang the bell. They waited but there was no answer.

Temple lifted the letterbox and called through it. 'Mr Reese. It's the police. Please open up.'

No response.

The next door neighbour – a plump woman somewhere in her fifties – appeared on her doorstep.

'I'm sure he's in,' she said. 'He had a visitor about half an hour ago.'

Temple creased his brow. 'How do you know?'

She shrugged. 'I was putting the bin out when I saw some bloke ringing the bell. George opened the door to him and I heard voices. Both male. Then the door was shut.'

'So how do you know Mr Reese didn't go out?'

She stepped closer and Temple got a strong whiff of cheap perfume.

'Well, about ten minutes later, I heard his front door being shut again,' she said. 'I looked out the window and saw the same bloke walking away. But George wasn't with him.'

'Can you describe this man, madam?' Temple said.

'I don't think so. It was dark, and he was wearing a hood and didn't look in my direction.'

Temple felt something twist inside him. Could it be the same hooded man who had ridden down in the lift at the Riverview apartments? The same man they suspected of murdering Daniel Prince?

'Can you tell me how tall he was?'

'Average height, I reckon,' she said. 'Five eight or nine.'

'What did he sound like? Did he have an accent?'

She shrugged. 'Sorry, I didn't hear him that clearly. It was like they were whispering to each other.'

He decided there was just cause to break into the house. Luckily it was a uPVC front door with a frosted glass panel in the middle.

The uniformed officer was dispatched to fetch his baton from the patrol car, and then use it to smash the glass and open the door from the inside.

Temple went in first, calling out Reese's name as he switched on the hall light.

His first impression was that the place was well looked after but nothing special. He walked along the hall, followed by Angel and the uniform.

The first door gave access to a downstairs toilet. The second to a small living room stuffed with furniture that looked old and worn. There was a TV on a stand, two leather armchairs and a coffee table. A shelving unit stood up against a wall and contained books and various ornaments.

The third door led to the kitchen and when Temple turned on the light, a chill erupted in his gut.

George Reese was lying face down on the floor between the units.

The handle of what looked like a large carving knife protruded from his back, high up close to his right shoulder.

CHAPTER 53

THERE WAS A lot of blood. It soaked Reese's yellow T-shirt and formed a puddle that was still spreading across the laminated floor.

Temple knelt beside him, careful not to touch anything. The man's eyes were closed and he wasn't moving. But when Temple put two fingers against his neck he felt a pulse.

'He's alive,' he said. 'But only just. Call for an ambulance.'

As Angel made the call, the uniformed officer got out his radio and requested back-up. Then he went to get Vaughan.

Temple put his ear close to Reese's mouth and detected a faint breath.

The guy had obviously been left for dead. Maybe the attacker had fled in a panic for some reason before making sure he'd done a proper job.

The knife in the victim's back matched the set in the block on the worktop. Temple didn't dare touch it for fear of disturbing any evidence. And there was also the possibility that the blade was helping to keep him alive. God only knew what would happen if it was suddenly wrenched out. It wouldn't be sensible to remove it until Reese was at the hospital.

177

There was nothing Temple could do for him. Whether he'd live or die would depend on the extent of the internal damage, the amount of blood lost, and how quickly the paramedics could get here.

Temple stood up and looked around the kitchen. It didn't appear as though anything had been disturbed. There was a dirty dish and some cutlery in the sink. A bottle of unopened red wine stood on the worktop.

Temple stepped back out of the room to where a white-faced Angel stood in the hallway.

'You OK?' he asked her.

She nodded. 'It was a bloody shock, though. I didn't expect us to stumble on this little scene.'

'What about an ambulance?'

'On its way.'

'Good. We need to check the rest of the house. But let's tread carefully. This is now a crime scene.'

They both pulled latex gloves from their pockets and went upstairs. There were two bedrooms and they were both empty. Only one of them had a bed that was made up and Temple assumed that was where Reese slept.

There wasn't much in the way of personal paraphernalia, and very few clothes in the wardrobe. No photos in frames, and only a few Ikea-type prints on the walls.

Back downstairs, they were joined by Vaughan and together they explored the living room. They spotted a pile of betting slips on the coffee table.

'You'll remember that according to his employers, Reese has a gambling addiction,' Vaughan said. 'Maybe someone tried to off him over an unpaid debt.'

Temple shook his head. 'No way. The bloke who was here earlier must have been the attacker. And it's a sure bet he's the same man Clare Brennan saw in the lift. I'm guessing he came here to stop Reese exposing him.'

'So you reckon Reese was helping the killer?'

'Well, I can't think why else he would have disabled the security cameras for two hours on Sunday. It could be the other guy's now in a panic because things have started to unravel. First his bid to make it look like suicide didn't work, and now he probably realizes we're closing in.'

Temple heard the approaching sirens and went back into the kitchen. He wanted to make sure that Reese was still alive. He was.

While he was kneeling over the body, he spotted part of a mobile phone poking out of Reese's trouser pocket.

He carefully removed it and found that it was still switched on. He carried it back outside just as an ambulance pulled up and two paramedics got out.

'Victim's in the kitchen,' he told them. 'Knife in his back but he's breathing. Please try to keep him alive.'

Temple stood in the front garden examining the phone. It was a simple, easy-to-operate device, and he was quickly scrolling through the call list.

He was immediately struck by the fact that Reese had made and received very few calls. And all those he'd received over the past few days were from the same mobile number.

There were five calls in all from that number. The first was received at seven on Sunday evening, followed by a second five hours later. Then on the Monday there were two calls, followed by three today.

The last one Reese had answered was timed at 6 p.m. this evening, and the conversation lasted less than a minute.

Temple got one of the uniforms to use his radio to run a check on the number. Ten minutes later he was told the number was attached to an unregistered pay-as-you-go phone.

'Shit,' he said.

'Not quite that bad, sir,' said the female voice on the other end of the line. 'I've talked to the mobile network and they say the phone is still switched on.'

'Can they triangulate the signal?' Temple said, unable to keep the excitement out of his voice.

'They're already done it, sir. It's weak apparently, but they have managed to get a rough location.'

CHAPTER 54

THE ONE CALLED Anton vacated the fold-up chair and told Beth to sit in it.

When she didn't move he inhaled deeply on his cigarette so that the red ember at the tip flared and crackled.

'If you like I can show you how it feels to have a lighted cigarette pressed against your flesh,' he said.

She sniffed and swallowed and tried to be brave. But the fear filled her veins like liquid.

Anton pushed his lips into a shape that almost resembled a smile. There was something unsettling about it. Something unbalanced.

He means what he said, she told herself. *He won't think twice about inflicting pain.*

She tried to switch off mentally, shut down her feelings. How else was she supposed to cope?

'You really don't want to make me angry,' he said.

Beth glanced at his accomplice, Yuri, who stood to one side with his arms crossed and his head tilted.

'Don't be a fool, Miss Fletcher,' Yuri said. 'We've been told to offer you this lifeline. It's an opportunity to save yourself. The alternative is to suffer a very painful death. And it won't be quick and easy like being thrown from a tenth floor balcony.'

She fought the urge to scream because she knew it'd be pointless. But the ferocious anger that suddenly rose up inside her was more difficult to control.

'Did the pair of you kill Daniel?' she said.

Yuri blew out his cheeks. 'It may surprise you to learn that we didn't.'

'But you know who did?'

'Of course.'

'So why was he murdered?'

'Because he posed a serious threat to my country and my people. Just as you will if you pursue these reckless campaigns on his behalf.'

Beth let her shoulders sag, and then mouthed a single word: 'Russians.'

Yuri planted a mirthless smile on his face. 'I thought our names would have given the game away at the start.'

And they would have if her mind hadn't been in a state of near-paralysis.

Now it made sense. Daniel had been planning to call for a boycott of Russian goods and services across the world. The campaign had provoked a fierce reaction even before it was officially launched on the blog.

She remembered Daniel showing her a newspaper report about the Russian president condemning it as totally irresponsible. But she also recalled what Daniel had told her at the time.

'The Russians have become a serious threat to world peace, Beth. The western-imposed sanctions aren't tough enough. The bastards need to know that they can't continue with their unjustified aggression. If I can add to the pressure then perhaps they'll eventually see sense and back down.'

The voice in her head was so clear she felt he was in the room with her. But he wasn't, of course. He was dead. Killed on the orders of a cruel and corrupt regime that above all else feared for its own survival.

She could feel the scream building inside her again, the rage coursing through her body.

'Your man was a victim of his own success,' Yuri said, his voice raised and edgy. 'We couldn't have allowed him to spread his poisonous rhetoric. My people are already suffering severe hardship. He was determined to inflict more damage. And so will you if we let you.'

'Daniel wanted what everyone else wants,' Beth said, her tone defiant. 'And that's to make the Russian government realize that it can't bully and threaten the rest of the world.'

Yuri stiffened, and his expression became dark and hostile.

'We're the ones under threat,' he said. 'And we won't allow the west to dictate the terms of our existence. You're out to rob us of our dignity.'

'That's bullshit,' she snapped.

He let out a sneering laugh. 'You stupid, pathetic woman. You have clearly been brainwashed by your smug, arrogant boyfriend.'

Beth felt the fire in her belly.

'Go fuck yourselves,' she shouted.

In the same instant she sensed a movement to her left. She turned just as the other thug, Anton, lashed out at her with his fist.

He punched her hard in the stomach and she doubled over, gasping for breath. The blow sent a white flash across her vision and the pain was explosive.

'What makes you think you can show us disrespect, bitch?' he yelled. 'You're at our fucking mercy and if it was up to me, I'd never let you walk away from here.'

He then seized Beth by the arm, pulling her across the room and shoving her in the chair.

She clutched at her stomach as the pain throbbed. Her breath came in short, rapid gasps and her gut had to fight waves of nausea.

Anton gritted his teeth and shook with rage.

'We don't have time for games and pointless conversation. And if there's any fucking to be done, it'll be us doing it to you.'

He then reached into his jacket pocket and to her astonishment, produced an automatic pistol.

'You need to understand that we mean business, and we're professionals,' he said. 'We're not a couple of amateur yobs, and we'll do what we've been instructed to do, whatever it takes.'

It was the first time Beth had seen a real revolver up close, let alone had one pointed at her. She stared at it, one eye squinting, and felt the fear weaken her resolve and drain the energy from her limbs.

'Don't imagine that if I use this it'll be over in an instant,' Anton said. 'I can still make sure that you suffer a slow, agonizing death.'

She lifted her eyes to look at him and sensed that he was

itching to hit her again. Or maybe even shoot her.

She realized then that she had no choice but to play along if she didn't want to be badly beaten, and perhaps even sexually assaulted, before they finally put her out of her misery.

She sat up straight, sniffed back a sob, and said, 'Let's get it over with then. What is it you want me to do?'

CHAPTER 55

THE POLICE POOL car with Temple at the wheel raced out of Southampton along the M3 towards Winchester.

Beyond the cathedral city, they would turn onto the northbound A34 and head for the roadside services at Sutton Scotney.

That was the present location of the mobile phone that was emitting a signal which was being picked up by two transmitters. It wasn't a strong signal apparently, and had an accuracy radius of between 500 and 600 metres. In a built-up area that would have been a problem, but at a service station in the countryside it was a result.

Whoever was in possession of that phone had been making calls to George Reese, right up until shortly before he was stabbed in the back.

The mobile service provider had confirmed that it was a pre-paid phone that had been activated only days before and had been switched off for most of the time. They were now examining previous usage and trying to determine who else the owner had called and from where.

Temple experienced a burst of energy, and his senses were thumping.

His gut told him that this was the breakthrough they'd been waiting for, that the man in the hood who had stabbed George Reese was the phone's owner. The same man who had murdered Daniel Prince.

With luck things would now quickly come together. If George Reese survived – and it was a big if – then he would surely uncover his attacker and reveal why he had switched off the cameras in the Riverview building on Sunday night.

Had he been paid to? Was that the reason three cash sums of £2000 each had been deposited in his bank account?

By now Reese would be at the hospital under the care of a trauma team. Armed officers had also been sent there to ensure that he remained safe.

Beth Fletcher's phone, meanwhile, was still not transmitting a signal, although it must have been switched on at some point because she'd sent the text to Joseph Kessel.

Temple was still perplexed by Beth's message.

You and everyone else will hear from me soon. There's something I have to do.

What on earth did she mean? Was she planning another big announcement? Had she found something out about Daniel's murder?

Temple discussed it with Angel and Vaughan in the car, and they were just as mystified.

'Maybe she needs to be alone to properly grieve,' Angel said. 'And I suspect she's trying to get her head around the fact that her boyfriend had actually been cheating on her.'

The affair that Prince had confessed to was something that Temple had pushed to the back of his mind. They still hadn't identified the woman involved or unearthed any details.

But it was a line of inquiry he would gladly stop pursuing if Prince's killer was about to be collared.

CHAPTER 56

IT WAS A typical A-Road pit-stop, with a petrol station and a food and beverage service centre.

The pool car with the detectives arrived at the same time as two armed response units.

Temple maintained contact with them by radio, and he told them to stay in their vehicles until he gave the order to move.

Temple knew the place well. It was only about twenty miles from Southampton and a popular stop for motorists. The services and petrol station were separated by a large car park. He did a quick count. There were only twelve parked vehicles – ten cars and two vans. They all appeared to be empty, but they would all be checked.

As soon as confirmation came through that the phone signal was still being picked up from this location, Temple spoke into the radio.

'OK, listen up, everyone. There's a mobile phone around here somewhere that may belong to a man who tried to murder another man in Southampton a short time ago. We don't know the suspect's identity, but he's of average height and may be wearing jeans and a blue, hooded cardigan.

'A man answering to the same description is also wanted for questioning in connection with the murder of Daniel Prince on Sunday night. So he's highly dangerous and might well be armed.

'The phone signal is being monitored and it's been stationary for some time. It's accurate within a radius of 500 or 600 metres. So let's get to it.'

They'd lost the element of surprise, of course, by drawing attention to themselves as the convoy entered the car park. Now Temple spotted several startled faces at the restaurant window as the armed officers rushed towards the single-storeyed building.

He didn't know what to expect, or even if he'd made the right call in attaching significance to the phone number.

But there was no turning back now, and if the gods were smiling down on them, then he would soon be face-to-face with Daniel Prince's killer.

The service building consisted of a restaurant, coffee shop and book store. At this time of day it was thankfully quiet.

The tactical teams spread out and once they were inside, the reaction was predictable. A man shouted, a woman screamed, and there were several raised voices. But it didn't get out of hand because there were only about thirty people inside, including staff, and most of them were in the restaurant and adjoining kitchen.

A couple in their twenties were in the coffee shop, and a man in his seventies was in the toilet. They were approached, then ushered into the restaurant where Temple got everyone's attention and told them not to be alarmed.

As he spoke, he surveyed the room, looking for a man in a blue cardigan. But of those present only half were men and none of them was wearing a blue cardigan.

Most were dressed in crumpled suits and looked as though they were salesmen heading home from a hard day on the road. Luckily there were no children among them.

'I'm Detective Chief Inspector Temple and I'm sorry about the surprise entrance,' he said aloud to the gathering. 'But we have reason to believe that a man suspected of a serious crime is on the premises. He's of average height and when last seen, was wearing a blue hooded cardigan and jeans.'

The reaction he got was muted. They all looked at each other and several of them voiced their anger, including a man who identified himself as the assistant manager. He said, 'Are the weapons really necessary? You're really scaring my customers.'

'We can't afford to take chances, sir,' Temple said. 'It's highly likely that the man we're after is armed.'

'Well, as you can see for yourself, he's not in here,' the assistant manager said.

Temple asked if anyone had seen a man matching that description, but the only response he got was a lot of shaking of heads.

He clenched his jaw and felt the bitter taste of disappointment. Around him, the team started carrying out a methodical search of the building. Angel stood to his right, monitoring the mobile signal which had been patched through to her phone.

'It's still transmitting,' she said.

To his restless audience, Temple announced that he wanted everyone to be quiet. He explained that he was going to call a mobile phone number and he wanted to know if the phone was in this room.

'It's important,' he said. 'And the sooner we can get this done the sooner you can all get on your way.'

Then he used his own phone to call the number. He held it to his ear, heard the connection being made, and then heard it ringing.

But not in the restaurant.

There were no bells, or chirping sounds, or bursts of music.

'It could be on mute,' he said, and then asked everyone to take their phones out of their pockets and handbags and to place them on the tables. Only a few said they didn't have a phone.

He tried again and left it ringing as officers went from table to table checking the phones, only to confirm that none of them was receiving a call.

'I'm afraid it means we have to search everyone before you leave here,' he said. 'We will also need to examine your vehicles.'

Some of them raised objections, but most of them didn't. Temple left Vaughan and Angel to oversee things in the restaurant and went outside to the car park.

Beyond it the petrol station was empty, but he saw two uniforms entering the shop to question the staff there.

He decided to check it out for himself and walked over there. There were no cars at the pumps and no people around.

He stood in the middle of the forecourt and took out his phone. He spotted a sign prohibiting the use of mobiles, but chose to ignore it.

Then he called the number again and listened as the connection was made. He braced himself for more disappointment.

And was shocked when he heard a high-pitched ringtone coming from close by.

CHAPTER 57

THE ONE CALLED Yuri held out the sheet of paper from his pocket and said, 'Just read it. Then we'll start recording.'

A cold dread flowed through Beth's lungs, but at least the pain in her stomach had subsided. And the revolver the other man had threatened her with was back inside his jacket.

So it was less of an effort to breathe.

Her hand shook as she reached out to take the sheet of paper. She unfolded it and squinted at the words that were scrawled in black ink.

I'm Beth Fletcher, Daniel Prince's fiancé. I made a statement earlier in which I said I'd carry on the People-Power blog on his behalf. But that was before I found out that he was a liar and a cheat. And not the man his followers thought he was. So as far as I'm concerned, the blog has died with him. That's all I have to say. Thank you.

As she finished reading it, the veins in her temples started to pulsate. She raised her eyes to look at Yuri, who stood in front of her.

'Daniel wasn't a liar or a cheat,' she said. 'He was an honest man. A good man.'

Yuri shrugged. 'That's irrelevant. This is about saving yourself.'

'So why can't I just say that I won't take on the blog? Why do I have to rubbish Daniel's name and reputation?'

'Because it will sound more convincing that way.'

Beth's head swam with emotions. Fear. Terror. Pain. Disbelief that she was suddenly confronted with an impossible choice.

She shifted her gaze to Anton, who was standing next to the tripod ready to operate the camera. She could tell from his expression that he was running out of patience. His jaw was set tight, his eyes burning holes in the air.

'So shall we begin?' Yuri said. 'Or are you going to make us hurt you?'

She looked again at the words on the sheet of paper. This time she read them aloud to herself, not once but twice.

'That'll do,' Anton said. 'You're not trying to win an Oscar.'

She cleared her throat, felt the tension grip her body.

'I'm ready,' she said after a beat.

'Then look directly at the camera,' Anton said. 'And try to relax.'

Yuri went and stood behind him, and the pair of them watched her like she was an actress about to give an audition.

Anton pressed a button on the camera and a little red light came on.

'Recording,' he said.

Up until that moment she was going to do exactly what was expected of her. But suddenly an image of Daniel's broken body reared up in her mind, and she realized she couldn't go through with it, regardless of the consequences.

No amount of physical pain could be as bad as the grief that already gripped every fibre of her being. And if she was going to die anyway, then she didn't want her last words to be those dictated by the very monsters who had destroyed her life.

As she stared into the camera, everything inside her turned cold. She took a long, deep breath and spoke slowly and clearly, accentuating every syllable.

'I'm Beth Fletcher, Daniel Prince's fiancé. I want the world to know that he was murdered on the orders of the Russian government. Now the bastards are going to kill me as well. They're terrified that—'

She didn't get to finish the last sentence because Anton shot out from behind the camera and rushed towards her.

She scrambled to her feet and raised her arms to cover her face.

But he slammed his fist into the side of her head, twice, powerful blows that sent her crashing face-down on the floor. The pain spiralled through her as he reached down, grabbed her by the hair and wrenched her to her knees.

She screamed and tried to seize hold of his jacket. But he knocked her arm away with his free hand and then slapped her face.

'Do you think that was funny, bitch?' he shrieked at her. 'Well, we're not laughing and neither will you by the time we've finished with you.'

'Go to hell,' she shouted. 'I don't care what you do to me. I don't care if I die. You've already destroyed my life anyway.'

His response to her outburst was to hit her again, a punch that connected with her jawbone and ignited an explosion inside her head.

He let go of her hair, and she fell to the floor, where she lay still, her body numb, her brain on fire.

She heard voices, an angry exchange between the two men, but she couldn't make sense of anything through the darkness that swept in and consumed her.

The last thing she heard before passing out was a groan that came from deep inside her own throat.

CHAPTER 58

THE SHARP, CRISP ringing led Temple to a rubbish bin next to one of the petrol pumps. Inside it, resting on top of plastic cups and wads of screwed-up paper towels, he saw the mobile phone that had been emitting the signal.

He tapped the red key on his own phone and the ringing abruptly stopped. Then he speed-dialled Angel, and when she answered, he said, 'I found it over at the petrol station. It's been dumped in a bin. Don't let anyone leave there just yet. And get Dave to come straight over.'

He hung up, put on disposable gloves, and reached inside the bin to carefully lift the phone out.

It was a cheap-looking Nokia and when he checked the call list the only number on it was George Reese's. That told

Temple the phone had been purchased for the sole purpose of communicating with the concierge. When there was no longer any need to do so it was discarded.

But whoever had owned it for that brief period had neglected to switch it off before lobbing it into the bin.

Temple placed the phone in an evidence bag. By this time he'd been joined by the tactical officers who had ventured inside the shop. He told them he'd found the phone and they told him that the station attendant had seen the man in the hooded cardigan.

Temple rushed into the shop. The attendant was a girl in her late teens, with heavy make-up and a tattoo of a heart on her neck. Her name was Cheryl, and she was standing behind the counter alongside a middle-aged man, who said he was Clive Deakin, the manager.

Temple held up his warrant card and asked the girl to tell him what she'd told the other officers.

'Well, there was a bloke in here about fifteen minutes ago wearing a blue hoodie,' she said. 'He bought twenty pounds worth of petrol, paid in cash and walked out.'

'Did he say anything to you?' Temple asked.

'Only hello and thank you.'

'But you got a good look at him.'

'I suppose. He was white and thirtyish. Not bad-looking.'

'Accent?'

'Don't think so.'

Temple turned to Deakin. 'What about you, sir? Can you describe him?'

'I'm afraid not. I was out back checking through the stock.'

Temple gestured towards the security camera mounted high on the wall behind them.

'That's working, I assume,' he said.

Deakin nodded. 'It should be.'

'Good. Then we need to have a look at it, along with the footage from the cameras outside on the forecourt.'

Dave Vaughan joined them as they crowded into a small back room where the digital recording equipment was stored.

Deakin was all fingers and thumbs as he fiddled with the controls, but after a while he managed to scroll back to the point where a red Honda Civic drove onto the station forecourt. The picture was in colour, but of poor quality, with everything slightly out of focus.

The driver got out and Temple's heart rate leapt when he saw that it was a man in the blue cardigan. Unfortunately the hood was up and they couldn't see his face.

The man had his back to the camera as he put petrol in the tank. Then he strolled into the shop, all the time keeping his head lowered.

Even in the shop he managed to avoid showing his face to the camera, which had both Temple and Vaughan cursing.

He walked out straight after paying. When he got back to the Honda, he paused for a moment and took something out of his jeans pocket, which he dropped in the rubbish bin.

'That must have been the phone,' Temple said.

The guy then got back in behind the wheel of the Honda and drove off. Temple was expecting him to pull into the services, but instead he drove out onto the A34 and headed north.

'Bugger that,' Vaughan said. 'We didn't even get to see his bloody face.'

'But we've got his vehicle registration,' Temple said. 'So let's call it in and see if we can get his name.'

CHAPTER 59

BETH SURFACED FROM the darkness quite suddenly, pulled back to consciousness by the sound of angry voices.

She opened her eyes, which wasn't easy. They didn't want to open. The lids felt like they'd been weighted down with cement blocks.

'Our orders were not to hurt her until after we'd got her to do the recording,' Yuri was yelling. 'You really need to control that fucking temper of yours.'

'She wasn't going to do it,' Anton shouted back. 'You heard what she told us. The bitch thinks she's tough.'

'She was testing us, you idiot. Surely we can get her to do it without knocking her senseless.'

Beth was still lying on her side on the floor. She watched them squaring up to each other from behind a veil of stinging tears. Her head was clanging, and her face felt hot and swollen.

She had no inkling of how long she'd been out, but it was probably only a few seconds, a minute at most. She was actually surprised that she was still alive, and she wondered if she had Yuri to thank for that. It sounded like his psycho accomplice had lost the plot.

Yuri, it seemed, was the more level-headed of the two, anxious to ensure their mission was carried out with the minimum of fuss.

But whatever the twisted dynamics of the callous duo, Beth knew that her fate was still out of her own control, and there was more pain to come.

She could feel a lump blocking her throat, so she took deep intakes of air through her nose. It made her cough, and this gave away the fact that she was awake.

Fuck.

She opened her eyes and saw their heads snap towards her in unison. A long, blistering moment of silence passed, and then Anton smiled crookedly and said, 'This one is a glutton for punishment, Yuri. She's come back for more.'

As he moved towards her, Beth flinched. He grabbed her arm and yanked her to her feet.

'You've got one last chance to redeem yourself, young lady,' he said. 'If you don't read the script you'll get more of the same.'

Her legs felt weak and she almost lost her balance. Anton put his face close to hers and gave her a piercing look. She recoiled at the fierce intent in his eyes.

'Do you understand what I'm telling you?' he said, and his

accent was suddenly far more pronounced.

Her mind was a maelstrom as she stood there staring back at him. The fear was still thick inside her, but so too was the rage.

'If you're going to kill me you might as well get it over with,' she said defiantly.

His right hand shot up and he put a vice-like grip on her jaw.

'What is it with you?' he screamed. 'All you have to do is read a few fucking lines.'

Pain engulfed her again and her vision clouded. But she held his malevolent gaze long enough for the anger inside her to boil over.

Instinctively she lifted her knee and with all the power she could muster, rammed it into his groin. He gave a groan of agony and stepped back, his hand dropping away from her jaw.

Beth glared at him and got a small measure of satisfaction from the stunned expression on his face.

'You fucking bitch,' he yelled.

Yuri stepped forward and put a hand on Anton's shoulder.

'Keep calm, my friend. He'll be here soon. After that you can do what you want with her.'

But Anton was too fired up to listen. As Beth backed away from them, he launched himself at her.

As he seized her sweater, he growled like an animal. Beth lost her balance and fell backwards onto the floor with a heavy thud.

The Russian leaned over and stretched forward with his arms to get at her. But as he did so, his jacket fell open to reveal the butt of the pistol poking out of his inside pocket.

Beth's window of opportunity lasted no more than a split second. But it was enough time for her to grasp the gun and whip it out of the pocket.

Anton realized too late what had happened, and by then he was in no position to save himself.

Both his hands were reaching for her throat, leaving his

belly exposed. At the same time his knees were bent at an awkward angle so they were straining under his bodyweight.

Beth wasn't even aware of her finger squeezing the trigger.

Bang!

The shot sounded like a hammer hitting a tin roof.

The bullet's impact sent Anton sprawling backwards and as he hit the floor, he let out a primal scream.

Adrenaline dropped like a bomb into Beth's bloodstream. She sprang up, still clutching the gun, and aimed it at the bastard writhing on the floor.

Her hand shook and her mind spun out of control. She was tempted to fire off another shot, but then she caught a movement to her right and Yuri's voice cried out, 'Drop the gun now.'

But she was too scared to respond, so she swung her body towards him – along with the weapon.

And there he was, aiming at her with his own revolver. He was holding it in both hands and squinting along the barrel, deep furrows appearing across his brow and the bridge of his nose.

'I promise I will shoot you if you don't put it down,' he said.

The fact that he hadn't already fired told her that he wanted to keep her alive if possible, despite the fact that she had just shot his partner.

So she didn't move, and by some miracle she managed to hold herself steady even though her blood was on fire, and her stomach was pitching and rolling.

Anton's groans started to fade as the life left his body. Beth could see him out the corner of her eye, lying on his back and leaking blood at an alarming rate.

'You need to see sense, Miss Fletcher,' Yuri said. 'I'm not like him. It won't give me pleasure to kill you.'

Beth found herself gulping short gasps of breath. She was holding it together through a mixture of raw fear and panic.

'I heard what you told him,' she said in a shaky voice. 'I know you were going to kill me, whatever happened.'

'That's not true.'

He shifted on the balls of his feet and she saw indecision in his eyes.

She remembered what Anton had said about them being professionals. She didn't doubt that they were. But she wasn't. She was just a petrified amateur who now found herself as part of a crazy Mexican stand-off. She knew that if it continued for much longer, she'd crack first and he would come out on top.

And she couldn't allow that to happen.

Which was why she decided to throw caution to the wind.

And fire before he did.

CHAPTER 60

THE BULLET TORE into Yuri's right shoulder. It caught him completely by surprise, but he did manage to get a shot of his own before his gun clattered to the floor.

Luckily for Beth, the shell went wide and pummelled into the ceiling. The impact was hard enough to throw him off his feet. He crashed into the wall behind him and his legs gave way.

As he fell to the floor, he clasped at the wound, but the blood sprayed out between his fingers.

Beth staggered to her feet and was hit by a wave of dizziness that caused her to sway slightly. Her world started turning to liquid, and she had to shake her head and breathe deeply to stop from passing out.

All the time she kept her eyes on Yuri, even though his blood-spattered body moved in and out of focus. He was still conscious and able to move, and she watched as he tried desperately to crawl towards his revolver.

She jumped forward and picked it up. Now she had a gun in each hand.

'I want to know where we are and what you've done

with my phone,' she said in a voice that sounded strangely unfamiliar.

Yuri rolled up against the wall and his face contorted in pain. Beth pointed both guns at him, and her hands shook so much it seemed as though she was waving them to get his attention.

He looked up, muscles twitching under each of his eyes. She could tell he was trying to think, mental gears whirring, but he was finding it hard to focus.

She gestured towards his partner-in-crime, who was no longer moving and was either dead or soon would be.

'You don't have to end up like him,' she said. 'I can phone for an ambulance.'

He shook his head slowly and started foaming at the mouth. Then his eyelids began to close and his head lolled to one side.

Beth stood there transfixed. The terror and exhaustion had drained her of the ability to move.

She couldn't believe what had happened. She had shot her captors and she was still alive. How the hell was that possible?

The relief was like warm blood passing through her veins, and she felt a flutter of hope in her chest.

She was still in a bad place, though. The Russians had spoken of another man they had been waiting for. The one they'd reported to. The one who had ordered them to get her to record the speech they'd written.

He might turn up at any moment she knew. And there might be others with him.

Her reaction to this thought was all instinct and panic. She stepped over Anton's body and hurried over to the open door. Before going through it, she paused to glance back into the room she had turned into a bloodbath.

Her mouth dropped open and her lungs heaved. It was like a scene from a Quentin Tarantino movie.

A wave of anguish swept through her, and she had to force herself to turn away. Now was not the time to reflect on what she'd done.

She went into the hall and her first instinct was to head for the front door. But she wanted her phone. If she could find that first, it would surely improve her chances of escape.

The corridor which led to the room with the mattress was to her right. Directly opposite was another door that was closed. She figured it must be the kitchen and she was right.

But when she opened it she got a shock. On the tiled floor between the teak units was a rolled up sheet of black plastic. And resting on top of that were two shovels.

'Oh my god,' she gasped.

The bastards had been planning to bury her. The realization sent her head into a buzzing frenzy and she had to lean against the doorframe to stop from falling over.

Despite what they had said, their plan all along had been to kill her after getting her to do the recording. They had never had any intention of showing her mercy. She'd suspected it, of course, but it was good to have it confirmed. It more than justified what she'd done to them.

The adrenaline drained out of her, leaving her trembling. She clamped her top lip between her teeth and looked around the kitchen, which had spanking new fittings.

And that was when she spotted her handbag. It was lying on the worktop next to the sink.

She stepped over to it, put down the guns, and pulled it towards her.

As soon as she plunged her hand inside, she found her phone. It had been turned off. She switched it on and waited for it to come to life, praying she would have a signal.

But before it did she heard a sound behind her. She whirled around and watched in disbelief as a zombie-like Yuri staggered towards her through the doorway.

She instinctively reached for one of the guns she'd placed on the worktop. But before she got to it he slammed into her with all his weight and they both collapsed in an untidy heap on the floor.

CHAPTER 61

THE IMPACT OF Yuri's body drove the air from Beth's lungs. As she was pushed over, she hit her head against a unit and a flash of white exploded inside her skull.

Yuri landed next to her on the tiles, and he was cursing and spluttering like he was possessed by the devil.

Despite his wound and the loss of blood, a flood of endorphins had obviously given him the strength of desperation. He shoved a fist into her gut and used the other hand to grab her by the throat. She started to gag and seized his wrist to try to get him to loosen his grip.

Their faces were only inches apart. He was gritting his teeth, and his eyes were flickering and rolling in their sockets.

She felt her own vision start to tunnel, becoming black around the edges as it began to fade. But she couldn't dislodge the hand from her throat and the pressure of his fingers on her windpipe was becoming unbearable.

As a last resort she let go of his wrist and hammered the side of her fist against his shoulder wound.

That did the trick. He cried out in pain and let her go. Beth struck the wound again and this time his mouth opened, but nothing issued forth other than a horrible gurgle.

Beth then gave a roar of effort and tried to crawl away from him. But he wasn't quite ready to give up the fight. He pitched himself forward and sank his teeth into the side of her arm. The pain was excruciating; deep, sharp, intensive, and it spread through her entire body.

Beth's response was swift. She thrust her thumb into his right eye, forcing him to open his mouth. And she continued pressing until he couldn't take it anymore and rolled away from her.

Mustering one last burst of energy, she reached up, grabbed the edge of the worktop and pulled herself to her feet. She then stumbled over his legs and got herself clear of him.

She saw then that he was finally a spent force, too weak

to get up and come after her. It was all he could do to push himself up against the sink unit. His eyes were large and unfocused, the pupils wildly dilated. The bullet and the blood loss had at last sapped his strength.

Beth picked up her handbag and placed the two revolvers inside. As she backed out of the kitchen, she checked her phone and saw that it was now on and she even had a weak signal.

She moved into the hallway, her breathing heavy, her chest heaving. Tears tingled the backs of her eyes and her head and body were a riot of aches and pains.

But she'd survived against incredible odds and once she was free of the house, she'd call the police and get as far away from here as possible.

She reached the front door and pulled it open.

Then stopped dead in her tracks.

There was a man standing on the porch, his body lit from behind by a car's headlamps. The shock of seeing him hit her like a bolt of electricity.

'Hello, Beth,' Joseph Kessel said. 'Looks like I got here just in time.'

He then placed a hand on her chest and shoved her back inside.

CHAPTER 62

'How in God's name did we miss it?' Temple said.

Angel and Vaughan were standing with him in the car park at Sutton Scotney services. They had just received information on the car being driven by the hooded man.

It was a lease vehicle that for the past nine months had been in the charge of one Joseph Kessel, who lived at the Riverview apartments in Southampton.

Temple's shock was almost palpable. Joseph Kessel had

been Daniel Prince's drinking buddy, the only person Prince had confided in about his affair. He had even accompanied Beth to the mortuary, for Christ's sake.

It was therefore hard for Temple to accept that he wasn't the concerned friend he had made them believe he was.

'He wasn't a suspect for the simple reason that he wasn't in the building at the time of the murder,' Vaughan said. 'Or at least that's what we were led to believe.'

Temple remembered being told how Kessel had left the building at about seven on Sunday evening – three hours before Prince was pushed from the balcony. This had been confirmed by the security footage. And he hadn't re-entered the building until the following morning, fresh from a business trip.

That was why the team had left him off the list of suspects, which included all those who had been in the building the previous night at around ten. After all, why waste time on someone who was supposedly nowhere near the scene of the crime?

But, of course, that was before it became clear that the concierge, George Reese, had been lying to them.

'I can see what might have happened,' Angel said. 'Let's assume Kessel was colluding with Reese. For whatever reason, the concierge was being paid to help him. On Sunday, Kessel made a point of leaving the building and being seen to do so. Then, by arrangement, Reese disabled the security cameras at the rear so that Kessel could sneak back in. Reese left them off long enough for him to go up to Prince's flat, carry out the murder, and then leave by the back door. The cameras were then switched back on and as far as everyone was concerned, Kessel had never been back there.'

It was a plausible theory, Temple thought, but it still left a lot of questions unanswered.

What had been Kessel's motive? Was he a lone wolf or was he working with an organization or a foreign power? Why had he tried to kill Reese? And was he the person who had emailed the death threat to Beth?

Temple took out his phone and had another look at the text that Kessel had received from Beth a little earlier.

Joseph. Got your voicemail. Don't worry. Am OK. You and everyone else will hear from me soon. There's something I have to do.

'I don't understand why he felt the need to tell us about it,' Temple said.

Vaughan pursed his lips. 'He probably thinks we're monitoring her phone and we'd get suspicious if he didn't pass it on.'

'That's one explanation, I suppose,' Temple said. 'But I've got a bad feeling about it. I'm not even convinced it's genuine.'

'What do you mean, guv?'

Temple shrugged. 'Well, what if he has her phone and he sent that message to himself? A ploy to stop us worrying and to distance himself from any involvement.'

'But why would he have her phone? He wasn't around when she walked out of the building to go into town.'

'But he went looking for her,' Temple said. 'Perhaps he found her.'

He felt a ball of anxiety expand in his chest. His concern for Beth was mounting with every passing second.

They hadn't seen her in Kessel's Honda Civic when it pulled into the petrol station. But that didn't mean he hadn't stashed her in the boot and was now planning to make her disappear for good.

Temple tried again to call Kessel's number, but it failed to connect, just as it had a few minutes ago. He'd switched it off, presumably so it couldn't be traced.

He probably still didn't know they'd identified him. Or that they'd found George Reese. And he was hopefully oblivious to the fact that they were closing in.

Temple reminded himself of what little they knew about the man. He was a 38-year-old Israeli who had lived in the Riverview apartment block for nine months. He worked as a freelance IT consultant and had apparently been Daniel Prince's confidante as well as his friend.

But Temple wondered now if Kessel had struck up a friendship with Prince just to get close to him, in much the same way as William and Faye Connor had. If so, then he had probably been another part of the extraordinary surveillance apparatus that had been constructed to monitor the blogger's every move.

But then on Sunday, he had suddenly progressed from watching Prince to killing him. Was that because he'd been ordered to? Or did something happen that prompted him to act by himself?

Temple looked at his watch and said, 'Why the bloody hell is it taking them so long to get back to us?'

'It's only been a few minutes, guv,' Vaughan said. 'We should hear any second.'

They were waiting for confirmation that Kessel's Honda Civic was fitted with a GPS tracking device. It would have been unusual if it hadn't been, given that it was a fairly new lease vehicle.

Once they had a fix on it, they'd know where he'd driven to after leaving the service station.

It was a tense wait and Temple was stamping up and down on the spot impatiently.

They were so close and yet so far. For all they knew, Kessel was about to dump the car and ride off into the sunset in another vehicle. Or maybe he was on his way to do Beth harm.

All they knew for sure was that he was a jump ahead of them and he had one murder and one attempted murder to his credit.

Vaughan's phone rang and he answered it. He nodded as he listened and then allowed himself a small smile.

'We've got it,' he said. 'They're patching it through.'

'So where is the car now?' Temple asked.

'About five miles north of here. A house in the middle of the countryside.'

CHAPTER 63

JOSEPH KESSEL PUSHED Beth back into the hallway with such force that she dropped her handbag on the floor.

She then watched with sickening dread as the contents spilled out – including the two guns and her mobile phone.

Kessel stooped to pick up the guns, one of which he placed inside his belt. He then retrieved the phone, checked the display and switched it off.

Beth stood frozen to the spot, not quite able to believe the evidence of her own eyes. Every nerve ending in her body was vibrating and she felt a flash of heat in her chest.

It just didn't make sense. Joseph Kessel was her friend. He'd been Daniel's drinking mate; a kind and thoughtful man who had been there to offer comfort in her time of need.

So why is he here and why did he just push me?

'Where are they, Beth?' he said. 'Where are the two men who picked you up in town?'

Her mind had been slow to respond, but it clicked now that he was the one Yuri and Anton had been waiting for. The mystery man they had reported to.

'What's going on, Joseph?' she said, finding her voice.

He pushed the door shut behind him and pulled down the hood of his cardigan.

'I won't ask you again, Beth. Where are they?'

His mouth was set in a determined line and he slowly raised the gun so it was pointed at her stomach.

She was shocked by his demeanour. He had adopted a persona that she was entirely unfamiliar with. This wasn't the man she had got to know over the past nine months. He seemed different in every respect. There was a hardness in his expression that alarmed her.

'I shot them,' she said.

His brow peaked. 'Are you kidding?'

She didn't answer. Just shook her head.

He flicked the gun. 'Show me.'

But she didn't move straight away. She couldn't. It was as though the soles of her shoes were stuck to the floor.

This can't be happening, she told herself. It's not real. Surely I'll wake up soon from the longest and most horrific nightmare I've ever had.

Kessel stabbed her shoulder with the muzzle of the revolver.

'Get on with it, Beth. Show me where they are and then we can talk.'

Her breath hitched in her throat. She turned around slowly and started walking back across the hall towards the living room. Questions were swamping her mind. Why was Joseph involved with a pair of Russian henchmen? Did he kill Daniel? What was his plan for her now?

He followed her into the living room and let out a sharp breath when he saw what was in there.

'I think he's dead,' Beth said, pointing to Anton.

Kessel told her to stand with her back against the far wall. Then he knelt beside the body and checked for himself.

'Dead all right,' he said. 'How did you get the drop on him?'

Beth swallowed. 'He was attacking me. I managed to grab the gun from his pocket. It went off and he was hit. I didn't mean for it to happen.'

Kessel stood up, looked at the camera on the tripod.

'Did they record you reading from the note?'

'I wouldn't let them,' she said. 'And I'm not going to let you.'

He studied her for a moment. There was no emotion in his slate-grey eyes. They remained flat and unblinking.

'Where's Yuri?' he said.

'In the kitchen.'

'Then lead the way.'

She felt a cold shiver run through her back and her heart thumped in her ears. She had a sudden urge to break into a run and head for the front door. But she knew she wouldn't make it that far. She would either be gunned down or brought to heel some other way. Once again she had lost control of her own destiny.

'Move along, Beth. We haven't got all night.'

She shuffled back across the room without looking down at Anton's body. Then back across the hall to the kitchen.

'This one is still alive, I think,' she said.

'Then go stand at the far end.'

She did as she was told.

Yuri was still sitting up against the unit, his chin resting on his chest, his blood everywhere. On hearing Kessel's voice, he lifted his head and murmured something unintelligible.

'You really fucked up, Yuri,' Kessel said, standing over him. 'You were told to do a simple job. How did it go so wrong?'

Yuri licked his lips and tried to focus on the figure before him.

'I'm so … sorry. Anton … lost it. He let her …'

Kessel shook his head. 'That's a pathetic excuse, Yuri. And it's going to reflect badly on me, which I'm especially not happy about.'

Yuri sucked in a rasping breath that rattled in his throat.

'Please … I … need an ambulance …' His voice trailed off and his head fell forward again.

'There's no need for an ambulance, Yuri,' Kessel said. 'Even if you could be saved, you're no longer of any use to us.'

Kessel pointed the gun at the back of Yuri's head and pulled the trigger.

CHAPTER 64

YURI'S HEAD EXPLODED like a pumpkin at a shooting range. Blood and brain matter splashed across the floor and some of it landed on Beth's skirt. She closed her eyes as a bolt of nausea hit her.

'I'm not sure why you can't bear to look,' Kessel said. 'Based on what you've managed to achieve here, I'd say you were a natural born killer.'

Her eyes flicked open. 'What I did wasn't out of choice. You know they were going to kill me.'

'That wasn't the intention. If you'd simply done as they asked—'

'You're lying, Joseph.' She pointed at the shovels and black sheeting on the floor close to Yuri's body. 'They were planning to bury me as well. On your orders, no doubt.'

He didn't bother to deny it and that told Beth all she needed to know.

'You'll never get away with it,' she said. 'You'll be made to pay.'

He shook his head. 'No one knows we're here. In a little while, this house and everything in it will be going up in flames. There'll be no evidence left to reveal what happened and no Beth Fletcher to make things more difficult for my fellow countrymen.'

They stared at each other for several long seconds. She saw now that a dark light burned behind his eyes. She wondered if it had always been there and she simply hadn't noticed it. And neither had Daniel.

'I thought you were my friend,' Beth said.

'That's what I wanted you to think.'

'And what about Daniel? Were you his friend?'

He shrugged. 'Up to a point, I suppose I was. But it's probably more accurate to say that it was an arrangement that served a purpose.'

Beth cleared her throat and said, 'Are you the one who killed him?'

To her surprise he gave a simple nod. 'For what it's worth, it gave me no great pleasure. It was just something that had to be done. I was the one who was tasked with doing it.'

He spoke as though it was no big deal, like throwing someone from a balcony was an everyday occurrence.

His attitude chilled Beth to the bone and made her hate him even more.

'I think you've earned the right to be told everything before you die,' he said. 'So I suggest we retreat to a place where there are no dead bodies to distract us.'

He settled for the hall and told her to sit on the floor while he sat on the stairs. He made sure there was a distance of about eight feet between them.

Then he rested his arms on his knees and held the gun so it was loosely pointed in her direction.

His relaxed composure unsettled her even more. It made her realize that the man she had regarded as a decent friend was really a callous killer without a conscience.

'Let me put your mind at rest on one particular issue,' he said, and she thought she detected the faint trace of a smile on his lips. 'To my knowledge, Daniel never had an affair with another woman. It was a rumour I put about to make it seem like he had at least one reason to want to kill himself.'

'You bastard.'

He shrugged. 'In any event, it wasn't necessary because the police didn't buy the suicide bit anyway. Which I accept was my fault because mistakes were made.'

Beth had never believed that Daniel had been unfaithful anyway, and she was glad now that she hadn't been swayed by the rumours and vicious online comments.

'You've probably guessed by now that I'm not really the person I've been pretending to be,' he said. 'Joseph Kessel is not my real name and I'm not an Israeli. I emigrated with my parents from Russia to Israel twenty years ago. We were part of that huge exodus that followed the break-up of the Soviet Union.'

Beth was well aware of how almost two million Russians, mostly Jews, had fled to Israel looking for a new life. And how Russian speakers now accounted for almost fifteen per cent of Israel's 7.7 million-strong population.

'But my heart remained in the country of my birth,' Kessel said. 'So I returned there five years ago and joined the army. From there I moved into the intelligence services and that's how I came to be part of the surveillance operation centred on Daniel Prince. We knew we weren't the only ones watching him. The British, as always, made it obvious. The Chinese and the Americans were more discreet.

'We all deployed different methods and levels of intensity. For instance, I was told to move into the building and befriend Daniel. And it was me who planted the bug under your breakfast bar. The Brits chose to install those two clowns calling themselves the Connors next door.'

Beth was mortified. Was it really possible that William and Faye had been spying on them too? Was that why they had been accumulating information on Daniel? Was their claim that it was for a scrapbook a complete fabrication?

'Daniel's success as a blogger posed a serious threat to a lot of people,' he said. 'We acted when we did because he decided to target Russia in his forthcoming campaign. The original plan had been to wait and see what happened, but then when he forced those politicians to resign we saw an opportunity.

'My superiors in Moscow took the view that if he committed suicide amidst all the fanfare and fuss he'd created, then suspicion wouldn't fall on us. His followers would either accept he killed himself because he was depressed, or they'd think he was the victim of a government-inspired conspiracy. Either way we believed we would benefit from the demise of the blog.'

Beth wasn't sure how much more she could take. It felt like her mind was being overloaded with too much information. She could imagine that soon the sheer pressure would open up cracks in her skull.

'And then just when we thought we had done all we needed to do, you went and told the world that you were taking over the blog to carry on where Daniel had left off,' he said. 'That gave us a problem as you well know. I was hoping you'd be persuaded not to go ahead with it after I sent you the death threat in the email. But it quickly became obvious that there was no stopping you. So I was instructed to sort you out.

'Anton and Yuri came down from London yesterday and have been watching you. I told them to pick you up and bring you here. It's true that we weren't going to let you live once you'd recorded the message, but I didn't think it would turn into such a bloody mess. Now I have to put myself into damage-limitation mode. Luckily there'll be nothing to link my two comrades with the Kremlin, assuming that they can even be identified after the fire.'

'And what will you do?' Beth said.

'Well, my job here is done. I'll go back to the flat, pack up and slip away quietly when the time is right.'

'And you think the police won't track you down?'

'I know they won't,' he said. 'Detective Temple and his team are out of their depth. They've no idea where you are and they're clueless about my involvement. As far as they're concerned, I wasn't even in the building when Daniel was pushed from the balcony.'

'Was he conscious?' Beth asked.

The question surprised him. He inhaled a large breath and shook his head. 'No, he wasn't. I had to hit him first. I went to your flat armed with a rubber-headed mallet. He didn't see it coming.'

'And you wrote the note too,' she said.

He nodded. 'I typed it out, yes. But that was where I made a mistake. I didn't know he'd cleaned the keys.'

It felt like a dagger was being plunged into her heart. The pain was like nothing she had ever experienced. In her mind's eye, she could see this bastard attacking Daniel and then pulling him across the floor to the balcony. It brought tears to her eyes and caused her stomach to flip.

Kessel glanced at his watch and got to his feet. Then he raised the gun and aimed it at her.

Beth lifted her head and looked at him, her face firm, stoic.

'I want you to know this is not personal,' he said. 'I actually like you. But it's got to be—'

He stopped mid-sentence, snapping his head towards the front door. Beyond it came the sudden sound of sirens, and through the glass panel could be seen the flashing of coloured light.

'Looks like you were wrong about no one knowing we're here,' Beth said.

CHAPTER 65

THE HOUSE WAS a two-storey, red-brick affair close to the village of Whitchurch. It was set back from the road and had a driveway that was big enough for half a dozen cars.

There were two cars already parked on it when the police convoy arrived. One was Joseph Kessel's Honda Civic and its headlamps were still on, even though the car was empty. The other was a silver Land Rover.

The pool car was the first to come to a stop and Temple got out. The two tactical response vehicles pulled in behind.

He made a quick visual assessment of the scene as the armed officers piled onto the driveway.

There were lights on inside the house, but the curtains were closed so they couldn't see in. The place was surrounded by trees, and the nearest other property was a good 300 metres away.

Temple gave the signal for the armed officers to surround the house and told them to be careful. There was no way of knowing how the next few minutes were going to pan out. Kessel obviously wasn't alone inside. He might well have had a small team of accomplices with him. And there was every chance they were armed.

'How do we play this, guv?' Vaughan said.

Temple twisted his lower jaw, considering. Then he said, 'I don't want anyone rushing in. Have we got a megaphone?'

'I'll check.'

As Vaughan walked away, Angel approached.

'Just got confirmation that George Reese is still alive,' she said. 'Our man at the hospital reckons he should pull through.'

'That's good news.'

'Meanwhile, a team is about to descend on Kessel's flat to see what they can find.'

Temple kept his eyes on the front door some fifteen metres away. The fact that whoever was in the house hadn't yet appeared made him nervous. They must surely have known by now that they had visitors.

Vaughan came back and handed him a police megaphone. Temple put it straight to his mouth and aimed it at the house as he spoke into it.

'This is Detective Chief Inspector Jeff Temple with a message for Joseph Kessel. I know you're in the house, Mr Kessel and I'm here to talk to you about a knife attack in Southampton earlier this evening. The property is surrounded by armed officers so I would advise you and anyone else in the house not to try to run away. It'll be best for all concerned if you come out of the front door with your arms raised.'

Temple lowered the megaphone and took a breath. He locked his eyes on the front door and felt beads of sweat sparkling above his upper lip.

They had to wait another half a minute before anything happened. Then all eyes were drawn to a window to the left of the front door.

The curtains were pulled open to reveal a figure framed in the window. It was Beth Fletcher and she was standing as if to attention.

A man wearing a hood stood behind her with one arm around her neck, while in the other he held a revolver that was pointed at her head.

CHAPTER 66

HAVING MADE HIS point, Kessel pulled the curtain back across the window and dragged Beth away from it.

'How the fuck did they know we were here?' he raged.

'You're obviously not as clever as you think you are,' Beth said.

He led her back along the hall and told her to sit on the stairs. He was sweating now and in a panic. As Beth watched him pacing the room, he looked like a caged animal.

He must know the game is up, she thought. There's no way he's going to walk away from this situation.

'You should give yourself up,' she said. 'It's over.'

He stopped pacing and looked at her.

'I'm not letting them take me,' he said.

'Then you'll be shot.'

'I'd rather that than spend the rest of my life in a prison cell.'

'It's what you deserve for killing Daniel.'

He shook his head. 'That's not how I see it. I had just cause. Your boyfriend's blog was set to inflict more misery on millions of Russians. I did what I was ordered to do.'

'That doesn't mean it was right. You got to know Daniel. You saw that he was a good man. What you did was wrong.'

Kessel started to respond but was interrupted by DCI Temple's booming voice from outside.

'Switch on your phone, Mr Kessel,' he said. 'I'd like to open up a dialogue with you. I'm sure we can work this out. And please release Beth Fletcher. She's done you no harm.'

Kessel took a step towards her and she saw that he was shaking. She also saw something else. The dark light in his eyes had faded, and it was like looking into a pair of black holes.

Beth felt her muscles tremble. Instinct told her that he wasn't going to prolong the agony; that he would rather go out in a blaze of glory than surrender to the police.

She tried to resign herself to her fate, but it wasn't easy. Her mind swirled with a rush of thoughts and images. She saw Daniel, her father, the little hotel in the New Forest where they'd been planning to tie the knot.

All the while, she maintained eye contact with the man who had shattered her world and was about to end her life.

He was gripping the gun so hard his knuckles had turned white, and sweat was now trickling down across his cheeks.

Suddenly a sound came from the back of the house. It could have been one of the cops trying to open the kitchen door. Or maybe they had found an unlocked window.

She wondered if they were preparing to storm the house and how Kessel would respond if they did.

His eyes darted right and left. Beth could see his mind working. He was trying to decide what to do, weighing up his options.

Then, after a couple more seconds, he said, 'Close your eyes, Beth. It'll be easier that way.'

But just then someone knocked hard on the front door. Kessel's head jerked towards it.

And in that split second Beth found a last reserve of strength and threw herself at him.

Kessel grunted in surprise and fell back. The blistering sound of the gun going off pierced her ears. But the bullet whistled past her head and smashed into the nearest window.

They hit the floor together, kicking and flailing and cursing.

Beth tried to wrap her arms around his waist, but he reacted by butting her hard in the face with his head. She choked out a scream and her body went limp.

In a flash, Kessel pulled away from her and hauled himself up. He still held onto the gun and his eyes burned like mercury as he levelled it against her forehead. Her skin went cold and the air in her throat turned to ice.

And the sound of gunfire filled the room.

CHAPTER 67

JOSEPH KESSEL WAS blown off his feet by a bullet that slammed into the side of his head.

The cop who fired it was the first of the tactical team to rush through the front door after it was kicked open.

He was just in time to save Beth Fletcher's life.

Temple had given the signal to storm the house after the first shot smashed the ground floor window. He entered himself a few moments later and was appalled at what he found.

There were two other bodies – one in the living room and the other in the kitchen – and Beth herself was in a terrible state. Her face was a swollen mass of cuts and bruises. Her jaw was badly discoloured, and blood was dripping from her nose and from a gash across her left cheek.

And no doubt there were injuries he couldn't see, deep psychological scars that would probably never heal.

But at least she was alive and that, given the circumstances, was nothing short of a miracle.

An ambulance was called and while they waited, Beth was taken outside. Temple got her to tell him what had happened in the house. She explained how she had been abducted in the park by the two men.

'They drugged me and brought me here,' she said. 'They called themselves Yuri and Anton. They worked for the Russians and they reported to Joseph.'

She told him what they had wanted her to do and how they had ended up dead. And as she spoke she began to cry, and Temple put a blanket around her shoulders and told Angel to take her to sit in the car.

'You're in shock, Beth,' he said. 'So try to relax. You can tell me more later. But rest assured you're going to be OK.'

But Beth wasn't convinced that she would ever be OK. Her heart was broken and her mind had been ravaged beyond repair.

As she sat in the back of the unmarked police car, the tears continued to flow. She cried for Daniel and for herself. And she cried because over the past few hours she had seen and done things that would always be the stuff of her nightmares.

She had shot and killed two men she had never met before. Two government-sponsored assassins who had planned to bury her in an unmarked grave. And for no other reason than to stop her writing a blog.

She had also discovered that part of her life had been a lie. William and Faye Connor had never been her true friends. And neither had Joseph Kessel. They'd been part of a vile conspiracy to control and ultimately to destroy Daniel Prince.

And it was a chilling thought that the train of events that had brought her to this point had begun years ago. On the day Daniel had started to write his blog, his destiny had been decided. Each successful campaign had drawn him closer to his untimely death.

And the manner of that death had been horribly cruel. Kessel's description of what had happened played over in Beth's head again and caused a great torrent of anger to well up inside her.

A bullet to the head had been too good for him. He hadn't been made to suffer and that would always be a source of regret. As would the fact that she hadn't been the one to end his life.

Revenge might have offered a small crumb of comfort. As it was, the police officer's bullet had denied her even that.

CHAPTER 68

TEMPLE SPENT TWO hours in what the team started to call the 'house of horror'.

He stood at the living room window and watched the ambulance arrive to take Beth to the hospital. He told Angel to go with her and said he'd be along later.

He then briefed the scene of crime officers when they turned up to carry out the forensic sweep. They had three dead bodies to process and what seemed like gallons of spilled blood. It was nothing less than total carnage.

The evidence spoke for itself. Beth Fletcher had been through a terrible ordeal in this house. The fact that she had survived was a testament to her strength of character and her will to survive.

This belief was reinforced when he was shown a piece of paper that had been found on the floor in the living room. It was the little speech that Beth had been told to read out for the camera.

Her captors had planned to release it on the internet before making her disappear. It prompted Temple to examine the video camera perched on the tripod. It was still switched on and there was plenty of life left in the battery.

He pressed the play button and Beth appeared on the little screen. She was sitting in the fold-up chair and holding the note in her lap. But the words it contained were not the words that came out of her mouth.

'I'm Beth Fletcher, Daniel Prince's fiancée. I want the world to know that he was murdered on the orders of the Russian government. Now the bastards are going to kill me as well. They're terrified that—'

The camera continued to record, and Temple stared in amazement as the man Beth had identified as Anton rushed into shot to attack her.

What followed was a dramatic sequence that showed in blood-curdling detail how she had defended herself against Anton and then his accomplice. It was an irrefutable piece of evidence that supported Beth's account of what had happened.

But it was a shame they wouldn't be able to use it to bring about any convictions.

CHAPTER 69

THE STORY GOT out during the night. Not every gruesome detail was leaked, but enough to provoke another media firestorm.

By the early hours, reporters were turning up at the house and TV camera crews were laying siege to the city hospital.

Temple also had to contend with a flurry of calls from the top brass. Two senior officials – one at the Home Office and the other a spook at MI6 – even bypassed the usual channels to phone him directly on his mobile phone.

Everyone wanted to know the identities of the dead men and whether what had happened was likely to cause a major diplomatic incident.

The potential was there, of course. The men were all Russians who had been working together to kidnap and murder British citizens. It was too early to know if there would be a direct link between them and the Kremlin, but somehow Temple doubted it.

Beth was sleeping in a private room when he arrived at the hospital. Her wounds had been treated and the good news was that she had no life-threatening injuries. She did have mild concussion and a fractured cheekbone, however, and a facial trauma specialist was being called in to see what needed to be done.

Temple stayed at the hospital with Angel so that he could be there when Beth woke up. From there he liaised with the chief super, the media department and the rest of his team. With so many people involved, the information flowed in without delay.

The house of horror was owned by a Ukrainian business-man who claimed he had no knowledge of anyone gaining access. According to him, it had been taken off the market a few months ago and he had the only set of keys. He was now the subject of a full background check.

The two men Beth had shot did not appear on the criminal records database. They'd both been carrying wallets contain-ing cash and driving licences in the names of Yuri Demidov and Anton Pankin. But the licences were fakes which had been used to hire the Land Rover they'd been driving from a company based in London.

The search of Joseph Kessel's flat had also uncovered a wealth of fake documents used to create his own false identity.

None of it came as a surprise to Temple. All three men had been part of a world that exists in the shadows. Where nothing is ever what it seems and the usual rules don't apply.

When Beth woke up, Temple was at her bedside. He told her

he had phoned her father to inform him that she was all right. And he told her about the recording on the video camera.

'The one who called himself Anton didn't bother to switch it off,' he said. 'It recorded most of what happened in that living room.'

'Then you saw that I was given no choice,' she said.

'That was pretty obvious, Beth. And for your information, when Kessel said he was going to burn the house down, he wasn't bluffing. We found two cans filled with petrol in the boot of his car.'

Temple informed her of what they'd discovered and she listened attentively. Then Beth fleshed out her account of events and revealed more of what Kessel and the others had told her.

'He made up the story about Daniel having an affair,' she said. 'It was a lie to support the claim that he was suffering from depression.'

Temple felt stupid for having fallen for it. He should have known that there was no truth in it when they failed to uncover a single scrap of evidence.

Beth also revealed what Kessel had said about planting the listening device in the flat and about timing Daniel's death to coincide with the resignations of the politicians over the tax scandal.

'The Russians believed it would ensure that suspicion didn't fall on them,' she said.

Her eyes then filled with tears as she told how Kessel had described killing Daniel.

'It meant nothing to him,' she said. 'He reckoned he was just doing his job.'

CHAPTER 70

GEORGE REESE WAS in a different part of the hospital. He had also been given a private room and a police officer was stationed outside.

Temple went to see him after leaving Beth. He had recovered enough for the doctors to allow him to be questioned.

Reese was sitting up in bed with a bandage wrapped around his torso and a drip plugged into his arm. He was surprisingly coherent – and responsive. He confirmed that Joseph Kessel had been the person who stabbed him and left him for dead.

'He kept phoning to warn me to keep my mouth shut,' he said. 'He was convinced I'd crack and tell you everything. Then he suddenly turned up at my house and invited himself in. He asked me to put the kettle on and as I walked to the sink he stabbed me in the back.'

Reese went on to confirm that Kessel had approached him soon after moving into the Riverview apartments nine months ago.

'He offered me money to keep an eye on some of the residents, including Daniel Prince and Beth Fletcher,' he said. 'He wanted me to monitor their comings and goings and to tell him if and when they had visitors. He knew I had big gambling debts and a criminal record that my employers weren't aware of. So I agreed to help.'

Reese said he was asked to disable the cameras for two hours on Sunday night, and told to leave the service entrance unlocked.

'He said he wanted to come back into the building but he didn't want anyone to know about it. When I asked him why he told me it was none of my business. So I did what he asked and then he called me after Daniel fell from the balcony. He said it was nothing to do with him, but warned me not to tell the police what I'd done. He said if I did he'd have me killed. That was why I was afraid to tell the truth.'

By midday, Temple was in a position to give a full briefing to a roomful of senior officers, including Beresford and the Chief Constable. Officials from the Home Office and MI6 joined in via video link from London.

Three hours later, the Chief Constable staged a press

conference at which he explained how Beth Fletcher had survived a vicious attempt on her life by three men who had claimed they were acting on behalf of the Russian government. Their motive, he said, was to prevent her taking over Daniel Prince's People-Power blog.

The proverbial shit hit the fan after that. The Russian ambassador in London was called to a meeting with British government officials and the Kremlin was quick to deny any involvement or knowledge of the three dead men.

The Russian president issued a statement saying the story had been fabricated as part of a campaign to denigrate his country.

But the news spread across the various social media platforms like wildfire and before the day was out, Beth Fletcher was the most talked about person on the planet.

CHAPTER 71

Two weeks later

THE SUN HUNG low in the sky, shining through the clouds and casting long shadows over the grounds of the crematorium.

Thousands of people had gathered in the Garden of Remembrance and the roads leading up to it. They had all come to pay their respects to Daniel Prince who was being cremated on this day.

More people stood inside the little chapel as a tearful Beth Fletcher read the eulogy.

She hadn't expected so many to turn up and she felt overwhelmed. But at the same time she was also proud of Daniel for having had such an influence on so many lives.

She said as much in a voice that cracked with emotion as it was carried outside the chapel through loud speakers.

'Daniel was a man of immense integrity who stood up for

what he believed in,' she said. 'Through his blog, he inspired millions of people to believe in themselves and to try to make the world a better, fairer place.

'I announced shortly after his death that I would take over his blog and drive it forward on his behalf. Well, I want the world to know that this is still my intention, despite the efforts that were made to stop me.

'In fact, this very evening, the People-Power blog will be updated for the first time in two weeks.'

It was welcome news for Daniel Prince's millions of followers and they waited eagerly to find out how Beth would set about exacting revenge on the Russian government.

And she didn't disappoint them, even though her approach took most by surprise.

'It would be wrong of me to seek retribution against the people of Russia for what happened to Daniel and for what was done to me,' she wrote. 'Vengeance in the form of sanctions will result in the wrong people suffering. I therefore reject the need for a wider boycott of Russian goods and services. Instead, I'm calling on the people of Russia to rise up against the country's oppressive and corrupt regime.

'It is time you used people power to topple a dictator who routinely violates human and civil rights and quashes opposition. Regime change is the only way to free yourselves from the tyranny that blights your lives and poses a growing threat to world peace.'

The message got through despite the level of internet censorship in Russia and despite several successful attempts to shut down the People-Power blog.

Activists and bloggers within Russia lent their support to the campaign to topple the government, as did opposition parties who adopted the people-power slogan themselves.

A head of steam built up during the months following Beth's first blog posting. Massive street protests took place across the country and one demonstration brought the centre of Moscow to a complete standstill.

Finally, the Russian President and his cabinet bowed to the unrelenting pressure and resigned. The team who took over promised a new beginning – an end to rampant imperialism and more freedoms for the people of Russia.

The incoming president said during his first speech to the nation that it had been shown once again that it was possible to change things for the better when enough people insisted on it.

He made no mention of the part Beth Fletcher had played in bringing about what was being described as a social revolution.

But she didn't mind because by then she was busy promoting a raft of new headline-grabbing campaigns through the People-Power blog – and making a lot more enemies along the way.